Stowaway to Trouble . . .

"Do you know what the masters of ships long ago did with stowaways?"

"I'm sure I don't care to know the dreadful details, Captain St. Simon," she replied, her pride returning at his taunting.

"Some of them would throw the wretches overboard. Kinder ones set them adrift in a skiff with a few fishhooks and a keg of water. But the most accepted practice was to give them the lowest, meanest, hardest, dirtiest jobs." There was a menacing quality in his voice, though it was soft.

"That's assuming they couldn't pay for their passage!" she said triumphantly.

"And what form of payment have you?" he asked, his eyes roving over her trim figure.

CHRISTINE SKILLERN
lives in California with her husband and two children. She works full-time as a legal secretary, but readers will be glad she found the time to write *Moonstruck,* her first Silhouette Special Edition.

Dear Reader,

Silhouette Special Editions are an exciting new line of contemporary romances from Silhouette Books. Special Editions are written specifically for our readers who want a story with heightened romantic tension.

Special Editions have all the elements you've enjoyed in Silhouette Romances and *more*. These stories concentrate on romance in a longer, more realistic and sophisticated way, and they feature greater sensual detail.

I hope you enjoy this book and all the wonderful romances from Silhouette. We welcome any suggestions or comments and invite you to write to us at the address below.

Karen Solem
Editor-in-Chief
Silhouette Books
P.O. Box 769
New York, N. Y. 10019

CHRISTINE SKILLERN
Moonstruck

Silhouette Special Edition
Published by Silhouette Books New York
America's Publisher of Contemporary Romance

SILHOUETTE BOOKS, a Simon & Schuster Division of
GULF & WESTERN CORPORATION
1230 Avenue of the Americas, New York, N.Y. 10020

ISBN: 0-671-53571-4

First Silhouette Books printing January, 1983

10 9 8 7 6 5 4 3 2 1

Map by Ray Lundgren

America's Publisher of Contemporary Romance

Printed in the U.S.A.

To my daughters,
Lisa and Laurie

Moonstruck

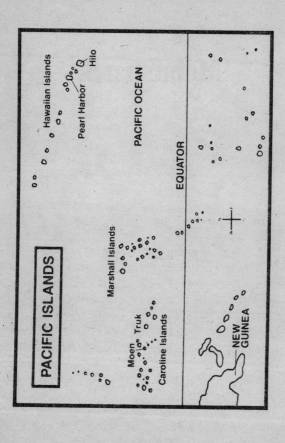

PACIFIC ISLANDS

Hawaiian Islands
Pearl Harbor
Hilo

PACIFIC OCEAN

EQUATOR

Marshall Islands

Moen
Truk
Caroline Islands

NEW GUINEA

Chapter One

The early morning light caught the outline of a ketch tacking leisurely around the green headland of Leleiwi Point toward the shelter of Hilo Bay. A man clad in cutoff jeans and a red sweatshirt was winching down the white jib sails on the vessel's forward mast. A boy at the tiller expertly aided him by tacking into the wind to take the strain off the billowing sails. The trim ketch soon drew near to a huge white yacht anchored among the many small boats in the harbor.

From the rail of the yacht, a woman watched the combined efforts of the pair sailing the ketch. Her expression was one of bored disinterest with the arrival of yet another small sailing craft in the already overstuffed harbor of Hilo, Hawaii.

She wore a skimpy white bikini despite the early hour of the day and the slight chill of the wind. The garment enhanced her golden tan and did little to hide her lovely body. High full breasts strained to be free of their two tiny restraints, long shapely legs and slender arms added to her wondrous symmetry.

A delicate well-pampered hand reached up to push back a wisp of shoulder length golden red hair. Her face was accented by delicate cheekbones, a perfect straight nose, a wide generous mouth and a firm chin with an angle of determination. However, it wasn't any one of these features that intrigued people; it was her lovely eyes generously framed with deep russet lashes. The color? There wasn't a color under the sun that some hapless male suitor hadn't called them. Her passport listed them as hazel, but it wasn't an accurate statement. It was her mood that determined their color: green fire in anger, deep blue in thought, violet in passion, silver in laughter.

The ketch drew within ten yards of the yacht. She could hear the low purring of the auxiliary motor as sail power was abandoned for the close maneuvering required in the harbor. At the precise moment she looked down upon the deck, the man in the red sweatshirt looked up, freezing her with a pair of sea green eyes against a deeply tanned face.

She felt the shock of his gaze down her spine, and an unaccustomed feeling of excitement raced over her body as he slowly appraised each part of it.

She was suddenly aware of the scene she presented—rich, spoiled, bored, uncaring and totally self-centered.

As if he had read her mind, he made a slow, formal, mocking bow to her. It was as correct as if he were formally attired in black tie and tuxedo and standing in a continental drawing room instead of barefoot on a bobbing teakwood deck.

She flushed in anger. Anger at him and anger with herself for presenting an image that wasn't at all like the real person she was. Even though he couldn't know this, she was enraged with him all the same for thinking the worst of her. She would be darned if she would give him the satisfaction of knowing his opinion was of any importance to her! As he raised his dark head from the low bow, she looked down on him with a bored, haughty expression on her beautiful face. She turned away, failing to notice a crewman passing right behind her with a large silver breakfast tray—and both crashed to the deck in a shower of orange juice, scrambled eggs, toast and marmalade.

She rolled quickly to her feet with the grace of a circus acrobat and involuntarily turned to look at the man in the ketch. He struggled mightily to contain his amusement. On seeing her stormy face, his silent laughter became merry rolling thunder which seemed to reach across the small space of water separating them and wash against her skin in sensuous ripples of delight. The boy's laughter, a light falsetto joining the man's rich baritone, completed her humiliation.

She flashed green eyes filled with fire at the pair, subduing the boy's laughter, but adding fuel to the man's total enjoyment of her antics. She turned on a bare heel and stalked away, almost upsetting the crewman who had just regained his feet and was trying to clear away the debris from their collision.

Behind her she heard the boy say in a southern American drawl, "Jake, she sure is beautiful."

A deep voice answered in the same accent, "Her lines are too long. You'd have to be an oil sheik to afford the upkeep on that one, boy."

The double meaning of his words was crystal clear to her! How dare he speculate on her upkeep? Storming into her cabin, she peered into the antique Florentine mirror on the sitting room wall. The image staring back at her wasn't pleasing. Egg was stuck to the left side of her face; orange juice, broken toast bits and marmalade plastered down her hair. In spite of herself she began to smile at her sorry reflection. The picture of casual glamour she worked so hard to project was under a mask of breakfast.

The anger vanished. It was rather funny. She had tried to be sophisticated and failed rather badly. She chuckled to herself and a burst of riotous laughter bubbled to the surface. She hadn't experienced such a feeling of unabashed joy since she'd left her college days behind her to return to England and the gray late spring of Wales.

Her thoughts returned to the handsome man who had caused the accident. Strangely, there was no more anger left against him. Anyway, she reasoned, it was highly improbable she would ever see him again, and she couldn't stay mad at a stranger. Still, she couldn't stop her natural curiosity about him.

His image came easily into her mind. The mocking salute, the deep booming laughter, the hair so black it flashed blue in the sun, the appraising eyes the color of a sheltered lagoon. His wide shoulders and heavily muscled arms and legs indicated years of physical labor. His slow lazy speech had stroked her senses like an ermine cape, caressing and soft, even while the words he had used were uncomplimentary.

He wasn't at all like the pampered men who now followed her every move since she had reached the age of consent for marriage. Her father's wealth had only increased the number of men pursuing her, and the position in society a marriage with her represented further sweetened the deal.

She wondered if the laughing sailor would care about the wealth of the Conal family, or the social prestige of marrying into a family whose lineage could be traced to Welsh kings. Even now, in the twentieth century, they were received as peers by every remaining royal family in Europe.

She sighed heavily. Being Lady Caroline Blythe Mary Elizabeth McPherson Conal wasn't as easy or enviable a position as it looked. Caroline knew she was considered a pretty woman in some circles. But by English standards she was a misfit. Depending on the season, her skin was amber to bronze instead of the fair creamy complexion prized by English women and their men. Her hair was too far to the red side of blond to be acceptable. Her mouth was wide and generous, not a small cupid's bow. She was much too tall at five feet six inches. What had that man Jake said? Her lines were too long.

"Well, Lady Caroline, I'm sure someday a man will come along and love you for all your faults. However, it's more than an even chance he'll love your daddy's money and position," she told her bedraggled reflection. Shrugging her shoulders, she quickly stripped off the food-stained bikini and stepped into a hot shower.

Her merry laughter and high spirits of just moments ago had been effectively squelched by gloomy appraisals. In the past she had never given much thought to money or social position, until she had been thrust from the comparatively austere life at school into the grandeur of her father's world. She had just begun to realize the full impact of his life, a life of trivial dinners and frivolous parties, where all business contacts were made by the men, and the latest and most expensive fashions were displayed by their women. It was a life of mandatory summer cruises without really seeing the beauty of the waters and lands being cruised. It was a life of winter skiing trips to luxurious European resorts without seeing the surrounding countryside or mixing with people other than their own kind—the wealthy. And most of all, it was surrounded by a constant awareness of the opportunists who were ready to prey on any weakness and take full advantage. She frowned at herself for this newfound cynicism.

She turned her mind away from these thoughts and let the warmth and tingling pulses of the water relax her taut muscles and mind. Again her mind wandered back to the little yellow ketch and her master. She suddenly remembered the boy. He was probably the man's son, but hadn't he called the man by name? Jake. Still the boy had the same black hair and general appearance as the man. Where was the boy's mother? Probably chained in the galley by the masterful dad or home minding the rest of the babies! She was sure this man, every advertiser's dream of the man's man to promote their products, would have a devoted slave for a wife.

She lathered her hair with fragrant shampoo and

scrubbed the egg, toast, orange juice and marma-lade out of the silken strands with vigorous strokes, as if the man Jake, his son, his laughter, velvet voice, bold eyes, and sleek trim boat would also wash out of her mind and disappear down the drain with the bits of food.

As she stepped from the shower, she heard a heavy rapping on her door. She hurriedly wrapped her hair in a plush golden towel bearing the large red coat of arms of the Conals in the center. Struggling into a short gold velour coverup with the same red coat of arms on the pocket, she muttered to herself that her father certainly couldn't be accused of underplaying his family heritage.

"Come in," she called impatiently. Her mind was still on her humiliation of this morning at the hands of an unprincipled pirate. Her anger suddenly rekin-dled as she thought again of those laughing sea green eyes and his unsavory comments.

As her father entered the room, a frown of disapproval crossed his face at her scanty attire. He said nothing. Behind him was the crewman she had fallen over. He smiled nervously at her and glanced worriedly at the silver tea service in his hands. Caroline gave him a quick reassuring smile and backed away from him in the opposite direction.

Caroline's eyes slid to her father, and noticing the frowning scowl on his face, her russet eyebrows drew together in a frown of her own. He rarely spoke to her, let alone called on her with morning tea. She asked, "Was there something you wished to speak to me about, sir?"

"Do you mind if I sit down?" he asked. Without waiting for a reply, he moved into one of the overstuffed velvet chairs which flanked a low table in the sitting room of her cabin.

"Please Caroline, sit down," he ordered, having taken charge of her sitting room. "Tim, please pour the tea, or would you prefer coffee? That's a disgusting habit you've picked up at your American college—black bitter fluid to greet the day with."

"I've already had my coffee, sir. Tea will be fine, thank you," she answered with the curtness that always seemed to be just below the surface when he was near. His thinly veiled criticism didn't dampen the readiness on her part to reply with tartness.

"So Tim informed me." He paused, then asked with an inquisitive note in his voice, "Is it your habit to rise so early each day?"

"Yes, it is, sir," she answered defensively.

"Why?" he demanded sharply.

"I . . . I learned to study best at school in the early morning hours," she retorted. Defiance covered her lovely face and a challenge filled her eyes. What motive was behind his sudden interest in her habits? She had been aboard the *Caroline* for a month now and this was the first time he had acknowledged her presence, other than an occasional nod at meal time or when introducing her to the friends and business associates he had entertained in Hong Kong before they sailed for Hawaii.

"Was it really necessary to leave your own country for an education? England has quite a number of excellent schools." He tried to sound amused but his ruffled attempt fell short.

"Yes, sir." She tried to smile. The attempt fell short too.

She studied him under her lashes. He really was a

proper Englishman to the core. Even in a casual, red knit polo shirt, white slacks and canvas deck shoes he was stiff and correct. She decided he was quite distinguished and handsome. His dark brown hair was still thick but liberally sprinkled with silver and completely white at the temples. Caroline's tall, rake handle thinness had come from him. It was the only feature of his she had received. The black Welsh features that refused to be bred out of the Conal line were always passed to sons, never to daughters. His eyes were the piercing blue about which poems had been written over the ages. His smile was quick and easy at times, a compensation for his forbidding austerity. But with his only child the smile was less apparent than with others.

Caroline could easily have admired and cared deeply for him if he had permitted it. In true British tradition, he had turned her early care over to a succession of capable nannies, then had sent her off to boarding school at age nine to emerge at eighteen a complete adult. Even then he seemed unprepared to deal with a high-spirited young lady of eighteen. It was Caroline herself who had postponed his paternal responsibilities for a while longer. After her graduation from Miss Calvert's Academy for Young Ladies, she had asked to attend Radcliffe, in Cambridge, Massachusetts. He had appeared relieved when he granted her the required funds and permission to attend. The years had passed slowly. Now they were faced again with the decision of whether to become a family of two or to travel their separate paths.

She was surprised and delighted upon returning to England to find an invitation and travel arrangements waiting for her to fly to Hong Kong for an extended cruise with her father on his yacht the *Caroline*. She had hoped to establish a relationship with him, but on the voyage to Hawaii he had conducted his business with his customary intensity.

Caroline wondered if he would have been a different man had her mother lived. Lady Anne McPherson had died trying to deliver a son and heir to the Earldom of Conal Keep less than a year after she had borne a disappointing girl. The only evidence that Anne had ever existed was Caroline's Scottish coloring, the McPherson name and a dusty trunk in the tower room at the Keep in Wales.

Robert had remarried three years after Lady Anne's death, only to have his young wife run off with a young Italian count who worked for Robert. The count's family, impoverished but proud, promptly disinherited the offending man for having betrayed his benefactor so disgustingly. Caroline had been only four at the time and couldn't remember the woman at all. Later, gossiping servants told an impressionable teenage Caroline the tale. She had thought it wildly romantic, but later realized the embarrassment and perhaps the hurt her father must have felt.

Robert had been thirty-one when his second wife had run away. Upon his father's death a year later, he became Robert Edward Albert James, sixteenth Earl of Conal and heir to one of the largest fortunes in England. After losing his wives at such a young age, he vowed that women would never become a serious part of his life again. Instead, he surrounded himself with his financial empire and built it into a power base few men on earth would dare to challenge. In doing so, he cut himself off from his only child, Caroline.

An uncomfortable silence lay between them as they sipped their tea. When she could not stand the waiting any longer she asked, "Is there something . . . was . . . What is it you wanted to speak to me about, sir?"

"Would it be so hard for you to call me father, Caroline?" he asked with surprising gentleness, his blue eyes enticing.

"Father," she obeyed, feeling moved by the request, but confused and slightly cautious of his motives.

"I want to be sure you have suitable attire for this evening. I'm having some friends aboard tonight for dinner; it will be a black tie affair." His voice was still gentle but his face had a small worried frown as he appraised his daughter's crestfallen face.

"Yes, I've something suitable," she said dully, her hopes dashed. What had she been expecting? A confession of paternal love and affection?

"Good."

"Is there anything else I should know?" she asked him. He usually had her briefed as to the likes and dislikes of their guests, and she was always given a proper seating chart, lest she make the unforgivable error of putting people together who detested each other. The duty of this briefing usually fell on the capable shoulders of Miss Starr, her father's quiet, efficient personal aide and secretary.

Jean Starr had been Robert's personal secretary for years, although she couldn't be much over thirty-six years of age. Caroline had always suspected that the woman's devotion stemmed from a carefully hidden love for Robert rather than a strong sense of duty. Caroline had on several occasions tried to tactfully suggest to the woman that she change her hairstyle from the knot of dark hair at the back of her head to a softer style around her finely sculptured face. Once Caroline had even suggested Jean switch from glasses to contact lenses while working. In Hong Kong Caroline had taken the reluctant Miss Starr shopping and tried to talk her into purchasing some informal clothing and discarding the severely tailored and drab suits she had worn for years—navy, black and brown for winter, tan and light gray for summer. Caroline had even suggested a bikini for the cruise, but Jean had smiled slightly, mumbled her thanks for Caroline's interest, and continued to wear her hair, glasses and suits just as she had for years.

"I'll have Jean come in later with the guest list." He paused and scrutinized her face so closely she dropped her eyes.

"Thank you, sir," she mumbled.

"Caroline, a young Englishman, actually a distant cousin of yours, will be flying into Hilo today from England. . . ." He paused, seeming to have some difficulty explaining the purpose of this mysterious relative's visit.

"Yes, si—Father?" she prompted, genuinely interested now. She had never seen him so reluctant to speak. He had a well-deserved reputation for blunt words.

"Caroline, a girl in your position is subject to a great many undesirable attentions, people who will flatter you insincerely, fortune hunters, the kind of men who wouldn't hesitate to play on your emotions—"

"Sir, give me some credit for dealing with that kind of man!" she cried, angry that he wouldn't acknowledge the fact she had been doing just that for years.

"I have credited you with the good intelligence to recognize that kind of man, and you've conducted yourself admirably since you've graduated from school. I was, however, worried while you were in America. Fortunately, you formed no serious attachments . . ."

"How do you know I formed no serious attachments, Father?" she interrupted with astonishment. To her knowledge, he had received only her marks from school and her address but knew nothing else about her life in America.

"You spied on me?" she cried, jumping to her feet, her face accusing and very angry.

"Really, Caroline, there isn't any reason for this outburst." His voice was low and slashing at her unexpected outcry.

"Outburst? I'm mad as hell!" she shrieked at him.

"I'm your father, and as such responsible for your conduct," he stated firmly, as though it were perfectly natural to have his daughter watched.

"What a fool I've been! Pretending I was on my own and free! All the while you've had me on a long leash!" she cried, raising her voice to him for the first time in her life.

"Caroline, that's quite enough. It's obvious that you are much too upset to continue this discussion. I will speak to you at lunch, after you have regained your composure." His voice was icy as he closed the door behind him and left her sputtering in hopeless rage.

She stomped around the room hurtling pillows in fury and frustration at her father and at herself for being so naïve. Was she going to be pampered and protected all her life? Kept on a jeweled leash? Would she ever be allowed to live her own life?

Not while she lived in the Earl of Conal's shadow! Not while she accepted all the fringe benefits of being Lady Caroline—the lavish allowance, clothes, cars and the deference due her lofty position. It was time she started a life of her own! Today!

"I'll leave!" she decided, her usual conservative nature overruled for once by an impulse to change her life, to stop being her father's daughter and start becoming her own person. She would call the airport and book a seat on an airplane home to England. She had a small trust fund from her mother's family, which she could survive on until she was able to put her education in business administration to good use. If there wasn't a company brave enough in England to employ the Earl of Conal's daughter, she would go back to America, where such prejudices were not even given a second thought. If need be, she would take her mother's maiden name, McPherson. The name would fit well among the melting pot ancestry of America's citizens. She could even alter her British accent to a fair imitation of her former New England classmates.

With each plus in her favor she began to form a stronger plan. She would go to Wales and Conal Keep, open the dusty trunk that held the name of the agents who administered the trust she had never

needed—until now. She would seek an anonymous
solicitor to send monthly checks to her in America
until she became established in her own right. By the
time her father had traced the money to the solicitor,
she would be independent and safe from his smothering tentacles.

The excitement of the challenge began to take
hold. She picked up the ship to shore telephone to
call the airport, then put it down remembering that
every call going off the yacht went through her
father or Jean Starr. She would have to go ashore to
arrange her travel.

She went to the chest of drawers, removed some
lacy underthings and put them on her slim body.
Hurriedly, she went into the bathroom and dried her
hair without styling it. She returned to the bedroom
closet and grabbed the first outfit in her wardrobe
that came to hand, a white linen skirt, red raw-silk
blouse and navy blazer. She pulled them on without
really seeing them or caring about her appearance;
now that she had reached her decision, she was
impatient to carry it out.

She took a quick look in the mirror. The results
weren't exactly pleasing. No makeup. Her hair hung
in limp waves and her face was taut with nerves. She
wound her hair into a careless knot on top of her
head, thrust a few hairpins into it, and then mashed
a wide-brimmed white straw sunhat over the whole
thing. Only a few errant untameable strands hung
beguilingly around her face. She applied a wisp of
red lip gloss and put on a pair of sunglasses. She
started through the door, then remembered she
hadn't put on shoes. Since she'd moved aboard she
had rarely worn shoes, as there had been no need.

She dug into the dark recesses of the wardrobe until she found a pair of white pumps. She stepped into them; the three inches added to her height would give her an imposing appearance which sometimes intimidated the people she encountered. She fervently hoped it would have that effect on her father's crew when she gave the order to take her ashore.

She removed her passport and health certificates from the top drawer of the dresser where she had put them after the customs officers had come aboard yesterday to inspect them. She opened her handbag and put them in. Checking her funds, she realized that she had less than a thousand dollars—not nearly enough to get her home. She couldn't ask her father for money. She wouldn't! She crammed her jewelry into the handbag. She didn't stop to think that it was her father who had given her most of the jewelry.

She left the cabin and strode purposefully toward a crewman working near the launch. In a voice with just the right degree of authority she said, "I want to go ashore to do some shopping. Would you lower the launch please?"

"Of course, Lady Caroline," he responded instantly and moved quickly to do her bidding.

"Where are you going, Caroline?" came the question from behind her.

She whirled around to face her father. Had she not taken the precaution of hiding her face with the hat and sunglasses, her guilty eyes would have betrayed her without her having uttered a single word.

"Where are you going, Caroline?" he repeated in a firmer voice when she hadn't answered.

"Ashore to shop. I inspected my dinner gowns

24

and I have nothing suitable for tonight. You didn't say it was a special occasion, but I gathered from your attitude that this dinner party might be somewhat different than those we've had in the past." She realized she was running on needlessly to hide her nervousness.

He ignored her comments on the party and answered, "You'll have to wait until after lunch to use the launch. Jean will be needing it in a few minutes to go ashore to meet the man I spoke of earlier."

"Couldn't I go ashore with her?" she asked with a calm she didn't sincerely feel.

"Not until I've had the opportunity to speak to you." His voice was cold as steel.

"I think you and I have said . . ." she began, as fresh anger washed over her. But her determination to get away without arousing his suspicions made her squelch the rest of her sharp retort. She answered meekly, "Yes, sir."

"Tim, have luncheon served in my study. This way, Caroline."

The room was entirely functional, which told of Robert's character. In one corner stood an ebony desk. A raised lip around its curved edge prevented the two radiotelephones, dictation machine and several stacks of papers from sliding off in heavy seas. On the opposite side of the room was Miss Starr's desk. It was a mirror image of his with the exception of a typing table on which stood an electric typewriter. The telex machine behind Robert's desk, which usually chattered away, was silent. There was a small table with two chairs for dining while working. Two brown, velvet tub chairs were the only concession to comfort in the room. Even the hardwood deck underfoot was stark and bare of rugs. On the paneled walls were several Flemish paintings of the fifteenth and sixteenth centuries, Robert's only indulgence in life.

Caroline took off her sunglasses and drew off her hat slowly as she dropped her lithe form into one of the brown chairs. She carefully tucked her bulging handbag into the crown of the hat. She tried to appear careless, relaxed and unconcerned on the outside, while on the inside her stomach was knotted in fear and anxiety. She cautioned herself over and over to remain calm and keep her conversation limited to the facts instead of telling elaborate stories she could trip herself up on.

Robert moved with effortless grace to his desk, picking up the black telephone receiver. This instrument was used for intraship communication; the other, a red telephone, was his ship to shore radiophone. Caroline heard Jean's voice answer the bell at the other end.

"Jean, the launch is ready. A limousine is waiting for you on the dock. It shouldn't be too long a wait for Edward at the airport. He's been through customs in Honolulu and his airplane is a private charter which will eliminate groveling around for his baggage." There was a long pause, then, "Yes, she is here with me now. Jean, I am going to tell her now." He glanced at Caroline; a trace of annoyance was on his austere features and a little light of anger flickered in his blue eyes.

Caroline could hardly believe that her father was receiving a dressing down from his secretary. Had she been drastically wrong about her opinion of the meek, mild-mannered Jean Starr? She could see

Robert's anger building and it surprised her that he could feel this strongly. As far as Caroline had observed, he had always used Jean in the same emotionless manner he used the telephone or dictation machine. She was just another extension of his work. And most confusing of all to Caroline was that this disagreement had to do with her. What could she have possibly done to cause this strife between them? Her plan of leaving wasn't more than an hour old. Neither could have found her out already!

"Good-bye." The curt ending to the veiled conversation brought her back from her wild guilt-ridden speculations. Her firm chin tilted in defiance. The hazy blue color of her eyes remained neutral, but threatened to turn to green and betray her anger at any provocation on his part.

"Caroline, a matter of great importance . . ." A tap at the door interrupted his words. "Come in," he said impatiently.

Tim came in and in less than two minutes deftly set lunch for two on the table, complete with crisp white linens, gleaming silver and crystal. Robert turned back from the porthole where he was standing and dismissed the man. "Thank you, we'll serve ourselves."

The man withdrew. Together, father and daughter, awkward, angry and proud, approached a luncheon that would have equaled any dining establishment in the world. A salad containing several varieties of lettuce, raw mushrooms and fresh shrimp was followed by a light fluffy spinach omelet with fresh asparagus on the side, hollandaise sauce and crusty French rolls with avocado butter. A delicate, delicious white wine accompanied the meal. But in spite of the efforts of Robert's chef, neither father nor daughter managed to eat much.

Afterward the two of them moved back to relax in the easy chairs, although to Caroline they felt as hard as the cold marble bench in the office of the headmistress of Miss Calvert's, where students waited to be reprimanded for some minor infraction of the school rules. A swiftly moving anger rushed over her at Robert for being able to create this situation. She was on the defensive and he, naturally, was the far superior of the two at this form of baiting. She wasn't his daughter for nothing; her chin came up, she stiffened her back, and her nimble mind raced in readiness to parry any thrust he could make at her. Instead he turned to face her with a look which Caroline could only translate as a plea to hear his words with understanding.

"Caroline, this morning I was perhaps offensive. It wasn't my intention to upset you. I didn't have you spied upon in America. I merely inquired about you from friends who had met you or had children at the same college. And for their pains of speaking about you to me, I'm afraid they had to suffer my rather boorish tales of your brilliant marks, acceptance onto the debating team, your sorority; things I had learned from your reports and your school newspaper."

"You boasted of me?" she squeaked out in a small emotion-filled voice. She was stunned by this totally spontaneous admission of paternal pride. It disarmed her and left her vulnerable.

"Caroline, I am very proud of you. I know I haven't been exactly a model father, something Jean hastens to point out to me." He paused, then frowned at his own mention of the woman who of late had been asserting herself in a way he found disturbing.

"I know your life has been too busy to include a bothersome child, but I *am* grown now, Father. If we could be friends . . . I studied business with the hope that one day you would. . . ." She stopped. Never had she admitted, even to herself, that her motives for her course of study had been to please him.

"The world of business is not for you, Caroline," he said firmly.

"But Father, there are many women in your business," she protested.

"Your future doesn't hold a career. With your loving, giving nature you would hand the profits away in a minute." He smiled at her, taking away the firmness of his words.

"How do you know I'm loving and giving?" she countered, disarmed by his smile. Her hopes were soaring, perhaps she could convince him. Although he was right, she did have a wide streak of generosity, but as far as love was concerned she had yet to suffer more than a mild crush in her relationships with men.

"You're like your mother," he answered simply.

"My mother? Please, oh please, Father, tell me about her," Caroline begged, rushing into the forbidden subject he had suddenly mentioned after all these years.

He began slowly, gathering the tale of his love. "I was a hellion in my twenties, what with women, gambling, running with a wild crowd. Your grandfather Conal called me a thoughtless rake. When he sought to tame me with a firm hand, I rebelled. He banished me, as the first Earls of Conal had done with their unruly sons. But there weren't any crusades to send me off to. I was sent to Scotland, to the estate of Laird Dougal McPherson who was my father's chief of operations in Scotland.

"Your mother was away at school for the first few months I was there. Your grandfather McPherson was very strong on education. She was his only remaining child; her brothers Hugh and young Dougal had been killed during the war in Africa. They fought against Rommel and were decorated several times over for their heroism."

"What happened when mother came home from school?" she asked.

He laughed at her dreamy face. His eyes were dancing as he said, "You think she fell immediately into my waiting arms, don't you?"

"I would have!" she answered truthfully.

His smile faded and he said in a husky voice, "Thank you, sweetheart."

"Well, what did happen?" she urged.

"She couldn't stand the sight of me!"

"What?" she cried disbelieving. He was still wonderfully handsome—what had he been then? And after having witnessed his personal charm, how could her mother have resisted him?

"It's true. I, in turn, was completely knocked over. You have only to look in the mirror to know what she looked like. She wasn't tall, as you are, but in every other way you are the same. Every time I spoke to her, she would upbraid me over the lifestyle I led. After a deep searching of myself, I decided I loved her and would change if that's what it would take to win her. I went home to England and assumed my responsibilities. My father, knowing that I had changed because of her, invited her and her father to Wales for a summer holiday. After some fancy talking on my part, she admitted that she loved me. We were married over the protests of her father and to the delight of mine. When you came, everything seemed complete. The rest you know. She died in childbirth, although I pleaded with her not to risk it again."

All her life she had blamed him for wanting a precious heir to the Earldom of Conal Keep. How wrong she had been! Caroline understood so much now. Why he had buried himself in work. Why all the traces of Lady Anne were gone. The memories were too painful. Had she been one of those reminders? She gathered her courage and asked, "Why did you send me away to boarding school? Because I look like she did?"

"No!" he exploded. His eyes silently but deeply searched the face that couldn't conceal the resentment and confusion she had felt all these years.

"I didn't feel I could give you a proper home. I didn't want you to be lonely, as I was. I sent you where you would have children to grow up with." Seeing the pain in her face his voice faltered. "Was I wrong?"

"I thought you didn't want me," she whispered brokenly. It was a painful revelation of her soul and a total release of the protective defense she had spent years building around herself. She was placing her heart in his hands.

And he responded, "Want you? Of course I wanted you. I love you. I tried very hard to give you the best."

"Why couldn't you have told me these things long ago?" she asked, with the impatience of youth.

"I don't have an answer, Caroline." He shook his head and looked at her with eyes filled with pain, realizing that he had caused her hurt.

Filled with compassion for his grief she got to her feet, her arms outstretched to him. At her movement he stood too. He put his hand out and she accepted it. He hesitated a moment, then hugged her to him, holding her tightly in his arms.

For the next hour, father and daughter asked questions of each other and tried to bridge the gap of years they had been strangers to one another. It wasn't until a discreet knock at the door brought them back from this mutual journey of exploration that they realized the time.

"Come in," called Robert.

The door opened to admit Jean Starr. She smiled at Caroline, although her liquid brown eyes were pitiful. When Caroline flashed a wide, bubbly smile, Jean frowned. Jean's puzzled eyes flew to Robert's. Out of the corner of her eye Caroline saw her father's silver head move imperceptibly negatively. Incredibly, Caroline saw the puzzlement on Jean's face dissolve into sparks of anger and a readiness to begin an argument. Jean suppressed her words, but her face was accusing as she said in stilted, clipped tones, "My Lord, Edward Ashford has been shown to the forward guest cabin. Will there be anything else?"

"Thank you, Miss Starr," he replied, his words as stilted as hers. "Yes, there is something else. Caroline wishes to go ashore to shop . . ."

"To shop?" Caroline interrupted. She had completely forgotten her earlier declaration and her elaborate plan for flight from her father. Just hours ago she had held him in the highest contempt and had labeled him a tyrant when he was only looking out for her interests! Her plan had now drastically changed. She wanted to stay near him and allow a normal father and daughter relationship to flower and grow between them.

"Caroline?" His voice cut through her thoughts.

"What, Father?" She smiled at him. "I'm sorry, I was wool gathering."

"Have you changed your mind?"

"No, I'd like to shop," she answered him truthfully.

"Good. I want you to accompany her ashore, Miss Starr." His voice lacked the emotion he had shown minutes before with his daughter. He was once again in complete control. The only sign of emotion was the tiny flame of anger burning in his blue eyes as he looked at Jean.

"My Lord, I have several last-minute details and plans to see to for tonight's dinner."

Caroline rushed forward to put her arm around the woman. Caroline cajoled, "Please come with me, Jean."

"I . . ." began Jean, clearly surprised at Caroline's display of affection.

"I need your help," pleaded Caroline.

Jean's eyes studied the excited, flushed face of the

young woman beside her. She felt her heart tighten, knowing the resounding thump in store for her, and suddenly wanted to protect and shield her.

"Please, Jean." Caroline appealed with her beautiful eyes.

"Very well, Lady Caroline," she agreed. Her eyes slid to Robert, the cold anger she felt against him shining in them. He returned her emotion in full silent measure.

In Caroline's present state, she didn't see this mutual anger; if she had, perhaps she would have realized she was the object of their anger. She remained blissfully ignorant of the impending dilemma.

The launch sliced through the sparkling waters of Hilo Bay. The girl at the wheel laughed with pure pleasure at the speed and power of the craft. She was oblivious to the powerful white rushing wake the launch created, jostling the small boats anchored nearby. She didn't even notice the ketch with the yellow hull that bounced on their wake like a cork on turbulent seas, or the skipper whose curses at her retreating cloud of golden red hair couldn't be heard above the throb of hundreds of horsepower.

In the seat beside her, Jean was clearly terrified. Her sable tresses came loose from their usual restraints and blew out around her face in wild disarray. Not a hand was raised in vanity to pull them into place because those hands were too occupied gripping the chrome handle in front of her on the bulkhead of the boat.

Caroline cut the power and instantly the launch slowed; by the time they reached the dock, they had to rely on the ocean's small swells to give them the necessary motion to glide into the slip Robert had rented at the public wharf.

As Jean began to rewind her hair, Caroline cried, "No, don't. Just for today, leave it loose! It's so beautiful, Jean. Just brush it."

The woman looked exasperated and grumbled, "All right. I probably couldn't find enough pins to do it up again anyway."

"Good! Let's shop our brains out! Father gave me tons of money!" she said in exuberance, linking her arm in Jean's and tugging her along faster.

Caroline looked carefree with her windblown hair, a glorious aureole around her smiling face. She hadn't changed from the clothes she had hastily pulled on this morning, but had discarded the navy blazer and sunhat, leaving only the white skirt and vivid, scarlet silk blouse.

Jean couldn't help but be drawn into her high spirits, even though she knew a black, threatening cloud was on the horizon. But for the moment she put aside her anger at Robert and joined Caroline's youthful fun.

Caroline tried on several gowns and finally settled on a dramatic, royal purple silk with a tight-fitting bodice covered with thousands of rhinestone sequins. She purchased an elegant pair of velvet dinner shoes with the highest heels she had ever worn, and a small, matching black velvet clutch bag to complete the outfit.

Caroline convinced Jean, who was still in a slightly angry and defiant mood, to try on a cardinal red, clinging jersey dress. Her full breasts and creamy arms were perfectly complemented by the plunging vee-shaped bodice and narrow shoulder straps, as were her shapely legs by the bold slit up the left front of the garment. It was a vast departure from her usual dinner dress of long black skirts and prim and proper white blouses with high lace collars.

"Jean! You are absolutely stunning," cried Caroline. "Tonight you will have legions of men vying for your favors!"

"No, I won't, Lady Caroline, because I can't purchase it." She started to remove the dress.

"Please call me plain Caroline. Now let me see it again," she pleaded, then a shrew look came on her face as she said, "You're probably right, Jean, father would be furious if you turned up in that dress and stole his thunder."

"Stole his thunder?" she asked in puzzlement.

"It's an American term for upstage."

"He would be angry, wouldn't he?" she answered. Her face was suddenly tight, and she said in a firm voice, "All right, I will take it . . . and some new accessories too."

"Wonderful!" exclaimed Caroline. She hadn't for one moment thought her father would be angry—stunned, maybe, but not angry. She hoped this dress would make him take notice of what a lovely woman Jean was and hopefully spark his interest.

After Jean had taken the first step and actually bought the red dress, Caroline had been able to wedge away some of her reluctance to build a new and different wardrobe. Several blouses of bright solids and prints along with slacks of white, summer checks and even two pairs of denim jeans were added to their parcels. Finally, Jean consented to buy a lovely ice blue, one-piece swimsuit with a bold white stripe running diagonally up the front, but that was the end of Caroline's success as Jean's Pygmalion. The older woman was frankly a little dazed at herself for these purchases and called a halt before her savings of a lifetime were completely flat.

The sun was low in the sky over the emerald green island, touching everything with mauve loveliness as they made their way along the sidewalk beside the seawall where a taxi had deposited them after a hair-raising ride through the evening traffic. The two women struggled with the boxes and bags as neither could see very well over them. Suddenly, Caroline crashed into the solid wall of a man's chest, and losing her packages, she tumbled to the pavement. The second time in one day!

She cursed, "Oh bloody hell!"

A huge brown hand reached down to her, and she accepted it without thinking or looking at its owner. She felt the strong arm attached to the hand effortlessly draw her to her feet. The forward momentum she had gained propelled her again into the chest which had upset her in the first place. Her eyes traveled upward noting the expensive, hand-embroidered, linen peasant shirt, the black wiry chest hairs exposed by the deep vee-neck of the shirt, a small gold medal nestled among them. When her eyes reached the strong brown neck and firm chin she was about to deliver some well-chosen words on watching where one was going. The words were frozen in her throat, murdered effectively by a pair of sea green eyes framed in thick inky lashes.

"You . . . you!" she managed to stammer, her face flushing to the roots of her flaming hair. Her eyes narrowed into hard chips of angry green.

"You do seem to have a penchant for falling down, don't you, ma'am? Does this happen all the time?" drawled the deep, familiar voice above her.

He still held her close to his hard muscular body. Through the thin silk of her blouse and the gauzy linen of his shirt, she could feel the warmth of his skin and the slow rise and fall of his breathing. Caroline's heart was racing, her breath short and irregular. She felt part of him! A shiver of shock at his nearness raced up her spine, just as it had this morning when only his eyes had touched her. She stepped away from him in panic and stumbled over a shoe box. A strong arm shot out to steady her; then as quickly as it had righted her, it dropped away.

She couldn't suppress a racing thought. Had she really wanted his touch to end? A myriad of uncontrollable, imaginary curiosities presented themselves to her disorderly mind: his lips full and soft against her own, his strong arms holding her close to his long body. He was the first man who had ever made her feel small and feminine. Instantly she remembered that her body had fit perfectly to his, thigh to thigh, breast to hard chest, her face even with his throat. She had only to tip back her head to allow their lips to meet. Her face burning at these thoughts, she mumbled, "Oh, my God!" as she stooped down and began stacking her scattered parcels together.

"Here, let me help you, ma'am," the deep voice drawled solicitously. He knelt down and gathered her bundles into a neat stack, then lifted them and himself to his lofty six-foot-plus height.

Seeing the laughter in his eyes, Caroline found her tongue. "Thank you, I'll take them now."

She put out her arms for the packages, but he ignored her and smiled slowly into her face, his white teeth bright against his sun-darkened face. The image of him as a pirate appeared in her mind.

"Allow me to escort you ladies to your launch. I believe I remember it, in fact I'm now docked next to it." His voice fairly oozed with charm as he spoke directly to Jean, ignoring Caroline's fuming face.

Caroline had completely forgotten Jean until he spoke. She turned to look at Jean who had observed the exchange between the two of them with interest. She couldn't decide if Caroline and this handsome stranger were friends or combatants in a private war.

"No!" exclaimed Caroline when the tall figure turned in the direction of the dock.

He stopped and turned back to face her, an impatient frown creasing his forehead between his thick, dark brows. With patience that didn't show on his handsome face, he said, "Come on and be a good girl. You can't negotiate the careful footing of the wharf with these bundles. Besides, Miss Bumblefoot, I don't relish the idea of having to fish you out of the bay! I'm in a hurry and in my best clothes to boot!"

"Why you . . ."

"Careful, or I'll change my opinion of you being a lady."

"You needn't be concerned! I can walk, and should the need arise, I can also swim quite well, thank you!" she said coldly. The rage of her humiliation from the morning was now boiling within her.

He didn't respond to her verbal challenge, but instead stepped lightly over the seawall, forcing her to follow him and Jean. She stared in silent loathing at the broad back into which she could have, at this moment, cheerfully put a knife!

After helping Jean over the side of the launch, he slowly handed her all the packages, one by one. Caroline wanted to scream, Hurry up for pity's sake, at his smiling face.

At last he turned to her, hands on narrow hips, a challenging look in his light eyes now. It was so unbending it suddenly made her want to quake in fright! She offered none of the resistance she had planned, instead meekly accepted the hand he offered and allowed him to help her into the bobbing craft.

He clicked the heels of his hand-sewn sandals and bowed mockingly to her as he had this morning. The stiff smile on her face faded, and she hurriedly turned the key in the ignition and was visibly relieved when the engine roared to life.

Slowly and with extreme care she maneuvered the launch out of the slip and past the ketch in the next slip. She noted the bold black script on the yellow hull, *Sunflower.* Somehow she would have thought his boat would have a more provocative name than *Sunflower,* something like *Restless Wind, Wanton Lady,* or *Rogue's Desire . . .*

"Caroline?"

Jean brought her back from her silly musings. Her voice was strangely husky, her emotions tangled between curiosity and anger as she answered. "Yes?"

"What's his name?"

"Jake," she repeated the name she had heard the boy call him this morning. Her hand and elbow still tingled where his hands had held her when he helped her into the launch. Why did he, a total stranger, have this power over her?

"Have you known him long?" Jean asked gently. It was plain that Caroline had been deeply disturbed at his sudden appearance. Had there been a tempestuous love between them in the past?

"I don't know him at all," she answered curtly.

Wisely, Jean didn't pursue the matter. They rode the rest of the way back to the yacht in silence, each woman in deep thought, but each thinking of the same subject—the man, Jake.

Chapter Two

Caroline dressed hurriedly but with immaculate care. She brushed her hair until the long golden red lengths gleamed. A single gold chain with a large teardrop diamond encircled one slender arm. With one last check in the mirror, she quickly moved along to Jean's cabin. Caroline wasn't about to let her back down from wearing the new red gown.

"Enter," was the light reply to her tap on the door.

Jean stood before the mirror with a frown of consternation on her lovely face. She wasn't sure she should wear this dress or her hair up in the high crown of curls that Caroline had put it in earlier.

"Oh, Jean, you look so beautiful, and I don't know . . . serene. Yes, you look gorgeous!" breathed Caroline.

"I don't feel serene," Jean snapped back, then she

smiled half-heartedly and added, "I'm sorry, Caroline, I don't know what's come over me lately."

"Jean, I . . . well . . . I don't know how to ask this, but is it because you love my father?"

The deep silence that followed caused both women to shift nervously. The shock on Jean's face told Caroline she was right. Jean did love Robert but perhaps hadn't faced the fact until now. Caroline rushed into the silence. "I'm sorry, Jean, I had no right to ask you something so personal."

"Is it as transparent as that? Does the whole world see it, but him?" she asked quietly. She had to know if people were feeling sorry for poor, dull Miss Starr, in love with Lord Robert, Earl of Conal Keep, millionaire industrialist, member of Her Majesty's court. Tears of shame trembled on her jet black lashes. She could barely see Robert's lovely daughter cross the room and put her arms about her.

"No, Jean, it's not transparent," she whispered. "If it were, the staff and father's business associates wouldn't hold you in such high esteem. Do you think that all these years when father paid court to one of his mistr—, lady friends, that they wouldn't have demanded your immediate resignation, if your love were that obvious?" She paused.

Neither of them knew how often Robert had stopped seeing a young lady who, in a fit of jealousy brought on by Robert's indifference, made the fatal error of accusing him of being interested in his personal aide.

"Jean, the only reason I guessed your secret is that I've always loved him from afar too! I wish he would open his eyes and recognize what a lucky man he is to be loved by you!"

The tears that had only threatened before fell now, causing Caroline to groan, "Why did I have to open my big mouth?"

"It's all right, love." Jean answered with fond affection. "Now help me out of this dress. I can't wear it."

"Please wear it, for me," pleaded Caroline. "If you don't, Jean, I'll feel badly all night because I upset you. Do you want me to die of guilt?" she cried dramatically.

"All right, you win, now run along while I finish dressing," Jean said, giving Caroline a watery smile.

Caroline turned from the door and asked, "By the way, Jean, what do you think of the mysterious cousin? I have yet to see him. He seems to be hiding in his cabin." She laughed at the notion of anyone hiding from her.

The smile froze on Jean's lips and pity rose into her eyes. She suddenly remembered the man, Jake. The thought that he and Caroline would make a striking pair came to mind. She was sure the attraction between the two of them was strong. Jean recognized that magical, rare instant of mutual attraction. Often born on a first encounter, it had happened to Jake and Caroline without either of them being aware of it!

"What is it, Jean?" asked Caroline, alarmed at the stricken look on her face.

"Nothing. I just remembered an important detail I have to discuss with your father about the party." There was indeed an important detail she had to discuss with Robert! She was going to do everything in her power to see to it that Caroline and this man Jake had every opportunity to discover if they had a future together. She would have Robert investigate this man, and if he passed the muster, Robert would have to find a way of bringing them together. After all, if he could move great conglomerates about with the ease of a chess master moving pieces about a board, he could arrange a little thing like this! If he could be talked out of Edward Ashford as a suitor. "If, if—damn," she said silently.

"Tonight, let's forget business and have fun, Jean! I'll see you soon, and if you have on one of those dreadful black skirt and white blouse uniforms, I'll jump overboard."

"Go away, Caroline, or I will change!" Jean laughed, her mind carefully composing the conversation she was about to undertake with the sixteenth Earl of Conal.

With a small laugh, Caroline left Jean's cabin. She was tempted to knock on her father's cabin door, but she wanted to surprise him with her own beautiful gown. She would make him proud tonight, by showing him she could be as savvy about business as any sharp young executive on his staff. In six months she would be working for him! She was determined to make herself indispensable to him. She would start tonight, while the guests at the party talked about business. In the past she had always been unwilling to listen, but now she would gather information and learn about Robert's business world.

Back in her cabin, her eyes fell on a pair of winking diamond drop earrings that would be perfect with Jean's outfit. Gathering them up she went back to Jean's cabin. There was no answer to her knock. She had turned to go when she heard Jean's voice coming from her father's cabin. She smiled to herself as she stepped across the narrow companion-way and pushed gently on the door that had been left slightly ajar. She was about to call to them, when Jean said, "But my Lord, you can't expect Caroline to calmly agree to a marriage with Edward Ashford simply because he'll inherit your title and Conal Keep!"

"Caroline's a sensible girl. I'm hoping an attraction will build between the two of them," he answered coldly.

"But you can't govern affairs of the heart, my Lord! I know that better than anyone!" Jean shot straight back at him, determined not to be bullied.

"You, a spinster? What do you know about the affairs of the heart, Miss Starr?" he returned cruelly.

"I know more than you will ever know, Robert Conal, you cold, calculating . . ." she raged, magnificently beautiful. Her face was alive with color; her soft body in the new gown demanding a response from him, as did the fierceness of her new spirit.

His anger was an all-consuming fire. He advanced on her, but she stood her ground. Then incredibly, Robert pulled her into his arms and kissed her passionately. The combination of anger and years of unleashed love overwhelmed her; she returned his embrace wholeheartedly.

At another time Caroline would have jumped for joy at this development between them, but now she just stood on the threshold of the cabin in stunned shock, their words replaying over and over in her mind.

Her father had arranged a marriage for her! And he had arranged it to keep the precious earldom in the immediate family. His title meant more to him than her happiness. What had all his declarations of love and affection meant this afternoon? Had he only said those things to soften her for this marriage contract? Had he really loved her mother? Or was that another garnish on the plate of lies he had fed her?

She fled to her cabin. What was she to do now? She sank onto her wide bed and tried to bring some order to her mind. She was strangely dry-eyed; not a single tear penetrated her shock. The cabin walls seemed to close in on her. She had to get out of here—away. Her plan of this morning came to mind. She would leave. She would escape her father's domineering scheme!

She went to the chest of drawers and with calm deliberance again stuffed all her jewelry into her small evening bag, along with her passport and health certificates. She groped in her closet for a wrap, feeling terribly cold and shaking with chills as her body reacted to her deep pain. She didn't even notice the white ermine cape she wrapped around her shoulders.

Her movements were mechanical as she left the cabin and made her way up to the deck, passing crewmen busy with the preparations of the dinner party.

"Excuse me, are you Lady Caroline?"

She looked at the man who had spoken to her. He was dressed in a white dinner jacket and black tie which didn't complement his sallow complexion. He was probably around forty years of age, but that was hard to determine; he probably had looked the same way at twenty. Caroline was several inches taller than him. His hair was a nondescript blond brown color. His eyes were watery blue buttons in a long, narrow, pinched face.

"Yes, I'm Lady Caroline. Who are you, sir?" she asked in return, already knowing the answer to her question. Tonight's guests had not yet arrived, and there was only one stranger aboard.

"I'm Sir Edward Ashford." His eyes swept up and down her body as though appraising her worth. Was he privy to her father's plan? Was he adding up in his mind how much he would ask Robert for his sacrifice in taking her as a bride?

"Excuse me, Mr. Ashford. I want to greet the launches as they arrive with our guests."

"Of course, my dear. And it's Sir Edward, not Mister," he amended with stuffiness.

She opened her mouth to tell him what a pompous ass he was but changed her mind. She didn't want to jeopardize her plans with a display of temper, regardless of the pleasure she would have derived by bringing him down a peg or two. Instead she hurried to the other side of the yacht where the first of the launches was arriving.

Jean had arranged for two launches, in addition to those of the *Caroline,* to bring the guests to and from the dock. The pilots were not regular crew members, so asking for a ride to the dock wouldn't cause undue speculation.

Her request was easily granted by a smiling pilot who tried to impress her with a display of speed enroute to the dock. Approaching the dock she saw several people awaiting their turn to board the launches going out to the *Caroline.* She kept her head down in the shadows and tried to go unnoticed. But as she backed into the darkness of the wharf, a small group of people approached her. She started violently when she heard a feminine voice call out, "Lady Caroline?"

She quickly stepped away from the voice of a rotund matron she had met in Hong Kong. As the woman persisted Caroline stepped onto the neighboring vessel and ducked into the dark cabin.

She heard the voice again and again, but in a few moments the engines roared as the launches pulled away from the dock and at last, silence. She let out the breath she had been holding with a whoosh . . . and then froze again as a sleepy, childish voice asked, "Jake? Is that you, Jake?"

"Oh no!" she breathed. In her panic to escape she had blundered aboard the *Sunflower!*

"Jake?" called the boy again.

She stood frozen, praying he would go back to sleep. He did not. She started when she heard his feet hit the deck somewhere behind her.

"Jake, I waited a long time. I was reading *Captains Courageous,* and I guess I fell asleep. Boy, am I hungry. Jake, can we have dinner now?—Jake?"

The lights blazed on in the cabin and Caroline was caught. She whirled around to face her captor.

"What are you doing here?" he demanded bravely. Then he recognized her. "It's you! The lady on the big yacht!"

"I'm sorry. I seem to have lost my way," she apologized.

His face was a mixture of delight and suspicion. "Where were you going?"

"I wanted to—" She hesitated, then decided to tell him only a half-truth. "I wanted to get away from the party on the yacht. I didn't feel like being charming tonight." She smiled at him; he was a very handsome boy.

"Oh—" His suspicion seemed to be melting. "Does Jake know you're here?"

"No," she said. At the mention of Jake's name, she realized she had better go before he returned. She wouldn't put it past a man like that to insist that he see her back to the yacht. She moved toward the stairs, saying, "I'll be leaving now."

His eyes suddenly changed from wariness to loneliness. "Don't go. Please, ma'am, stay—unless you're in a hurry or something."

His face was forlorn and appealing, and she couldn't say no to him. "I'm not in a hurry or something."

Then a reality came to her. She really wasn't in a hurry. Where could she go tonight? She would have to sell her jewels for airfare to England and she doubted if she could find a shop open tonight. And after her spending spree this afternoon, she didn't even have the money to stay in a hotel! It probably wasn't a good idea to go to a hotel anyway; her father would search the hotels first. She sighed aloud, drawing off her cape and putting it on the bench of the built-in dinette, next to the open *Captains Courageous*.

The boy gasped as the light struck the jewels about her throat and arms and on her long fingers, creating a million rainbows in the cabin. She was like a beautiful apparition out of a fairy tale.

A slow smile covered his stunned face as he drawled fervently, "You are beautiful, ma'am!"

"Thank you, kind sir," she answered with a small curtsy. She couldn't help but wonder where he had learned this charm—certainly not from that awful man Jake.

She looked around the saloon, surprised at the compact, utilitarian furnishings. There was an alcohol stove with an oven, a small refrigerator under the Formica counter top, a stainless steel sink and above all this was a row of lockers with a high sheen of lacquer over the beautiful light wood. The built-in dinette was slightly forward of the galley, the tabletop the same beautiful wood as the lockers. The cushions were covered in the same warm, sunny yellow fabric as the settee behind her. The saloon was a very homey place, not stark or spartan as she would have expected from the harsh Jake.

"Ma'am," the curious young voice brought her back from her musings.

"Yes?"

"What's your name?"

"Caroline. What's yours?" she countered.

"Hank St. Simon. Well really it's Henri, but Jake says that too many Henris in our family were nothing but failures. He says he will be damned if I'm going to end up a decadent sot." He smiled at her.

It was clear Jake's opinions were valued highly by young Master Hank. She did not reply to Jake's assessment of the Henris in the St. Simon family. She said instead, "Well, Master St. Simon, I believe you mentioned something about being hungry. If you know how to light the burners on the stove, I'll see what I can do about filling your stomach."

"I can light the stove, ma'am, but . . ." he said, doubtfully eyeing her gown with a dubious expression on his face.

"Please, Hank, call me Caroline. I understand

what you're trying to tell me," she said spreading the wide skirt of her gown. "This isn't exactly a cooking apron, but for the moment it's all I have."

Realizing that she hadn't been thinking very straight when she ran away in this gown, she made a mental note to purchase more suitable clothing after she sold her jewels. In this attire she would be spotted in a minute.

"Yes, ma—Caroline. You know, I think you could wear a pair of my big cutoffs, and Jake has some tee shirts that would fit, well, cover you anyway." He raced into the master cabin, not waiting for her to accept or refuse this offer.

Caroline couldn't suppress her curiosity to see the place where Jake St. Simon lived—and slept. Looking around the open door she could see two built-in berths; one was larger than the other perhaps to accommodate Jake's very large body. Suddenly she remembered the feel of being held against his large body. She blushed, then abruptly brought her thoughts back to the present. A chest of drawers was between the berths. The front panels had been ventilated to allow the moist sea air to circulate. She could see shelves, stacked high with books and a variety of other objects: pictures, a tape recorder, stacks of cassette tapes and a violin case. Somehow she couldn't imagine Jake playing the violin.

Hank found what he was looking for in the drawers and returned to the saloon holding a bold blue and gold striped rugby shirt. He opened another door on the portside of the boat opposite the kitchen. This was obviously his cabin.

He called, "Come in here, Caroline."

She complied. His cabin was a neat little apartment. A smoothly made bunk was built into the port bulkhead along with a wardrobe locker. Opposite was a dresser that Hank was now rifling through. Shelves circling the cabin held dozens of books, pictures of sports heroes and snapshots of people. An enlarged photo of a horse and a big burly dog stood in the place of honor over his pillow, along with a smaller photo of Jake, whose young, laughing face looked tenderly at the dark-haired beauty at his side. She felt a strange pain of jealousy at the sight of the happy couple. The reminder of Jake triggered a fear in her that he could return at any moment and find her here, uninvited and about to put on his clothes.

"Here you are, Caroline, freshly washed at the laundromat this evening," he said proudly, offering her the faded but clean denim garment.

"Thank you, Hank, but perhaps I'd better be leaving, your fath—" she paused, then corrected her assumption that Jake was Hank's father, "Jake wouldn't like a stranger crashing in on you, let alone borrowing your clothes and his."

"You promised you'd stay for dinner, and, Caroline, down home folks don't go back on their word," he drawled, with the unexpected charm and poise she found disarming in one so young.

"All right, Hank, but after dinner I'll be leaving," she compromised.

He smiled at her answer. His teeth were white in his darkly tanned face, another reminder of Jake's mocking, speculative smile on his dark face. After Hank left her in the cabin, she unfastened the dress and was dismayed when she remembered the bodice of the dress had required no bra. She had worn only a black silk slip to protect her skin from the sequins, but she couldn't wear that with cutoff pants and a tee shirt. She hoped Jake's shirt was loose fitting and was relieved to find it more than loose fitting, it was downright monstrous on her! But the cutoff pants were not. They were so snug they were molded to her bottom like a second skin. But as Hank had said, they were covering.

She rejoined Hank in the galley. In her absence he had lit the stove and was melting butter in a frying pan.

"How about eggs, Caroline?"

"That'll be just fine, but may I cook them for you?" she asked.

"Sure! Jake says I make the worst omelet he ever tasted, along with lots of other things I've cooked." He grinned, his brown eyes dancing with merriment.

"Do you do all the cooking?" she asked him with surprise. She took over the cooking expertly; one of the requirements for graduation from Miss Calvert's had been to learn the fundamentals of cooking and meal planning.

"No, we share all the duties," he replied, cracking the eggs in a bowl with the sure movements of one with plenty of practice. "Do you like mushrooms in your omelet? I love them in mine."

"Yes, I do," she answered with surprise. Master Hank was an amazing boy to have acquired a taste for a food such as mushrooms.

He opened a tin of mushrooms, drained off the water and set it on the counter. Next, he took a hunk of hard cheddar cheese out of the small refrigerator along with a large, red tomato, a tray of fresh pineapple wedges and a carton of milk.

"I sure do like being in port. Fresh milk, vegetables and cold soda."

"Don't you have those things while you're at sea?" she asked, puzzled.

"No!" He looked at her scornfully. "We don't run with motors like you do. We're under sail."

"But why can't you use the refrigerator?" she asked, not understanding what being under sail had to do with the refrigerator.

"Because it takes power to run it. We have to run it off the batteries, not off the engine like you do, and it puts a heavy strain on the batteries. And besides the refrigerator, we have to run the lights, the seawater converter, the motor for the water pressure system and the hot water heater . . ."

"Okay, okay, I understand now. Something has to go and the refrigerator is it." She laughed.

"It's worth it. There's nothing like cracking sail and running before the wind, or sailing against a wind that's holding you back from where you want to go." His face was so adult she couldn't help but wonder if he had ever been a child or if he was simply repeating the words of someone else—perhaps Jake? Jake seemed as mysterious as the sea; they were a good match.

"You really love it?" she asked doubtfully.

"Yep! So does Jake." Again, it was clear that Jake was the center of his young life.

Within minutes she had dished up a light, fluffy, mushroom and cheese omelet, with tomato slices, milk and the pineapple wedges for dessert. And surprisingly enough, with all the turmoil she had faced this evening, she ate every bite of her portion with relish; so did Hank.

"Now, let's clear this mess away and wash the dishes," she said. Earlier as she was cooking, the fullness of Jake's tee shirt had hampered her movements, so she had taken the left corner of the shirt and gathered the extra material into a knot at a rakish angle on her left hip. Her feminine form was now charmingly revealed as she moved around the galley, but the boy didn't notice what his sailing companion would have seen in an instant—she was a very desirable young woman.

"Hank?" she asked, her hands in the soapy dishwater.

"Yeah?" He was busily polishing the stove to the high sheen it had before they used it.

"Why aren't you in school?"

"Oh, I'm taking lessons. Jake's teaching me math —it's important for sailing—and he's teaching me English. I have to write a story of at least five pages every week. Sometimes it's hard to think of something to say. And Jake makes me read at least two books every week. I have to read one classic, like *Captains Courageous,* and then one of anything I want."

She studied him under her lashes as he hopped around the cabin putting dishes away and tidying up. He was probably about twelve years old, for all his apparent adultlike ways. His long, loose-limbed body already said he would be tall but not slightly built; he would have a well-muscled physique like Jake's. His hair was black, not the inky, flashing blue black of Jake's, but with sable brown hues. His skin was the same dark warm tan color of Jake's, as were his facial features: straight nose, strong arrogant chin, pleasing full curving lips. Hank's eyes were a melting chocolate brown, whereas Jake's were light, raking, caressing—she shivered at the memory of them on her body. She remembered his hard body against her own this afternoon and another shiver raced over her. Why did he have this power over her? If she wanted to avoid another meeting with him at all costs, she had to leave, immediately!

"Hank?"

"Yes?"

"I'd better leave now. Thank you for the wonderful meal and your company. I'll go and change back into my own clothes now. Thank you for lending me these."

"Lady Caroline? Lady Caroline?" came the searching call of one of her father's crewmen.

She froze in terror. She looked wildly around for an avenue of escape, but the only one open to her was blocked by the crewman. She looked at the boy who instantly understood that she was in some kind of trouble. He quickly turned off half the cabin lights, took down a book from the shelf above the settee, opened it, and laid it on the cushion where it appeared he had just put it down. He opened the door to his cabin and with a jerk of his head signaled silently for her to go into his cabin and hide.

She hesitated, not wanting to drag him into her trouble. Her father could make anyone's life miserable—even a young boy's. A heavy rapping on the deck overhead swept away any doubts and propelled her into the cabin. The door closed quickly but silently behind her.

"Is there anyone aboard?" came a loud question. It was the voice of her father! She almost gasped as the door she had been staring at in terror opened.

Her white ermine cape flew in and landed at her feet in a silent heap. She made no move to pick it up but stood frozen, listening.

"Yeah?" Hank yelled, using a more childish voice than she had heard earlier.

There was another rap over head. Hank answered, "Whatda' ya' want?"

"Where are you?" demanded her father.

"Below. Just a minute, I'll come up. What do you want, sir?" Hank's voice was filled with bravado.

Caroline realized her father was standing in the saloon just beyond the thin flimsy protection of Hank's cabin door.

"Please excuse me, young man, for coming aboard without your permission, but something distressing has happened. A young lady of my party has become lost. By any chance have you seen her tonight?"

Caroline almost laughed hysterically. Even in his presumably distressed state, he politely apologized, and in a calm, uncaring voice named her only as a young lady of his party, not his daughter, or even a human being; just a minor annoyance who had interrupted his dinner party.

"No, sir, I haven't seen anyone this evening." Hank drawled, unshakeable firmness in his young voice.

"What's going on here?" asked a new, but all-too-familiar, voice.

"Jake!" croaked Hank; his unshakeable cool sounded as if it had deserted him now that Jake was on the scene. Caroline sighed softly; her refuge was over. She put her hand out to open the door.

Jake's question halted her. "What's going on here?"

58

"A young lady of my party, off the yacht *Caroline*, has lost her way and I've raised a search. I was asking your son if he had seen her," explained Robert.

Caroline could tell by the tone in Robert's voice that he had taken an instant dislike to Jake and, for the first time since their meeting this morning, she found herself on Jake's side. Her father hadn't the right to become imperious and high-handed with a total stranger, especially this American who wasn't accustomed to the Earl of Conal's way of interrogating people.

But if she thought Jake would be intimidated at Robert's cool, condescending attitude, she was mistaken. Jake's voice was just as imperious as he asked, "And what was the boy's answer?"

"He has answered in the negative." Robert's tone of voice cast doubt on Hank's truth-telling.

"I said, no, I haven't seen her, Jake." Hank interposed eagerly. Caroline could hear the over-enthusiasm in his voice. She cringed inside; Robert would instantly pick this clue up!

"You heard him. Now, sir, if you'll excuse us?" Jake's voice was soft but laced with the steel that indicated there would be no further discussion on the matter.

Robert said, "Pardon me, but earlier this evening a dinner guest of mine saw the young lady we are seeking go aboard a boat on this dock . . ."

"Hank's been here since this afternoon, and he says he hasn't seen her. I suggest you check with the skippers of the other vessels on this dock." Jake's voice was still soft, but now there was the barest hint of assertion in it.

"I shall! Thank you for your help." Robert's answer was curt with clipped anger.

Caroline heard the retreating steps on the deck overhead, then felt the *Sunflower* rock slightly as Robert stepped off the deck and onto the dock. A feeling of relief flooded her body, then as fast as the relief came it was gone, as she realized Jake had her as trapped as her father! She had wanted to avoid another meeting with Jake at all costs. Now she was in the perilous position of certain discovery in addition to the wrath he would shed on her for causing Hank to lie for her. She couldn't decide which was worse, facing her father or Jake! She prayed Hank wouldn't give her away in deed or word so that she could sneak off the *Sunflower* after Jake had gone to sleep.

"Hank?" She jumped at the deep voice.

"Yeah?" mumbled Hank.

"You don't know anything about that girl, do you?" came the question Caroline dreaded. Could he tell his beloved Jake a lie?

"Jake, I don't know a darn thing about that girl," he answered defensively. It was a thinly disguised fib; Hank really didn't know anything about her other than her first name. He had been content to ask only her name. She had asked all the questions.

"All right, Hank," Jake answered quietly. There was a long silence of several minutes and, had Caroline seen Jake's face as he picked up the open copy of *Blackstone's Commentaries on the Laws of England*, she would have come out of hiding and taken her chances with Jake, but she only heard him ask, "Have you eaten?"

"Yes. I had some eggs and pineapple," he answered.

Caroline could hear the edginess in his voice and was afraid Jake would begin to connect the stress in Hank's voice with her, but Jake interpreted Hank's mood entirely differently.

"Hank, I'm sorry I was ashore so long. I had to make several calls to the States and there is a five-hour time difference between here and New Orleans."

"Did you talk to *grand-mère?*" he asked Jake, eagerness pushing out the petulant tone in his voice.

"Yes, she sends you her birthday congratulations for next month and says she is airmailing you a surprise. It should be on Truk when we arrive."

"Terrific!" cried Hank.

Caroline's legs were beginning to ache from standing in one spot. She stiffly eased herself onto the edge of the bunk. She heard pots and pans begin to bang and lockers open and shut. Jake was preparing his own dinner. She couldn't sit like this for hours! She gently rolled onto her side, swung her tired legs off the deck and, lying back, settled herself in for a long wait.

She came fully awake with a scream which was stifled by warm fingers pressed against her open mouth. She saw Hank's worried young face above her. She opened her mouth to speak, but he shook his head vehemently and pointed up toward the deck. Suddenly everything came into focus for her. It was daylight! The sun was high in the sky and something else was different too. But what?

Then in a sickening revelation she knew—the *Sunflower* was at sea! The gentle rise and fall of the harbor had given way to the moderate pitch and roll of the open sea. Panic consumed her. What was she going to do? She was a stowaway! A stowaway on a small ketch bound for . . . for where? She didn't even know where the *Sunflower* was headed!

She rolled to her feet and stared at the young boy, as if he could automatically give her the answers she sought and calm her churning fears. But Hank just offered her some pilfered food from under his shirt, his eyes begging her not to speak or raise an alarm that would alert Jake.

She acknowledged him with a small nod of her head. He handed her a scrap of paper on which he had written a note, "I'll be back soon and bring the tape recorder with music to drown out our talking." He had added, "Do you have to use the head?" She nodded yes.

He whispered through clenched teeth, "Go when you hear Jake and me talking topside."

Then he was gone. Moments later she heard him talking to Jake in what seemed like an unnaturally loud voice. She quickly crept out of the cabin and into the head. She hurriedly splashed water on her face and scurried back to Hank's cabin, although she probably could have taken her time because she could hear Hank firing loud questions at Jake. The answers came back in one-syllable grunts. Among Hank's many treasures she saw a hair brush. She removed it from the drawer, then moved away from the cabin's skylight into a blind corner and began to brush her long tangled hair.

How she wished she could brush away the snarled

thoughts that crowded her brain as easily as she could the snarls in her hair. Jake St. Simon was not the kind of man that would take lightly her sudden materialization aboard his boat in the middle of the Pacific Ocean! He was going to be very angry at the thought of the time wasted taking her back to Hilo.

Back to Hilo! That meant her father and Edward Ashford. Even those two seemed tame compared with the dark foreboding figure of Jake St. Simon. Suddenly she heard the sound of heavier footsteps approaching the cabin. She panicked when she heard them move closer to the door. For an instant she almost tried to conceal herself in the wardrobe locker. Her gown, cape, evening shoes and bulging handbag lay at the foot of the bunk directly in the line of sight of anyone opening the door. There wasn't any point in hiding herself. Instead she stood still and prayed the door wouldn't open.

Several seconds elapsed. She heard his deep, soft slurring voice call out to Hank, who must have still been topside. "Hold her steady into the wind, boy. It's a good steady push today. Later we'll break out the spinnaker and make some real distance."

"Okay," cried a nervous Hank.

Caroline was amazed at the change in the sound of Jake's voice; it was carefree and light. She could almost swear she even heard a smile in it. Her spirits suddenly took flight; perhaps she had misjudged him. Would he understand her leaving her father to be free from his smothering protection and a forced marriage in the name of heritage? Would he forgive Hank's deception? And would he forgive her for hiding behind a twelve-year-old boy's fascination with her?

As these thoughts formed in her mind, his image came before her brain, his broad shoulders in the gauzy peasant shirt, his narrow hips in tight Levi's, the black crisp curls at the nape of his neck. Suddenly she felt a desire to touch those curls, to press her long form against his muscled length, to feel his hands on her back holding her, to experience the curve of his full mouth on hers.

She gasped as the cabin door opened, then closed just as swiftly behind Hank. Relief filled her. She blushed furiously, as though he could have read her mind and knew her wanton feelings toward Jake, his fath—. What was Jake to Hank? Only yesterday morning she had speculated on the adoring slave who must be Jake St. Simon's wife. She wasn't chained in the galley, that much Caroline knew. Was there a Mrs. St. Simon somewhere in America waiting for his return? Was she the woman in the picture over Hank's bed?

Her eyes turned away from the picture to Hank. He set the tape recorder down and pushed the buttons that started the music. She expected loud noisy rock music, but instead Arthur Fiedler's Boston Pops filled the air with John Philip Sousa's "Stars and Stripes Forever."

"Caroline, why didn't you leave last night?" he asked.

"I guess I fell asleep," she answered, sheepishly.

He nodded, but his face was bewildered and seemed to be asking her, "What are we going to do now?"

"Why didn't you wake me this morning before Jake sailed out of Hilo?" she asked him.

"I was asleep too."

"Where did you sleep last night?"

"Jake let me sleep in the other bunk in his cabin. He lets me do that all the time because the light is better for reading. I read a long time, waiting and listening for you to go. I guess I fell asleep too. And Jake didn't wake me up when we sailed. He said he just couldn't take another day of port, and since we had stocked our provisions, washed our clothes and he had made all his calls, he didn't see any reason for staying. He took the *Sunflower* out this morning before the sun was up."

"Hank, what am I going to do?" she cried piteously. Her attempt to be brave, calm and strong was at an end.

"You can stay hidden until we reach our next . . ." His voice trailed off as he realized the impossibility of what he was suggesting. A person just couldn't remain hidden for two months on a small sailboat!

"Hank, where are we going?" she asked him.

"The Truk Islands next, then Australia, New Zealand, South Africa, the Bahama Islands, Key West, Florida, then home to New Orleans," he finished proudly.

"My God! Hank, that's halfway around the world! It'll take a year!" She stared at him, stunned at the enormity of a voyage like that.

"A year and a half. Jake's taken two years off from his work," he told her.

Caroline wondered what kind of work Jake did that allowed him just to leave for two years. She also wondered what kind of situation at home would allow his absence for two years. And Hank too! What kind of mother would let her son and husband go off for two years?

"But your mother . . . Hank, didn't she object to you being away for so long?" Not to mention her husband, she thought. Caroline had vowed to herself not to ask about his mother and Jake's wife, but it had slipped out before she could stop it.

"She's dead. Besides, she didn't care about me anyway. She left me with Jake and *grand'mère* and went away when I was a baby. Then Jake wouldn't let her come back—at least Sulkie, our maid, says he didn't let her—but I don't believe it because Jake's face is sad and hurt every time her name comes up." Caroline could see the hurt in Hank's face. Jake wasn't the only one with a decipherable face.

"I'm sorry." She stopped her hollow-sounding words of sympathy and said instead, "I know it hurts, Hank. My mother died when I was a baby and until yesterday I only knew her name. My father wouldn't or couldn't talk about her," she said gently over the riotous cymbals, drums and cannons of the music as it built to a crashing crescendo.

"Hank?" yelled Jake from overhead, bringing them back to the present with a sharp stab of fear.

"I'm coming, Jake," Hank yelled.

His chocolate eyes pleaded with her as he leaned forward and whispered, "Before you come up and tell Jake you're here, think about what you're going to tell him. He has a terrible temper!"

"I won't come up until I've talked to you again. I'll tell you what I'm going to say to him," she promised.

"Thanks, Caroline," he breathed, deeply relieved. He turned off the music and left her alone with her thoughts.

She sat down on the deck in the blind corner, her back against the solid bulkhead. She tried to relax but tension filled her stomach with a hard, tight knot which refused to allow her physical or mental comfort. She stood up and took a pillow off the bunk and put it between her back and the bulkhead. It wasn't much help but it forced her to try to think logically of what she could say to Jake to avoid arousing his terrible temper.

Jake and Hank were on a world cruise. They hadn't any deadlines to meet so putting about and returning to Hilo wouldn't spoil any plans. And if Jake refused? Their next destination was somewhere called the Truk Islands. Where and what were they? Did the islands have an airstrip or were they too remote? She had thought that geography was one of her strongest subjects at Miss Calvert's. At least she recognized the rest of the places Hank had mentioned. If she could get Jake to take her to Australia or New Zealand, she could fly to England from either of those places. Perhaps he'd agree if she offered him a straight business proposition, whatever he wanted in the way of money. Her jewels and cape would bring a handsome price if he would accept them as payment. She decided this was exactly what she would propose to him.

Her mind involuntarily moved on to the question of Hank's mother. Was she really dead, or was this a story Jake and *grand'mère* told the boy? She instinctively knew Jake was the type of man who would tell the truth because he couldn't stand subterfuge or false hopes. Not at all like her father, she thought bitterly. Suddenly tears trembled on her lashes, but anger surged through her and she fought back the tears. She wouldn't fall prey to self-pity. She would have to stiffen her spine and gather all the wits she possessed to face Jake and talk him out of putting about and taking her back to Hawaii and her father. She sighed, feeling as if she had lost control of her life. Then another bitter thought rose. She was putting her fate into the hands of a very disturbing stranger—she *had* lost control!

The day wore on interminably, but Hank didn't come back to converse. He came in briefly from time to time, once to bring water, once an apple and once to tell her he was going to use the same method of distracting Jake as he had this morning while she used the head again.

Sometime in the late morning, Jake had winched the spinnaker into place and she had felt the *Sunflower* increase in speed dramatically, taking her further and further away from the Hawaiian landfall.

As dusk came, her muscles cramped and she was forced to alternately stand and sit to ease them. It was of little use. She felt as if she had been forced to sit in a closet for days on end.

At last she heard them hauling down the spinnaker and reefing the mainsails for the night. Next she heard the two of them preparing their evening meal. They talked about inconsequential things: *Captains Courageous,* Hank's math lesson, the calculation of the sun sightings. She felt her stomach rumble at the delicious aroma coming from the galley.

Hearing that they had nearly finished dinner,

Caroline decided that now was the time to reveal herself and ask for help. Just as she was about to open the door, she heard Jake say, "Hank, I've thought about last night quite a bit today."

"Last night?" Hank croaked nervously.

"About the girl off the yacht. If you saw her or helped her, it's all right. But Hank, a woman like that is pure poison. In your life you'll meet many women, the fiery spirited kind, the soft and gentle kind; the kind with all these qualities is usually the best and, if you're lucky, you'll meet one with all these qualities and keep her." He chuckled a lazy, low sound, not the booming thunder of the previous morning when he had laughed at her.

Then his voice became slower and more deliberate, the humor gone. "But the girl on the yacht yesterday, so beautiful and cool, she'd spin a golden web of lies and promises to get what she wanted. Then once her needs were granted she'd discard you as easily as she does last year's fashions. That type of woman doesn't have a heart, Hank. Only a cool calculator to add up the money. She'd take your heart and rip it to shreds."

"No, you're wrong! Caroline has a good heart and . . ." Hank burst out in heated defense of her, then stopped when he realized he had given himself away.

"So you did help her?" Jake's voice was kind and understanding, with the tone of "I know you couldn't help yourself" in it.

"Yeah, Jake, I helped her. She was in trouble," Hank answered, a little reluctantly.

"Trouble of her own creation, no doubt. She probably wanted to cause a little fracas so she could make up with her—well, anyway she's probably back on the yacht which bears her name with a new piece of jewelry to soothe her ruffled feathers!" His words were drenched with bitterness and cynical humor.

"Yeah, maybe. Jake, can I sleep on the bunk in your cabin again? I'm almost finished with my book." His voice sounded petulant and bored with all this talk.

"Sure. Hank?"

"Yeah?"

"I'm sorry if I hurt your feelings, but someday you really will understand and realize my words are, unfortunately, true." His voice wasn't pious and didn't have the "when I was a kid" tone, but it sounded tired and wise.

"Can I go to bed now?"

"Yes, go ahead. I'll be in soon."

Caroline blanched, her stomach tightened into a ball of dread. Things were much worse than she had realized. She had been prepared to face Jake's anger but not this contemptuous loathing. Why had he prejudged her? Then she remembered her own cynical appraisal of the women and men who had surrounded her, and they were just as he had described them! Wasn't it ironic that she found herself judged as being the very type of person she loathed?

She fell onto the bunk. Hank's message that he was going to sleep in Jake's cabin tonight was clear—this wasn't the time to confront Jake. She was still cramped and tired, but her hunger was gone; cold fear had wiped it away. A tear slid down her face and she couldn't stop the next tear, or the next. She finally gave way to the turmoil of the past days' incredibly dizzying heights of happiness and unbelievably sad depths of disillusionment over her father's betrayal. Now she feared Jake St. Simon. How would she prove him to be wrong? What would she do to make him understand she wasn't that type of woman?

Chapter Three

When the gray light of dawn finally appeared on the horizon, Caroline was ready to open the door of her prison. Sometime during the night she had faced the reality of her situation; she had to confront Jake and suffer the consequences. And somehow she would prove to him she wasn't made of the cold, metallic mechanisms of a calculator.

She sighed wearily. Sleep hadn't claimed her as it had the previous night. She had tossed and turned trying very hard to shut out the sound of Jake's cruel words. All through the endless night they had taunted her, as he, himself, seemed to do. During the night she had heard his footsteps overhead every few hours, as he had checked the boat. Each time her heart would beat in fear, reminding her that he was so near and hated her for what he thought she represented.

She heard him making coffee and guessed that Hank was still sleeping. She vowed to ask nothing for herself, but she would plead for his tolerance and forgiveness of Hank's part in this mess.

She turned the latch carefully and opened the door quietly; Jake's shirtless broad back was to her as he poured coffee into a heavy pottery cup. Everything was so brilliant and clear in her terror-filled mind: the bright red of the cup, the satiny smooth locker doors, the gleaming chrome of the stove, the striking yellow of the dinette cushions. Caroline's eyes came to rest on Jake's warm brown skin, his midnight black hair curling on his strong neck, the muscles of his arm as he moved the hand holding the coffee cup.

Those same muscles froze and stopped the cup in midair, halfway to his mouth. His whole body was tense as he carefully returned the cup to the counter top. Somehow he knew, instinctively, that he wasn't alone and that it wasn't Hank behind him. He whirled around to face her.

His black winged eyebrows arched in amazement. The blue green eyes narrowed into slits as he assessed her presence. Then a look of disgust replaced the wariness in those terrible eyes.

He didn't need an explanation of what had happened. Her presence on his boat was explanation enough. Caroline stammered, "Mr. St. Simon . . . I know you think I planned to stow away with Hank . . . b . . . b . . . but it wasn't like that. He just fed me. Then my fa—friend Mr. Conal came aboard and Hank hid me. Then you came, right in the middle of all of that . . . I fell asleep and didn't wake until you were . . . had sailed . . ." She trailed off, realizing how lame her excuses sounded. He obviously didn't understand. Perhaps it was better just to remain silent.

"Are you quite finished? Would you care for coffee, Miss er . . ." He stopped, waiting for her to supply her name.

She just stared blankly at his handsome face. What had she expected, shouting, cursing and maybe—even physical violence?

"Well, what is is? Caroline what? Smith? Or Jones? Or maybe it's Conal, although I doubt very much if a man like Mr. Conal would marry a plaything such as yourself. After all, why marry what you can buy quite nicely on the open market? Tell me, what is the going rate these days?"

His eyes swept up and down, assessing her worth with a practiced eye that touched every part of her body. He raised an eyebrow at her outfit of Hank's cutoff pants and his own shirt. He nodded in satisfaction at the swell of her breasts, the slimness of her waist, the pleasing width of her hips and the shapely, long, tanned legs.

Her face was hot with color. She couldn't stop her arms from involuntarily crossing her breasts. If she thought she could stop his prying eyes, she was wrong. He walked a small circle around her, surveying her body. Her bare toes curled on the hard deck. Anger filled her, but remembering the vow she had made earlier not to utter a single protest, she dropped her arms and stared at the row of gleaming lockers. This was what she had expected from him, but it didn't make it any easier to take.

"What is your name?" he demanded.

"My name is McPherson and I am not a plaything," she replied in the icy calm voice she had rehearsed all night. She instantly decided to hide her identity from him. She had been prepared to tell him her true name and what had driven her to run away from her father. Now she knew he would not believe her. Let him think the worst of me. He loathed *her* kind of woman, but she could see that he also desired her. Perhaps his disgust would make him keep his distance.

"McPherson? Ah . . . at least it's an honest name." His implication was clear, her name might be honest but was she? He repeated his earlier offer, "Do you want coffee, Miss . . . aah . . . McPherson?"

"Please."

"Then get it yourself," he said curtly, challenging her with his eyes.

"All right." She moved slowly nearer him. He was blocking her access to the stove. She stopped in front of him, expecting him to move. He didn't. Instead, he smiled, knowing he was causing her acute discomfort.

Her stubborn pride came rushing through as she reached around him into the cup locker, taking extreme care not to touch his bare warm torso. She moved to one side, took the hot pot off the stove, and poured the scalding hot coffee into a cup, slowly, trying not to slop it as the ketch pitched. She succeeded with the first swell, but on the fall of the *Sunflower* into the trough of the wave, spout and cup didn't meet. A firm but gentle hand closed around her slender wrist. Not a drop of hot liquid spilled as he expertly guided her hand to finish filling the cup. He took the steaming pot from her with his other hand and set it back on the stove, all the while holding her wrist in a numbing vise of powerful fingers.

"You're hurting me, Mr. St. Simon," she said between clenched teeth.

"Oh, am I?" he replied pleasantly. He loosened his grip and gently kissed the place he had hurt on her wrist.

She shuddered as the shock wave of his lips on her smooth skin raced up her arm and over her body. She had a sudden desire to stroke the light furring of dark hair on his chest, to feel his sensuous lips against hers. Her dark violet eyes moved caressingly over his strong, handsome face up to his eyes. The icy depths were cold and filled with a contemptuous dispassionate fascination; such as that of a small boy observing a snake that had slithered into his field of play. Feeling the dinette against the back of her thighs, she sank down with relief, as her knees were not capable of supporting her any longer. Her insides trembled with fear at her weak reaction to his light caress and the hateful expression on his face.

He sat down opposite her, their bare knees almost touching in the cramped confines. Those terrible eyes still watched her. She laced her fingers tightly around the warm cup to conceal their trembling. She stared into the black depths of the cup to avoid his eyes.

"Miss Caroline McPherson?" he drawled her name, sweetly caressing each syllable.

"Yes?" Her voice sounded high and unnatural to her ears.

"Do you know what the masters of ships long ago

did with stowaways?" His voice was mild, yet nettling on her nerves.

"I'm sure I don't care to know the dreadful details, Captain St. Simon," she replied, returning to her rehearsed calm voice. She had emphasized the title captain with a dubious question mark in her voice, her pride returning at his taunting.

"Some masters, if the man was still alive after receiving his lashes from the cat-o'-nine-tails, would throw the wretch overboard. Kinder masters set them adrift in a skiff with a few fishhooks and a fouled keg of water. The most accepted practice was to give them the lowest, meanest, hardest, dirtiest jobs." There was a menacing quality in his voice now, even though it was still soft.

"That's assuming they couldn't pay for their passage!" she said triumphantly.

"And what form of payment have you?" His eyes roved lecherously over her trim figure.

She blushed scarlet, heated anger clouding her judgment as she blurted out, "I've jewelry worth thousands of dollars, an ermine cape . . ."

"No doubt earned for your many sterling qualities!" His sharp tongue cut her off abruptly.

She had known the instant the words had left her mouth that they were wrong! Jake St. Simon wasn't a man you could tempt with money or the trappings he perceived to be rewards earned through trickery and fake emotions. How would she ever convince him that she hadn't been a kept woman? Did she really care what he thought? No! I don't care! she thought recklessly. Anger filled a portion of her mind. That he could think such terrible things about her wounded the spirit inside her. But this voice was pushed aside by a false bravado. She would play his game and take his acid barbs as long as he took her back to civilization. She raised her eyes to meet his, and with the frayed reserves of the strength she had drawn on a great deal these past days, she asked evenly, "Am I to perform the lowest, meanest, hardest, dirtiest jobs, Captain St. Simon?"

"And anything else I tell you to do." His eyes flashed as he spoke. His bare body seemed so powerful and capable of punishing anyone or anything that failed to obey his every command. She would follow his instructions to the letter!

They were silently measuring each other when Hank came sleepily out of the master cabin. He stopped short when he saw her. He hadn't heard them shouting or fighting. His eyes flew instantly to Jake's face. His young face whitened at the anger he saw in Jake's eyes, but he was relieved to see that the two of them seemed to be drinking coffee together.

"Good morning, Hank." Caroline greeted him with all the congeniality she could gather.

"Good morning, Caroline," he croaked out, all the while searching their faces with bewilderment on his own.

"Morning, boy," greeted Jake, his voice carefully neutral.

"Good morning, Jake." Hank decided Jake's silence was a good sign, so he added, "Did Caroline tell you it was a mistake that she got trapped aboard?"

"Miss McPherson has explained herself very well. Both with words and her other attributes." The meaning of his words was quite clear. He believed she had beguiled Hank into helping her stow away on the *Sunflower* with her lies and beauty.

Caroline saw the boy's confusion and her heart twisted in pain. She could accept the low opinion Jake held of her, but she couldn't bear his tearing away at the affection and friendship she thought Hank felt for her.

"I don't understand, Jake," Hank said slowly. His usually open face contorted in concentrated thought at Jake's veiled words.

Caroline turned to Jake. From the crystalline depths of her multifaceted eyes, she pleaded with him silently not to hurt Hank. Her lower lip trembled slightly in weakness. It was an unconscious weakness, not intended. Something in Jake's face responded to the unexpected appeal. For a fleeting moment she glimpsed a small streak of compassion in this hard man. She knew he would keep his opinions of her to himself for the time being.

He said, "Hank, this discussion is closed."

He got up from the table and brushed by the puzzled boy who answered, "Okay, Jake." It was plain he didn't know *what* was okay, but the message was clear—the less said about Caroline the better.

At the sink Jake put his cup down. He turned to her and ordered in a flat voice, "Cook some breakfast—you *can* cook, can't you?" His eyes were hard and full of contempt as he looked at her face filled with gratitude at his handling of the situation between Hank and herself.

"I'll help!" Hank cried eagerly.

"No, you won't, boy." Jake's voice was still hard. "Go shower." He turned his back to them and went up to the deck.

"Caroline?" Hank seemed confused.

"It's okay, Hank," she repeated his own earlier response to Jake. "Go shower."

"Sure."

She nervously approached the lockers and assembled the food she would need for cooking breakfast. After several minutes of experimenting and testing she couldn't get the stove to light. Hank was still in the shower. She would have to ask Jake to help her. Her mind rebelled, but she could find no other way around it. She braced herself to face his mocking contempt and went onto the deck. She approached the man at the tiller. "Captain St. Simon?"

"Is breakfast ready?" he asked, annoyed at her intrusion.

"No . . ."

"Why not?"

"I don't know how to light the stove," she stated flatly. She added in the same stiff voice, "If you show me how to light it, I'll never need you to show me again."

With a curt nod he set the autopilot and followed her below. Asserting himself, he showed her the master cutoff valve, the proper way to prime each burner and finally how to light a match.

She thanked him, but instead of returning topside, he made her repeat the steps of lighting the stove like a school child. He admonished her on the importance of proper care of the stove. He explained the volatility of the fuel in the four liquid propane tanks concealed on the deck and went on to explain that if the burners were carelessly left on, unignited, the fumes would collect in the bilge of the ketch where heat or a careless spark would set these gases off and blow them into oblivion. Seeing her face whiten at this warning, his own softened slightly. Still, his words were cold as he left the saloon, warning, "I want my breakfast in ten minutes."

She didn't answer him. Instead she grimly cooked the oatmeal she had found in a food locker; it was lumpy. She made frozen orange juice, which was soft because the plastic packets of dry ice were melting. She toasted bread over the open propane flame with no success, burnt on one side, undercooked on the other. She reheated the nearly full pot of coffee, making it even stronger. She surveyed her efforts with dismay. It was hard to believe they were prepared by the same Caroline who had spent one summer on a whim with a friend at a cooking school.

She set the table, then reluctantly went to call Jake. Calling Hank wasn't necessary as he had been hovering near since he'd emerged from the shower, his chocolate brown eyes telling her how grateful he was that Jake's temper hadn't erupted.

Breakfast was eaten in silence. Hank's attempts at conversation were met with grunts and vague one-word answers from the two adults who stared at each other with challenge.

At the conclusion of breakfast, Jake said to Hank, "Go up and start the sun sightings."

As the boy left the saloon, he flashed Caroline an encouraging smile.

"Miss McPherson," drawled Jake.

"Yes . . . Captain St. Simon?" Her attempt at steadying her voice was a washout; it quavered and broke over these few words.

"Since you chose to become a member of my—er —crew, your duties will be: all of the cooking, try to improve on this mess, cleaning the head, making the bunks, but not Hank's, that's one of his duties, keeping the below decks clean and keeping the topside brass polished." His eyes held hers and seemed to be daring her to protest.

She nodded in agreement and in a steady voice asked, "Where are the cleaning materials?"

"In the locker under the sink."

He went topside and in the next few minutes she felt the tug of the spinnaker as Jake winched it into place.

As she set about her cleaning chores, most of her long nails split and broke off. As the morning wore on her arms ached, as did her back. Lady Caroline Conal, newly demoted to charwoman, cursed the day she had ever seen Jake St. Simon! Her only comforting thought was that he hadn't turned about and taken her back to Hilo and her father.

By midmorning all of the tasks were completed but one, the making of Jake's bed. In the master cabin, Hank's neat bunk was a big contrast to the tumbled confusion of Jake's larger bed. She took the pillow off the mattress; the blanket and sheet followed. The whole thing would have to be made over completely. As she smoothed the top quilt over the newly made bunk, she wondered if Jake's sleep was as restless as his bed showed it to be.

Picking up the pillow, she automatically brought it against her breasts to fluff it up. Jake's heady masculine scent rose to fill her head. Her arms hugged the pillow to her body, and the confusion she had felt the few times she had been touched by him suddenly overwhelmed her. Instantly, his cynicism toward her wiped away any confusion or tenderness she might have for him. She threw the pillow onto the bunk, slapped it into place and left the cabin feeling somewhat better for having hit the place he rested his dark head.

She opened a can of soup, expertly touched a match to the stove, and smiled in victory as the burner instantly flared to life. As the soup warmed for lunch, she made a salad with the wilted vegetables in the warming refrigerator.

Jake came down from the deck and stood very close to her as she finished pouring the soup into cups and putting the salad on the dinette. He seemed to know that his close presence annoyed her intensely. She gave him an irate look, her eyes cool as a glacial wind. He only smiled at her. She pushed the hot cups of soup into his hands, forcing him to move away and put them down while she finished serving the lunch.

Caroline had assumed that lunch would pass in silence as breakfast had. But Hank's questions about the Truk Islands brought answers to questions she also had about their destination.

"Providing we don't hit the doldrums, we should reach Truk in about six weeks." Jake smiled at Hank, his blue green eyes suddenly alight with teasing encouragement.

"Where are the Truk Islands?" Caroline asked.

"She has a voice after all," Jake said to Hank.

She hadn't meant to participate in the conversation, but she needed to know where these islands were if she was going to plan her return trip to England.

"Yes, she has a voice," answered Hank, eager to ease the tension. He looked from one face to the other, his eyes pleading with each of them to speak to one another.

"I'm surprised you don't know where they are, Miss McPherson. After all, they're part of an island group that bears your name, the Carolines, but perhaps only yachts that bear your name interest you." His eyes were mocking and his smile bitter as he taunted her.

"For your information, Caroline, the Truk Islands are a territory of the United States of America." He began in a professor's slightly patronizing tone. "A great Japanese naval base was constructed there during World War II. On the morning of February 17th, 1944, the United States Navy launched an air attack that caught a fleet of Japanese merchant vessels and warships by surprise in Truk Lagoon and they exacted the revenge they had been seeking since Pearl Harbor. Now, out of the ruins of that violence, nature has created an underwater wonderland of coral, schools of curious fish and beauty beyond words."

"You've seen this before?" she asked, surprised at his exciting description of this underwater spectacle.

"Yes, I've seen them before," he answered. His voice was curt and obviously bored with talking to her.

"Jake led an underwater exploration of the sunken fleet last year for the University of Louisiana! Jake's a marine biologist, even if he doesn't work at that, really he's a—"

"That's enough, Hank. Caroline isn't interested in the boring saga of Jake St. Simon." He halted the boy's prideful flow of words.

"What's a saga?" Hank's easy questioning personality had returned to normal. He seemed to be at ease with the two of them together now.

"It's a form of narrative prose written about the heroic figures of Norwegian and Icelandic history. It's rather long and sometimes boring." His face became stern and closed. "And speaking of sagas, you'd better get to work on *The Red Badge of Courage.*"

Jake was a surprising man, she thought. One minute he was patient, explaining and answering Hank's endless flow of questions; the next, he was a cold, remote authority, issuing orders in a stern manner that clearly said don't rebel or the consequences will be harsh.

"Oh Jake, do I have to read that?" complained the boy.

"You'll like it, Hank," said Caroline. "It's about your American Civil War and a young boy not much older than you who fought in that war."

"Really?"

"Really."

He raced off to his cabin to get the book.

"You amaze me, Caroline. I wouldn't have thought that Stephen Crane would be required reading for an English lady," he said mockingly. His aquamarine eyes were sarcastic, his upper lip curled into a scornful smile.

"I'm not illiterate. I did graduate from Radcliffe, Captain St. Simon!" she snapped at him. Instantly she wished that she hadn't fallen prey to her desire to take him down a notch or two. Now she had only given him one more weapon with which to taunt her.

"Radcliffe! I really am impressed. Mr. Conal must have grown weary of women who couldn't converse about anything more than the amount of carats in a diamond, but then I would imagine your observations weren't so crude. You probably have little trouble quoting the Dow and the *Wall Street Journal,* with your, er—brain." He sneered at her as his eyes traveled down then back up her body.

"You are contemptible," she rasped out, her voice almost lost in rage.

"Well, Miss Radcliffe alumna, I don't care for the job you've done on this deck, and I want it done over. After that you can start on the hardware topside. When you're finished, it should be time for you to cook supper. And the way you smell isn't very appetizing, so before you sit down to eat with me again, take a shower and wash those clothes," he ordered.

"But I haven't anything else to wear but an evening gown," she burst out. The high-handedness with which he ordered her to take a shower only added to her rage. She longed to scratch his eyes out! What did he expect her to smell like after scrubbing the decks? Perfume? Of course she smelled like disinfectant and perspiration!

"You really did run away prepared to meet every emergency, didn't you? Did you hope your lover would find you pouting at the Hilton and plead with you to come back to his bed?" He shook his head in disgust. "I've got a drawer full of shirts and Hank has more cutoff pants. Please feel free to clothe yourself at my expense." He said these last words with mock chivalry.

His eyes swept her body with the now familiar assessment as he continued in a cool voice, "And I guess I should explain about the sleeping accommodations. We don't have anything special—nothing like the satin bed sheets which usually pamper your body." He paused, his eyes holding hers with purpose. "My sheets are cotton. You won't find them so appealing, but you'll find the man between them infinitely more qualified to tame your desires."

"You . . . you . . . bast—" she started in shock, her eyes as green as grass, her skin burning red with bitter rage.

"Careful, Caroline, you're not in a position to vent your childish anger on the master whose ship you tricked your way onto!" he cautioned, in a voice that was menacing but softened with his drawl. His eyes noted her surrender with satisfaction, and without another word he turned on his heel and left.

It was several seconds before she could think properly. The words she longed to hurtle at his handsome face continued to rise to the surface, begging to be vented. If he thought she would sleep in his bed he was wrong! She would . . . she would . . . what would she do? What could she do? Tears of anger fell on the deck as she began to scrub, and her strokes were vigorous as she took out her rage at Jake St. Simon on his teak deck.

When she had finished the deck, she washed the lunch dishes, the counter tops, the stove, then looked around to find *anything* that would keep her below deck and away from Jake. But she had run out of tasks. Reluctantly, she found the hardware polish and rags and went up on deck.

Only Jake's brown figure was in the cockpit; Hank was still below, apparently finding more to like in *The Red Badge of Courage* than he had originally thought possible. She studied Jake under her eyelashes as she worked on the brass. His muscles rippled in the sun as he worked at his task, his long fingers sure and nimble as they moved over the piece of equipment before him. Suddenly his dark head raised and he caught her staring at him. He smiled sweetly; her heart did strange things. Then he dropped his eyes down over her body with a slow, leisurely appraisal.

She quickly turned away from him, almost upsetting the cleaning fluid. His thunderous laughter filled her with renewed frustration. She bent her head and worked more intensely on the hardware. The fresh air soon cooled her anger, but the disgust she felt for Jake St. Simon was firmly entrenched in her mind.

Filled with a full head of wind, the beauty of the canary yellow spinnaker emblazoned with a bold red cross was breathtaking to her. Later, when the sea and the sails became blood red in the setting sun, she didn't mind the fact that she shared this beauty with the man who had come to stand beside her. She looked up at him, his face distant while his eyes restlessly studied the flat horizon. He seemed to be very angry, and she was grimly reminded of her orders: make dinner and shower. She was sorely tempted not to take the shower, but she needed it for her own self-esteem. She went below, leaving him to his silent anger and the sunset.

Caroline surveyed the fresh meats in the warm regrigerator and decided to cook the chicken as it would spoil first. She searched the canned foods and found tomatoes, sauterne wine, dehydrated onion flakes and a large number of spices; the fresh vegetable drawer yielded a large green pepper. She browned the chicken, added the diced pepper, tomatoes, onion flakes, a little sauterne and some spices to the pan, turning the gas heat down to a simmer.

She was much more pleased with this dish than this morning's breakfast.

"Gee, Caroline, it smells wonderful!" complimented Hank from the door of his cabin.

"Well, I had given you up! I thought perhaps you had run off to join the Union Army!" she teased, as a tender smile came on her face. She had always wanted a brother, and Hank was beginning to fill that need; she had to admit to herself that she felt a little pinch of maternal emotion for him.

"Become a Yankee?" he cried, shocked at the very idea. His dark eyes were scornful.

She smiled at him, "I'm sorry, I had forgotten."

"What had you forgotten, Miss McPherson?" drawled Jake from the companionway behind her.

She whirled around and said scathingly, "I had forgotten, Captain St. Simon, that the chivalrous men of the South marched gallantly off to war and certain defeat because of slavery."

"Your Yankee education is sadly lacking," he drawled lazily. "Southern men went off to war because they believed in the individual rights of a sovereign state. Slavery was dying in the South, and had the North been patient, it would have been abolished without all the needless bloodshed. Now that your education has been amended, you may take your shower. Hank will watch whatever you're cooking."

She opened her mouth to reply to his taunting, but decided against it. She stalked into Hank's cabin to find another pair of cutoff pants. The photo of Jake with the laughing woman caught her eye, and she stuck her tongue out at it and immediately felt better. And when she came out of the cabin Jake wasn't in the galley. She didn't look at Hank as she went into Jake's cabin. She mechanically searched his drawers for a shirt. She found a tee shirt with NEW ORLEANS SAINTS in gold letters on a field of light blue. What in the world were NEW ORLEANS SAINTS? she wondered. And why did Americans always have writing on their tee shirts?

The shower wasn't warm, and it didn't invite lingering. Still, she washed her hair and body very quickly and felt human and decent again. She pulled on the cutoffs and the tee shirt which clung provocatively to her damp body. She blushed, angry with herself that she hadn't at least been wearing a bra when she ran away. Jake was right about one thing—she hadn't planned her escape very well. If she had, she certainly wouldn't be at the mercy of Jake St. Simon, modern day pirate!

She hung the towel on the rack next to the other two already there, and somehow the three towels hanging together made her feel part of a family. A strange, comforting feeling came over her, something she had never felt before. Looking in the mirror over the pullman, she couldn't help but notice that she looked healthy and happy. One would have thought she'd at least have the decency to appear pale and distraught at her plight. She brushed her hair until it fell in damp, red golden waves around her long slender neck.

When she returned to the galley, the chicken was almost finished. Jake and Hank were topside apparently preparing the *Sunflower* for the night. She found some instant rice and prepared it along with another salad. She dished up the dinner on plates when she heard them coming down.

She smiled wide and felt good inside when Hank said, "Wow, look at you, Caroline."

Jake said nothing, but his eyes told her he wasn't immune to her improved appearance.

As at lunch the three of them fell into easy conversation, Hank asking the questions and the two of them answering. Each was more than a little surprised at the extent of the other's knowledge on a wide variety of topics.

Caroline noted with satisfaction that both of them ate the dinner with obvious pleasure. After the meal the two of them helped with the cleanup, which surprised her. Jake scoured the stove, while she and Hank washed and dried the dishes. When they were done, Jake went silently topside with a canvas deck chair in hand.

"Come on, Caroline," invited Hank. He had found two more chairs and was waiting anxiously for her decision. She chewed on her lower lip and looked up toward the deck with doubt in her eyes.

"Please, Caroline."

"All right, Hank," she consented. She didn't know how Jake would receive her presence on his deck, but she was tired of looking at the galley where she had spent most of her day doing the chores. With anger aroused but held in check, she put her feet on the companionway behind Hank and went topside. She was ready to challenge Jake for her right to be there, but he said nothing.

The stars were brilliant on a canvas of black velvet sky. The gentle wind was so mild and warm it soothed her tired body. She soon relaxed completely, even if the carelessly sprawled form of her tormentor was just one foot away. She noticed Jake's bare feet propped up on the shiny side rail that she had worked so hard to polish this afternoon, but she couldn't stir any anger. Instead her eyes traveled from his long, strong legs clad in faded cutoff jeans, to his broad shoulders. Before dinner he had put on a clean red tee shirt. She noted the customary lettering appeared again, DUKE'S MARINE SALVAGE, in bold black script across the solid wall of his chest where he had held her just two days ago. Was it only two days ago? It was strangely disconcerting that she hadn't thought of her father and Edward Ashford at all today. As her eyes returned to Jake's strong, manly form she had to suppress an urge to chuckle when a vague picture of the wimpy Edward Ashford rose in her mind. His weak image couldn't hold a candle to the shockingly handsome man beside her!

The three of them sat under the dark sky and watched the thin crescent moon rise over the curved horizon of the earth. The ocean lapped gently against the boat providing a catalyst to the relaxation. They didn't chatter idly as they had at dinner.

Even Hank seemed to realize that now was the time for simply allowing the moonlit night to wrap them in relaxation and silent companionship.

Caroline's hard physical labor, combined with the previous restless night, made her very tired, and with a soft sigh she drifted off to sleep.

Chapter Four

Caroline, Caroline," a caressing voice called to her across the deep void of sleep. She struggled to her senses; a light touch on her cheek made her eyes fly open. Jake's face was less than an inch from hers. She realized the touch had been his lips! Panic assailed her and she struggled sluggishly to her feet.

When she gained them, she demanded, in fear born of her own wanting to surrender into his arms, "What do you think you're doing, Captain St. Simon?"

"Just playing the part of a chivalrous Southerner," he said, mimicking her English accent.

"You . . . you . . . bas—" she blazed.

"Careful, Caroline, you're going to get that word out someday, and I'm not going to like it one bit," he said flatly, his eyes cool.

"I'm going to bed," she answered.

"That's just what I had in mind," he said wicked-ly. It was obvious what he had on his mind as his eyes devoured her body.

"No," she gasped out in a frightened voice, her fear born of the fact that she knew he had only to take her into his arms and she would be lost—lost to the disturbing attraction she felt developing for this mysteriously desirable and handsome man.

"Are you afraid you couldn't be emotionally detached as you are with your other lovers?" He paused at her gasp. Had he guessed that she desired to be held in his arms? But all desire she felt was swept away as he taunted further, "It shouldn't be too hard; just think of it as payment for your passage. Mr. Conal receives your gratitude in this fashion."

"I'm not Mr. Conal's mistress!" she cried out, but she knew it was a hopeless denial.

He took her by the arm and drew her against his firm chest, his lips devouring hers. She forced her body to remain stiff in his arms, her lips slack and unyielding to his. With a muffled curse against her hair, he let her go.

She turned and ran down to the saloon, shaken and afraid. It had taken every ounce of strength in her not to respond to his kisses, to the hands that had moved over her back and round bottom, press-ing her close to him. What would she do the next time he touched her? And she was sure he would touch her again, his eyes told her he wanted her. Would she fall into his arms and beg him to take her into his bed?

His footfalls behind her made her move quickly toward Hank's cabin door.

"No." His sharp command made her freeze in flight.

"You . . . what do you want now?" she stammered, fear knotting in her stomach.

"You'll be sleeping in my cabin," he stated flatly.

"No!" she cried back at him.

"Quiet! Hank's sleeping," he commanded in the soft threatening tone she was beginning to know so well and dread.

He came forward, took her by the arm and pulled her into the master cabin. The smaller bunk Hank had slept in last night was empty. What had Jake told the boy before he had gone off to bed? Hank wasn't totally naïve about men and women! She felt warm color fill her cheeks.

Jake seemed to have read her mind and said, "Hank's delighted with you. All the qualities I've taught him to look for in a woman he thinks he sees in you. He has hoped I would marry for a long time now. Taking you to my bed brings reality to his hopes, even though you and I will still know the truth. I won't marry you."

"I will hate you forever for this, Jake St. Simon," she whispered between clenched teeth.

"I couldn't care less, Caroline McPherson," he replied pleasantly, his mocking smile back on his handsome face. "Now be a good girl and give me a good night kiss."

She wrenched herself out of his arms and hissed at him, "No, you swine."

"Careful, Caroline, I don't like to be called names," he warned.

Did he really expect her to kiss him? He advanced on her quaking form. He took her face in his rough hands and gave her a chaste kiss on the forehead. He whispered at her temple, "Good night, *chérie.*"

His French New Orleans heritage showed in the endearment, but she didn't stop her confused thoughts at this particular moment to wonder of his background. He released her and stepped away, his aqua eyes holding hers as he began to strip off his clothes.

"Oh." She turned quickly from him. Only when she heard the small bunk groan beneath his weight did she turn back. His brown bare back was to her, and he was apparently already falling asleep. She waited a long time, until his even breathing told her he was sleeping, before she slipped off her own clothes. She climbed into the large empty bunk. The cotton sheets against her naked skin served to remind her of his earlier comment about his bed. Well, she might be sleeping in his bed and between his cotton sheets, but he wasn't between them with her.

"Good night, Caroline."

She gave a startled gasp. He hadn't been asleep! She pulled the sheet and blanket tight around her body. She lay rigid for a long while, but try as she might, she couldn't stay awake as she planned and was soon adrift in a dreamless slumber.

A rude, rough hand on her bare shoulder shaking her brought her awake. She cried out, angry that her sleep had been disturbed twice in one night. "What do you want now?"

"Get up," came Jake's voice. Her sleepy mind

hadn't cleared. She felt no fear that Jake might have decided to come to her bed after all.

"Get up and get dressed," he ordered sharply.

She came fully awake at last. She sat up quickly, alarmed at the urgency in his voice. Was the boat sinking or was there some other danger? The sheet fell below her full bosom. In the dim light of the cabin's lamp she saw Jake's shadowy figure. Then she saw his face tighten.

"Caroline, you are too tempting, and unless you clothe yourself immediately you won't be alone in that bed for long!" His voice was ragged and full of barely checked passion.

With a protesting squeak, she pulled the sheet up. Her eyes were glacial green, her golden red hair tumbled about her bare golden shoulders, one slender arm was holding the snowy white sheet over her body, the other raised high over her head ready to strike if he should carry out his threat of joining her. Little did she know how desirable she was in her icy rage.

The luminous dials of the clock built into the bulkhead over his bunk indicated that they had been sleeping for only two hours. Was this some new form of torture he was inflicting on her?

"What do you want?" she asked again.

"Get up and get dressed. I won't tell you again," he warned darkly.

She knew that he was pushed to the danger point. She didn't care to start another fight with him in the middle of the night, but she'd be damned if she'd dress before his prying eyes. "Leave the cabin or turn your back."

He didn't argue with her. Instead he turned and

went to his wardrobe at the foot of the bunk. The open door screened her completely from his eyes. He was still searching through the wardrobe's contents when she finally finished struggling into her clothes beneath the sheets.

"Are you dressed?" he asked sarcastically.

"Yes," she answered curtly.

He turned and tossed her a windbreaker and said, "Put this on. It's cool topside."

"Topside?" she echoed while putting on his huge garment.

"I'm teaching you to stand night watch."

"Night watch?" she echoed his words again.

"You don't think that when night comes we simply stop dead in the water, waiting for the sun to come up so we can be on our way?" he said condescendingly to her.

"No, of course I don't."

"Good." He turned and went into the saloon as she trailed in his footsteps. Why was he so irritated with her? What had she done now?

Stopping at the companionway, he silently put on his safety harness. He took down another harness from a locker in the bulkhead and pushed it into her hands. When she held it before her in a confused tangle he took it back roughly, turned her around, and began strapping her into it as he would have a child. His touch was warm on her skin and lulled her anger at being awakened rudely and his scathing remarks.

"If I ever catch you topside at night or in heavy seas without this on, I'll lock you in your cabin until we reach landfall," he threatened.

"You . . . you won't need to, I promise," she

answered sincerely, realizing he was deadly serious about this; not to be mean or contrary with her but because he wanted to be sure she understood the grave importance of the safety harness.

"Good." He took the line of her harness with his own and together they went onto the deck. The air was cool. She shivered as it took away the last little bit of warmth she still had from her bed. He was leading the way, snapping the hooks onto the grabrail on the top of the cockpit.

When they reached the stern, he drew her close against him, her shoulder blades touching his hard chest. In his soft southern drawl, he began explaining the compass in analytical terms which were so very bewildering; she was sure she would never understand it. He moved on to explain the compass heading they were following and making notations on the chart, all without allowing her to voice the hundreds of questions that filled her mind. He pointed out and named the confusing array of other equipment in the sheltered cockpit—the depth indicator which was only needed near land but was vital around the sunken atolls which formed a deadly coral necklace about the Caroline Islands. He showed her the running lights' switch and explained that the lights were always turned on at night, green on the starboard side, red on the port, white on the main mast and the stern. Next he showed her the autopilot, which looked more like a weather vane. To her surprise Jake explained that it was just that. It paralleled itself to the wind and held that direction. This was perhaps the only thing she understood.

He took hold of their safety lines and pulled them back down into the saloon. He wrote their compass heading and the time in a log book and explained that unless something was drastically wrong this was all she really had to do on night watch.

He shrugged out of the safety harness and went back into the cabin without another word.

She stood in the saloon for several minutes, bewildered. Why was he so angry? She stormed after him, ready to demand an answer. Caroline's anger died instantly when she opened the door.

He was lying on his back, apparently asleep. The subdued light of the cabin played on his relaxed face. Her eyes involuntarily slipped over his masculine form, from the tumbled hair, closed eyes, the soft full lips, the strong neck, to the heavily muscled arms and masculine torso.

Suddenly she was consumed with a need to touch him. Before she could stop her hand, it went out and brushed the soft black hair back off his forehead. His eyes opened.

"Oh!" She jumped back as if she had been burned.

His eyes were not wicked or teasing but filled with a tender longing. His voice was gentle as he said, "Go back to bed, *chérie*."

He turned his beautiful body, presenting his back to her again. Caroline stepped out of the cutoffs and decided to wear the tee shirt to sleep in. Slipping under the sheet, she was quickly lost in a wave of sleep.

It seemed like only a minute had passed when she was again shaken awake. Her eyes flew to the clock and she was surprised to see that four hours had passed. She guessed he hadn't awakened her for the watch in between, and she was grateful. After he left the cabin, she scrambled out of bed and pulled on the cutoffs and windbreaker.

At the companionway she again put on the harness with his silent help, and together, as before, they made their way to the cockpit. This time he explained only the compass, their heading and the log entry. Her guess that he had let her sleep through the second watch was confirmed by the neat two o'clock entry below the one they had made at eleven.

Again they tumbled into their bunks; both undressing with their backs to one another. She was instantly asleep.

At five o'clock she was awake for the morning watch. She knew Jake was too, but she lay waiting for him to leave the cabin before rising.

"Caroline?" he whispered.

"Jake?" She realized how ridiculous it was to call the man you shared a cabin with captain.

"I'm getting up now."

She turned to face him. His sea green eyes were caressing, and his smile was actually teasing and tender. His face was shadowed with whiskers; he looked like the real buccaneer she had called him. His black hair lay in mussed curls on his forehead, and she had the same strong desire to touch him as she had last night.

"Stop looking at me like that!" he said, his slow lazy drawl, gentle and spine tingling.

"What?" she said, confused at the rush of emotion she felt for him. Her gray violet eyes touched his face, the bare chest with the light mat of dark hair, and all anger and resentment against him faded.

"*Chérie,* your eyes betray you. They tell me you are a passionate woman desiring to be kissed and loved. If you don't stop soon, you will get what your eyes are asking for—passionate wicked love." His eyes were alight with a strange gleam of daring and desire.

"I want . . ." She stopped horrified. What had she been about to say? Please, Jake, do make wicked love to me? The melting passion she felt for him every time he was near was overpowering, and when he turned his tender, teasing smiles on her, she couldn't think straight, let alone defend herself! Her eyes still beckoned to him, but his eyes turned hard and he warned again, "Please turn away from me, Caroline, or I won't be responsible for the consequences."

With an exasperated groan she turned to face the bulkhead, not realizing she gave him an unobstructed view of a shapely calf and thigh not covered by the twisted bed clothes.

When she heard him dress and leave the cabin she arose too, wincing at her stiff muscles, sore from her unaccustomed labor of yesterday. She dressed and went into the empty saloon. On the deck above her, she heard Jake's light tread, restless, as if he were longing to pace out more than just the eighty-two feet of the deck. She shrugged her shoulders; she could not possibly figure out the puzzle Jake presented.

She put on the coffee and went to perform her morning grooming. When she was finished she went back to the galley to find the coffee ready. Taking down two cups she poured the strong brew with a steady hand, now growing accustomed to the pitch of the sea.

Caroline was getting ready to go up to the deck with the cups when Jake came down. He sniffed the air appreciatively and smiled as she silently handed him a cup. By unspoken consent they sat down at the dinette opposite each other, their knees so close they could feel the heat of each other's body. They drank their coffee in comfortable silence, each forgetting the harsh words of the past day.

He got down the charts and the log and patiently explained the meaning of the previous night's log entries. He mentioned that he was going to run the auxiliary engine for a half hour to compensate for their slight drift off course and to charge the batteries.

She wondered at the change in him this morning. Had she misjudged him as he had her? Could they now be friends? She moved to the galley and began to take out the things she would need to prepare breakfast. She smiled at him when he stood up too.

His eyes were lightly appraising her figure, but she didn't mind until he said, "You haven't given me my morning kiss yet, Caroline."

"Your what?" she cried, shocked, having thought they had made some headway toward friendship; now he was ordering her to kiss him.

"Never mind, *chérie*, I'll kiss you," he said pleasantly. He folded her into his strong arms, and before she could protest, he soundly kissed her on the lips. She tried to remain stiff and indifferent, but his lips were soft and teasing and gentle as he extracted a passionate response from her.

He released her and, in the same pleasant voice, ordered, "Cook breakfast now. No oatmeal today. Then do the bunks, clean the head, scrub the deck in Hank's cabin, and in ours too."

He had emphasized the word ours. She groaned angrily, "You bas——"

"Ah, your vocabulary is limited, *chérie*." He went topside, and moments later she heard the rumble of the motor start and felt the speed of the *Sunflower* increase. How had she thought they could be friends?

She stormed about the galley, frying bacon and making biscuits, when she saw that the bread had already molded in the moist sea air. She was scrambling eggs when Hank came into the galley.

He was all smiles, but she impatiently snapped at him to go pester Jake with his questions. She was instantly sorry when a hurt expression came over his face, but before she could apologize for her sharp words, he had fled topside to escape her. Great! she thought. I've lost the only friend I have on this boat!

Breakfast met with their approval and soon Hank and Jake were back on the deck hoisting all the sails now that the auxiliary engine was shut off. By lunch she had completed all but one assigned task—the bunks. She made her own, then turned to his; it was roughly tumbled again. She thought she had heard him tossing about in the night. What made his sleep so troubled? Smiling ruefully to herself, she decided it was probably his guilty conscience.

Caroline picked up the red windbreaker he had loaned her in the night and went to the wardrobe to hang it up. Her hand came into contact with the silk of her evening gown and her lacy black slip. They were hanging among his clothes! Her ermine cape was sealed in a clear plastic clothes bag to protect it from mildew. Had Jake taken it as payment after all? Then she remembered her evening bag bulging with jewels, her passport and health certificates. Had Jake seen her full name on those papers? She searched frantically for the bag and was relieved to find it at the bottom of the clothes bag with her evening shoes. She opened it and found that everything was undisturbed. It seemed that Jake wasn't the type of man who searched ladies' handbags. If he had, she doubted that he would have remained silent on discovering her true identity. Reassured, she replaced the bag and went to make lunch.

When lunch was over and the mess cleaned up, she waited patiently for Jake to issue new orders—but none came. Instead, he went into the master cabin and returned with Hank's lessons. Hank had intentionally ignored her as the morning wore on, even though she had made several friendly overtures. She decided the best idea was to let his hurt feelings run their course and wait for an opening to say she was sorry.

She watched for a while as the two of them bent over the books, Jake the teacher, Hank the sometimes reluctant, sometimes eager student. Finally tired of their exchanges, she went into the master cabin and brought out her dirty clothes to wash.

"There're more clothes in the bottom of our wardrobe, and Hank's too," said Jake. It wasn't exactly an order, but it wasn't a request either.

She didn't answer him, but went in to get the

wash. In Hank's wardrobe she found a plastic laundry basket with his pile of laundry and brought it out. She washed and rinsed them vigorously and put them in clean heaps in the basket but was at a loss as to where to hang them to dry. Jake solved her problem by stringing a clothesline from the bow rail to the cockpit. Soon cutoff jeans, tee shirts, men's and boy's underwear and one pair of black lacy women's panties fluttered in the breeze.

As the afternoon went by, she prepared supper while Jake took a shower and Hank read at the dinette. Finally Hank said, "Caroline, I'm sorry about this morning."

His smile was impish and delightful. She went to him and brushed his hair playfully. "It was my fault, Hank."

He took up her challenge and tugged playfully on her long tresses. She put her hands in thick hair and messed it up.

"Hey, what's going on here?" asked Jake with mock severity.

Both of them turned guiltily from their horseplay. Jake's blue black hair glistened with water, his face cleaned of whiskers, his brown body still damp and clad only in white exercise shorts. She felt her pulse begin to hammer at his masculine scent mingled with the smell of soap.

"We were just teasing." Her voice was rough, her eyes couldn't stop caressing him.

He smiled lazily at her and then said with mock severity to Hank, "You need a shower if you're going to eat whatever that wonderful-smelling food is."

"I'll be out quicker than you can shout, 'supper's ready,'" he said, racing away to shower.

She turned busily back to the sink as the sight of him disturbed her even more now that they were alone. Her shaking hands worked on the last of the salad greens. The next thing she knew she had cut her finger and cried out in pain. Instantly Jake was beside her, holding her wrist and pressing the small cut. When the slight bleeding had stopped, he drew her against his warm bare body. Why does he always go around half-dressed? Her mind cried in protest at his nearness.

He tenderly kissed her temple, a russet eyebrow, the tip of her nose, then softly captured her lips in a way that was much more devastating than his angry passionate kisses. Her arms slipped around his slim waist, pulling him tightly against her. She burrowed her face into the damp, wiry hairs on his chest, her cheek feeling the cool metal of his medal. Her long form was a perfect fit against his, her face even with his strong throat as her long silken hair trailed over his shoulder and down his bare back. Sighing gently, she kissed the side of his neck, while they stood holding one another closely.

"My God, but you are beautiful, Carrie," he whispered in her ear, as his tongue circled its shell pink perfection, and he gently nibbled on her lobe.

"You are very pretty yourself, Jake," she whispered back.

He chuckled very low at her compliment. He kissed her again, then reluctantly released her. Her arms followed him, bewildered at his sudden withdrawal. Then she heard a happy humming that heralded Hank's return from the shower. Together the three of them went topside to reef the sails for the night and gather the dried clothes. She folded them, and they put them in the proper drawers while she served dinner.

Again, as on the night before, Hank and Jake ate hungrily and helped her with the cleanup; then all three went up on deck and watched the moon rise over the silver sea. Hank went to bed first, and when Caroline looked at Jake she couldn't suppress the apprehension in her face. Would her earlier willing kisses and returning caresses make him believe he could come effortlessly into her bed? What would she do if he demanded she make love with him?

"You go to bed, Carrie. I'll be up here for a while." His voice was strained with a hint of inner struggle.

She knew his light mood was gone, but it wasn't anger that had chased it away, for he had already adopted the casual use of the nickname he had given her earlier. She got up and went below, took off her clothes, including the tee shirt. She slipped between the cool sheets, not noticing their comfort as her mind dwelled on the man on the deck above her. What motivated this kind and tender display? She sighed and drifted off to sleep. A short while later she awoke slightly to realize he was in the cabin preparing for bed. She smiled to herself, comforted by his presence in the other bunk.

"Good night, Carrie," he said in a low voice.

"Good night, Jake," she whispered back sleepily.

Later she awoke instantly when he touched her shoulder to arouse her for the night watch. After he left the cabin she dressed and went topside. Together, as the night before, they did all the watches—each time dressing and undressing back to back in the dark, then returning to separate bunks.

Chapter Five

The next few weeks settled into a familiar pattern. The trade winds pushed them steadily in a wide arc around the Marshall Islands and toward their destination. Just as Jake had plotted, they were right on course. At breakfast one morning he announced that in six days' time, if his calculations were right, they would arrive at Moen Island, the largest island in the Truk group.

Caroline had learned from Jake that there was a small city on Moen, as well as an airstrip into which international airlines flew. She was sure she could sell her jewelry somewhere for airfare, but that didn't matter anymore. She no longer plotted her escape to England day and night as she had in the first days of their emotionally stormy passage.

Perhaps it was a telling statement of how much she

had changed in these weeks. Lady Caroline Conal was no longer! Her pampered hands were work hardened. Her body, which had never been soft, was somehow physically stronger now. To her surprise she actually liked making her own bed, washing her own clothes and preparing her own food. Most of all, she liked taking care of Jake and Hank.

Jake no longer issued orders for dirty jobs, but then she automatically did each of the tasks he had originally assigned her as part of the daily routine. Her cooking received daily praise from both of them. Her newfound efficiency as a sailor was complimented as well. She now alternated with Jake on the night watch and had even learned his routine of waking on the hour of every watch.

Jake kissed her each morning with growing familiarity and a lingering reluctance to release her. And she found that it was becoming more difficult not to press herself against his long hard body and return his affection. She made an effort to receive his attentions with all the forced coolness she could summon. It was a hard-fought battle with a cold hollow victory when Jake indignantly pushed her away after she stifled his caresses.

All this only added to the building and tormenting curiosity she had about him. It was strange that although the two of them lived in extremely close proximity, she knew very little about him. Or did she? She knew he read everything, from the classics to pure adventure novels; she knew he liked music from classical to jazz; but she didn't know what type of background had given him these qualities. She knew he was thirty-four years old but not if Jake was short for Jacob, or if it was short for anything at all.

She knew he liked his eggs fried, but she didn't know whether or not Hank was his son. She knew he lived in New Orleans but not what his occupation was when he wasn't sailing around the world, only that it wasn't marine biology—that was his hobby. She knew his French Creole heritage was a source of pride. She knew he had lived in Europe, not because he told her so, but because of his familiarity with places and customs found only in Europe. She knew that he did not have to worry financially, again not because he told her, but because Hank had often spoken of home and various maids, gardeners and *grand-mère*'s cook, Mona.

She knew Jake was quick to tease and laugh. He teased Hank gently with the affection of a friend, never talking down to him in any way. And once his initial anger toward her wore down, he teased her too. He laughed, as she did, at her silly blunders in seamanship, teased when she demanded a nail file for her broken nails. When he mentioned her former life-style now, he didn't jeer hatefully and accuse her of being a plaything but a rich girl on a "working" holiday. He even admitted good-naturedly that it was very nice to have a new member of the crew who could cook. The declaration inflated her pride and lifted her spirits as no other compliment had ever before.

Although these days had been idyllic in some regards, Jake slipped occasionally into one of his black, brooding moods. The laughter and gentle affections were wiped away. His answers became curt and clipped, and he withdrew to be alone within himself.

At first, Caroline thought she was the spark that

ignited these moods, but Hank told her in short painful sentences that Jake had always been like this. When she asked the inevitable question of why, he mumbled something about his mother and how much Jake had loved her.

His sleep was rough and restless, and more than once she heard mumbled curses and the name Therese clear and understandable; but she didn't dare ask who Therese was or what she had done to arouse such violence and hatred in him. Was she his wife? Hank's mother? These were thoughts that dominated Caroline's mind in her waking hours and occupied her dreams as well. Jake's handsome face brooding, smiling and kissing her haunted her nightly now. He wasn't the only one who slept restlessly.

On the day before Hank's twelfth birthday, Jake asked if she could make a cake and prepare a special evening for him. Caroline was delighted with the idea and immediately set about looking for the ingredients to set up a wonderful party. She found chocolate squares in the food locker, and with a little ingenuity made a chocolate cake with chocolate frosting. For dinner she planned spaghetti with clam sauce, something Jake said was a favorite of Hank's. It sounded terrible to her, but when she tasted the sauce she had made under Jake's supervision, she was pleasantly surprised; it was quite good. She baked fresh rolls in addition to the cake. Just as the sun was setting, everything was ready, except for one small detail which she was determined to remedy.

"Hank, go topside and help Jake, please," she said to the boy who was reading at the dinette.

"Help Jake?" he asked, puzzled, as she had never given him a direct order before.

"Yes, please. Would you take the tiller for a minute and send him down here? I need him to get something down that I can't reach," she lied blandly.

He cocked his head to one side and looked at her strangely but went to do as she asked without further question.

"What's up?" Jake asked her in a low, conspiratorial voice as he appeared. He had taken a shower earlier, right after Caroline, so they could take turns occupying Hank to be sure he didn't snoop. He had on his white shorts again; his tan had deepened into a golden bronze. He was smashingly handsome! As of late, he had a peaceful, contented look on his face, as if he had finally come to terms with whatever had been bothering him. Suddenly she realized his sleep had been peaceful for quite some time now. His black moods hadn't come on him in recent days either.

Jake's raven black hair was tumbled from the wind. It had grown longer on his neck since she had first seen him that morning on Hilo Bay. She smiled in remembrance of that fateful day.

"Carrie?" He brought her back from her happy musings.

"I'm sorry, I got sidetracked trying to remember everything for the party." She blushed at the lie because she could read in his smiling eyes that he knew she was lying. Quickly she asked, "Do we have any candles?"

"Candles? Let me think." He searched the lockers in the galley. She watched the play of his flexing muscles and remembered how they felt the few times, forgetting her resolve to be cool to his kisses, she had surrendered and caressed that smooth back with her hands.

Reluctantly she dragged her eyes away from him, catching her own reflection in the mirror on the door. She wished she had something more elegant to match the occasion than her NEW ORLEANS SAINTS tee shirt. She had learned from Hank that the Saints were a professional football team. She had toyed with the idea of wearing her evening gown, but she knew it would bring up unpleasant memories of her past and the kind of woman Jake had thought she was; she didn't want him to be reminded of those terrible thoughts.

Caroline knew she had earned his begrudging respect when she had accepted the tasks he had given her without a word of complaint. The thankful look in his eyes also indicated that the care and love she gave Hank was also appreciated. But did he still harbor doubts about her? Did he still think of her as Robert Conal's plaything?

She followed him into their cabin. She had stopped thinking of it as the master cabin or Jake's cabin weeks ago—it was theirs now. Out of habit she closed the door behind them. An open door in heavy seas spelled disaster, as it could do damage to the boat, or knock out a hapless crew member. She perched on her wider bunk and enjoyed the light playing on his back as he searched the chest of drawers. He smiled as he found two short, fat candles. He grinned up at her as he presented them with a flourish, his knee bent beneath him.

She giggled, then accepted them with all the reverence of a queen being presented the scepter of office. She looked down at his cocked head, her smile wide at his buffoonery. Then her silver, laughing eyes darkened to violet, meeting his gaze as he raised his head. She was suddenly caught in the blazing sea fire of his eyes. Her smile softened like soft petals ready to receive his full mouth. Her breathing seemed rapid as it roared in her ears.

Their hands met on the candles, which fell carelessly onto the deck. They were in each other's arms on the bunk. She was meeting his caresses with equal abandon. His hands drew off her tee shirt and she gasped in pleasure as her passion-hardened nipples tingled against his rough chest hair. His lips sought her throat while his hand caressed her back, pressing her closer to him with urgency.

He rolled off her and began a slow intense trail of kisses down her neck to her shoulders and down to the eager, pliant mounds of her breasts. His tongue began to tease and she moaned, revealing her need to release the sparks of a pent-up passion kindled by time and resistance.

Her fingers laced themselves in his black hair, tugging at his head until he left her breasts and raised his head to her face. Her lips kissed his broad forehead, the planes of his handsome face and the corners of his mouth.

It was his turn to groan with pleasure and longing. He muttered between the kisses he was raining on her fevered body, "I want you so badly, *chérie*."

She didn't answer with words, but held him closer. His desires were obvious, as were her own. His hard body was urging, tormenting and nudging her into greater wanting. His hands sought the fastenings of her cutoffs.

"Hey, can I come down now?" yelled Hank.

They withdrew from each other sharply, so lost in the heady draught they had completely forgotten Hank.

"Damn!" groaned Jake, moving away from her in frustration and anger.

She lay limply on the bunk, drugged with passion and bereft now that her arms were empty. He turned back to her, holding her tenderly as if he shared her emptiness. He stroked her hair and kissed her lips gently. He whispered, "I'll see to Hank, *chérie*." He drew away from her, his eyes caressing the lovely body, his reluctance to leave easily apparent on his face.

He went to the wardrobe and put on the peasant shirt that he had worn on that day long ago in Hawaii. Reaching again into the wardrobe, he removed a light blue silk dress shirt which he tossed onto the bed where she still lay. He grinned devilishly at her and said, "Put this on, it's always been a little small for me. Tie it up around your lovely smooth waist so I can see the places I kissed." She blushed at the hint of their shared intimacy.

She slipped her arms into the shirt as he was leaving the cabin. The shirt was smaller than his others, but still large for her. She rolled the sleeves up over her elbows and tied the tails around her midriff. The ice blue color was very striking against her peach skin.

While she tried to mend her ragged emotions, she brushed her tumbled hair into shimmering waves.

MOONSTRUCK

She had almost given her body to Jake and knew that, if Hank had not interrupted them, she would have given it gladly; in fact, she wanted him as badly as he wanted her!

Caroline went into the galley; it was empty. She heard the two of them talking on the deck.

She put the card she had made for Hank beside his plate. Inside the homemade envelope she put a man's gold circlet ring with the small crest of a bird in flight. She had found it among the things in her mother's old trunk at Conal Keep. She had carried it since she was a child as a link with her mother. The mystery of its owner had been solved by her father when he told her the name of her mother's dead brother. The initials H. McP. were on the inside of the ring—Hugh McPherson.

"Are you ready?" asked Jake from the companionway.

As she smiled shyly at him, her cheeks flushed happily. He came over to her, put his arms around her waist and kissed the tip of her nose as she looked longingly upward at him.

She put her arms around his narrow waist and leaned her face against his warm throat. This was the place she belonged. A happy feeling of contentment filled her. She realized that she loved this man deeply and forever. A deep, aching need for him rose within her. She didn't care if it was wrong for her to want him so desperately, or for the self-control of a lifetime to slip into the dark recesses of her mind.

"God, you're beautiful, Carrie," he murmured into her silken hair, then drew back to caress her face with tender eyes. His lips dropped to hers. At

119

last he ended the deep kiss reluctantly and said huskily, "Are you ready?"

"Yes," she whispered back. She was filled with such happiness and joy at the discovery of her love for him. Her hands traced the beloved face.

"Don't do that, Carrie, or you'll be back in that cabin with nothing to stop me this time from making you mine," he warned huskily. His large hands held hers firmly, stilling their restlessness. He kissed each one and frowned slightly at the new white calluses on them. His blue green eyes held hers and seemed to apologize.

She answered as though he had spoken, "Badges, for learning to be a competent and self-sufficient person."

"You're much more beautiful now than you were that morning in Hilo when I first saw you flaunting your charms in that flimsy little white bikini." There was a devilish gleam in his eyes. He grinned at her indignant face, then kissed her over the token protest she had begun to make. When he finally drew away, the protests were forgotten. He asked again absentmindedly as he rained light kisses on her neck, "Are you ready for the party?"

"Yes," she whispered again.

"Good, because after Hank's party, I intend to make you mine." He kissed her before she could answer, releasing her with reluctance.

She stared after him as he went into their cabin. Did he mean what he had just said? Was she ready to make love with him? Yes, I want him to love me, she thought, answering her own question.

He returned a minute later with three gaily wrapped packages. She had known of their existence in the wardrobe and had guessed their destiny from the conversation she had heard between Jake and Hank the night she had hidden in Hank's cabin. Now she was in love with the man she had feared so much that night!

He put the packages down beside her envelope. As he went by her to the companionway to call Hank, he kissed her lips lightly.

"Yeah?" was Hank's answer, plain that he was tired and grouchy with all this ordering about.

"Set the autopilot and come to supper."

They smiled at each other as they heard his feet scurry around on the deck, then clamber down the companionway. His handsome young face lit up with joy and his brown eyes burned with excitement when he saw the table.

"It's wonderful!" he cried, racing to the table, poking each package and shaking the envelope with the suspicious lump in it.

"All right, Hank, let's eat the supper Carrie has made. Then you can open the presents!" decreed Jake, his own face wide with a tormenting smile. Jake winked at Caroline as he lifted the spaghetti off the stove and onto the table.

She brought the rolls and sat down opposite Jake. Their knees and legs, which in the past weeks had politely avoided contact with each other, now secretly touched beneath the table. Every so often in the course of the meal, Jake would slip a large, warm hand onto her knee and squeeze gently, forcing her to meet his sea green gaze while his eyes devoured her own soft smile. She had never known such delicious happiness. Caroline felt as if it were her birthday and the moon had just been given to her.

The meal was eaten almost before she knew it, having been consumed in record time by an eager but appreciative Hank. He opened Jake's presents first: an exquisite book on underwater life which the author had autographed for the boy, a new brown shirt with a screen print of a yellow and orange sunset which Jake explained was only *one* of *grand-mère*'s presents and, in the smallest box, a very complicated and expensive watch for scuba diving. Hank was clearly delighted as he cried, "Jake, it's just like yours! Thanks! It's great!"

"You're very welcome, boy." Jake smiled at him, then resumed his slow tantalizing study of Caroline's face, her smooth stomach below his silk shirt, her long legs, her glowing eyes.

Hank opened Caroline's card and found the ring, his face solemn as he put it on his index finger and held it up to the light. He said, "Caroline, it's great!"

She smiled at him, then returned her silver eyes to Jake's beloved face. His answering smile was warm, his eyes alight with promise; she shivered, half in fear, half in excitement at the unknown delights promised.

"Thank you, Caroline."

"You're welcome, Hank. I've had that ring since I was around your age. It's been special to me and that's why I want you to have it—because you're special to me."

"Where did you get it?" he asked with his usual curiosity.

"It belonged to my mother's brother who was killed in World War II in the Africa campaign against Rommel. His name was Hugh McPherson."

"McPherson? If McPherson was your mother's name . . ." Hank stopped, his face crimson. He stuttered on, "Were you born without a father too?"

Caroline's eyes fastened on Jake, his eyes demanding an answer too. The moment she had spoken of her uncle, she regretted it. She had named herself a liar to Jake. His blue green eyes were now narrowed into cold speculative slits as he searched her face. She knew that he could sense her uneasiness.

Then the worst happened, that look of contempt returned to his dark features. She hadn't seen it in weeks, and suddenly it frightened her. His legs withdrew from hers. She felt cold dread race over her. Both Hank and Jake were waiting for her answer as she whispered dully, "No, Hank, I wasn't born without a father. My father's name is Conal. My complete name is Caroline Blythe Mary Elizabeth McPherson Conal."

"Oh." Sufficiently satisfied with her answer, Hank went back to examining his new watch.

Jake's expression was veiled in a mask of indifference; she jumped up and served the cake, decorated with the two candles that had earlier ignited the flame of passion between them. Now the twin flames seemed brassy and artificial.

Hank quickly blew out the candles and declared that his wish for a birthday party had already been granted. The flavor of the cake was a delight too, so much so that he helped himself to two pieces. In his happiness, he failed to notice the growing strain and tension between the two adults, who were merely pushing their cake from one side of the plate to the other.

"Hank, you're dismissed from KP duty, I'll help

Caroline tonight," Jake said, his voice flat and void of the teasing lilt which usually accompanied his soft southern drawl.

"Great! I'm going to my cabin to look at this book!" he said, disappearing into his cabin.

He'd called her Caroline! her mind cried—not Carrie or *chérie* or love. Her insides twisted and knotted with the old nervous fear. Her happiness of minutes ago was broken into a million fragments of shattered hopes; dreams of lasting love between them—gone.

They cleared the supper dishes in strained silence. She could feel the invisible anger in the air around them. When they had finished, Jake went topside without a word to her; she followed. She couldn't let the love she felt for him be destroyed so easily; somehow she had to explain, to try and make him realize how silly this was, throwing away the beautiful love that had grown between them. She didn't stop to realize until much, much later that perhaps Jake didn't feel anything for her other than a physical kind of love.

"Jake?" she said, when they reached the sheltered cockpit. Dusk had set in and she couldn't see his face in the shadows.

"Yes, Caroline?" he answered, his cold, polite tone telling her too clearly what she couldn't see on his hidden face. She winced as she recognized the same icy contempt he had harbored against her in those first terrible days. Surely she had proved to him that she was not a shallow, spoiled woman.

"Couldn't you please hear me out?" she pleaded.

"What's there to explain? Your mother's name was McPherson. Your father's name is Conal."

"Yes—"

"So instead of being Conal's plaything, you're his spoiled daughter; not his plaything but another man's—"

"No, I'm not anyone's plaything," she interrupted.

"A spoiled, rich man's daughter," he rasped out at her denial.

"I didn't tell you before because you wouldn't have believed me. You didn't believe me when I denied being his mistress. I knew you wouldn't believe me if I had told you I was his daughter. Jake, you've accused me unjustly. I've never been any man's mistress! I've not led the life of jetsetting you seem to think I have. I'm not the person you think I am!" she pleaded with him.

"Whose mistress were you?" he demanded, as though he hadn't heard her words.

"Please, Jake, listen—"

"Is that why you ran away from daddy?" he sneered. "Did he object to the money hungry man in your life?"

"Jake, I've never been anyone's mistress," she cried piteously, but the words fell on deaf ears as he went on relentlessly.

"Your body says otherwise, Carrie. A man only has to put his hands on your body, kiss your honeyed lips, and you respond eagerly, ready to fall into bed with him. You can't deny that you would have made love with me this afternoon if we had been alone. You can't deny it, can you?" he rasped out.

"No, no. I want you to make love to me, Jake. But *only* you," she whispered between sobs. Tears rolled down her cheeks.

"Chérie . . ." His voice was broken.

"Oh, Jake . . ." she choked out.

A groan emerged from his tight lips, and suddenly his eyes grew darker. "Get away from me, Carrie."

She fled below and into their cabin, sobs racking her slender body. She buried her head in the pillow to muffle the sound. The pain was deep in her, even worse than the pain she had felt when she had fled from her father weeks ago. She could at least understand her father's motives and maybe forgive him. But Jake's unwillingness to even listen or believe she wasn't an immoral woman who led a selfish and totally hedonistic life cut deeply into her. She had thought he loved her, but his prejudgment and unwillingness to accept her explanations forced her to realize that he must not. The tenderness and teasing he had shown her had been a ploy to get her into his bed without a fight. He had viewed it as a challenge to woo and bed her. How close he had come, and what a fool she had been!

Much later, when the storm of weeping had passed, she sat up. Crying had made her head hurt; she blindly got off the bunk, went into the head and bathed her face with cool water. Her eyes were swollen and her chest was tight with pain.

When she came out into the saloon several minutes later, Hank was hovering by the door of his cabin. His face was anxious, his dark eyes darting from side to side in apprehension. It was clear he had heard the two of them fighting.

They had managed to ruin his birthday! Suddenly she was furious with Jake. Previously, she had been bewildered and ready to appease his anger. Willing to humble herself and tell him just how much she loved him. Now, she decided with stubborn pride, she would be damned if she would humble herself. She had done nothing to warrant such treatment! She had never been selfish to the point of hurting, and never had she slept with a man for fun, excitement or what he could give her materially. In fact, she had never slept with a man at all! As old-fashioned as it sounded it was true. And if she responded to Jake, it was because he had the power to make her want him above all other men. His kisses and caresses had been difficult to ignore; but that was in the past. She would be free of him in six days when she would leave for England to start a new life, a life free of her father and of Jake St. Simon!

"Caroline?" Hank approached her timidly, as if he were afraid she would confirm what he already knew—Jake and Caroline were very angry. The happy bubble in which they had lived these past weeks had burst.

"I'm sorry that you had to hear Jake and me fighting. I could tell you that adults sometimes fight, Hank, and that we'll never do it again, but I think you're old enough to know that everyone fights. You can't stop differences of opinion or misconceptions." She smiled shakily at him, unable to stop the wobble in her voice or the pain in her face. He hugged her. It was the first time he had ever done more than give her a playful punch on the shoulder or tug on her long hair.

Caroline put her arms around him and smoothed his dark hair. Taking his face in her hands, she held his worried brown eyes with her own tender blue gray eyes and said, "The trouble between Jake and me has nothing to do with you. We both love you and wouldn't hurt you for the world."

"Why? Why did you fight?" he asked bewildered.

"The reasons are too many and too hard to understand." How could she explain it to him, when she really couldn't explain it to herself? She kissed his smooth cheek, gave him a quick hug and said, "Now I want you to go to bed and don't worry."

He searched her face and then agreed, but doubt and hesitation darkened his face.

Caroline woke at two o'clock, tumbling out of bed automatically as it was her watch. As she pulled on her clothes, she remembered the events of the past evening. She had lain awake for hours waiting in vain for Jake to come to bed but had finally fallen into a light, troubled sleep.

She looked at the other bunk; it was still empty. She went quickly into the saloon; it was empty too. Panic filled her heart—had he fallen overboard? She ran onto the deck, forgetting in her panic to find him that she hadn't snapped on the safety harness.

She found him in the cockpit. Relief flooded through her. He was sitting in a deck chair and from his position, she thought he was asleep. She turned to go below when he halted her.

"Carrie?" His deep voice caressed the pet name.

"Yes?" she answered him eagerly, despite all her earlier resolutions to be distant and cold.

"What time is it?" he asked, his voice tired and strained.

"Two," she whispered.

He stood up suddenly and turned to her. He put his arms out and she went into them willingly, snuggling against the solid, warm wall of his body in the black night. He kissed her forehead gently, while his hand stroked her back, catching in the silken tangle of her hair as a deep swell of contentment came over her.

When his lips traveled to hers, she responded with all the love and emotion she could find in her trembling body. Suddenly he drew away and scowled. "You don't have your harness on!"

"What?" she asked, uncomprehending in her euphoric happiness.

"I told you never to come up on deck at night without it!" he rasped out angrily.

"But . . . but you haven't yours . . ." she began stupidly.

"Shut up, you stupid, spoiled girl!" he ordered angrily.

"What? Why? Jake, what have I done that's so terrible?" she cried in hurt frustration.

"You're hopeless! Get below!" he said, his voice quiet, but so loud in her mind.

She fled from him for the second time in one day. She flung herself into her bunk, so angry that she couldn't even cry as a familiar pain flooded her senses. Pride and resolve grew in her as she said aloud to the night, "I've only to make it through the next six days . . . no, five." The pink of dawn was only hours away.

Breakfast was a silent affair. Hank didn't try to force conversation. His eyes watched Jake in youthful impatience, perceiving Jake's unbending, stupid pride. Caroline, on the other hand, didn't look at Jake at all unless it was absolutely necessary.

Her strained, pale face was the only outward sign of inner struggle. She went about performing her morning tasks as usual, mainly by rote. She was spared the chore of making Jake's bunk as it hadn't been slept in.

At lunch she heated soup and cut leftover cake for dessert. She asked Hank to call Jake down from the deck, and by the time he came down, she was in their cabin. Dinner was the same.

The nightly ritual of watching the moon rise wasn't observed. Hank went to his cabin, Caroline to her bed. Jake remained where he had spent the previous night, in the deck chair, staring out to sea.

Caroline woke at eleven, and taking care to don her harness, she went topside to take the compass heading and make the cursory check of everything. As she made the entries in the log, she couldn't help but wonder how he could continue without sleep.

When she made the watch at four, he was asleep on the settee in the saloon. She saw that he had made the two o'clock entry a half-hour late. He was human after all! She sighed softly and went back to her bed. Only four more days to get through—somehow she would do it! Jake's sleeping face, soft and vulnerable, was the last thing on her mind before sleep claimed her.

Chapter Six

The emerald green foliage of the island on the distant horizon stood out sharply against the white puffs of clouds in the brassy morning sky. Caroline stood in the bow watching the *Sunflower* gain the anchorage of Moen Island. They hadn't had any trouble navigating the treacherous coral necklace around the Caroline Islands. Jake had brought them through the shipping channel with practiced ease.

Caroline's eagerness for them to gain this safe harbor showed on her face. She wanted to feel solid ground beneath her feet and purchase clothes that were feminine. Most importantly, she wanted to get away from the silent man at the tiller. As she turned away from the horizon, her eyes fell to the strong hands on the wheel, which were expertly guiding her to freedom. They moved with lightness and delicate ease. Suddenly she remembered how those hands had moved over her slender body, extracting passion.

The strain between Jake and herself had been almost unbearable these past six days. She had performed her duties, cooked and served meals that she hadn't been able to eat in his presence. She had stood her night watch, lonely and miserable throughout the endless nights, knowing that one error could bring his ridicule. She had been alone in the master cabin for six nights as well, Jake preferring to sleep on the settee in the saloon, if he slept at all. His face was haggard, deep circles showing under his eyes; her own face was pale and drawn. They looked like a fine pair of refugees.

Hank had walked the thin line between them and perhaps it had been hardest of all on him. He loved them both and couldn't make up his mind to whom he should be loyal, though neither had asked nor tried to solicit his allegiance. So he was alternately civil, then cold and stubborn to Jake, while to Caroline he was a source of strength. He smiled reassuringly, helped her with chores and chattered incessantly to ease the lonely isolation Jake and she had created.

The rumbling of the auxiliary motor beneath the deck suddenly stopped, bringing her out of her unpleasant thoughts. Hank eased into Jake's place at the wheel, and with fluid graceful motions, Jake moved around the cockpit past the superstructure to the anchor winch in the bow. He let out the anchor with a noisy clatter as the chain went over the side. After several sharp tugs on the chain, he seemed to be satisfied that it was holding. He brushed past her without a glance and went below to radio the customs station.

Within ten minutes a white power launch, with the ensign of the United States Coast Guard and the flag of the United States of America fluttering on the stern in tandem, made its way at high speed toward the bright yellow hull of the *Sunflower*.

"Jake, Jake St. Simon, my old friend!" greeted a small brown man standing precariously amidship of his bobbing craft. Caroline was sure that at any moment he would tumble into the green lagoon and ruin his starched white uniform. From head to toe he was sparkling white: his officer's hat, shirt, shorts, long socks and oxfords. Only the colorful patches and silver emblems of the United States Customs Service broke the snowy effect.

"George Mekeni, you old pirate! I would have thought you retired to the easy life, letting those lovely daughters of yours wait on you hand and foot," Jake responded to the man who had just defied gravity and the gentle rolling of the sea by swinging nimbly onto the ladder Jake had put over the side.

"The daughters all have husbands," yelled the man. When he had gained the deck and restored order and dignity to his uniform, he looked up at Jake, his broad face splitting in a grin. The men shook hands and slapped each other on the shoulders as men who are good friends often do.

Spying Hank, he said to Jake, "The little man resembles you, Jake, but he's not your son!"

"You're right as usual, George. This is my nephew, Hank. Hank, this is George Mekeni, one of the best native divers in these islands. If he would only give up the Customs Service he could make a fortune by diving and guiding wealthy tourists underwater."

"Ah, Jake, I'm too old for diving, and tourists . . . ?" He rolled his eyes skyward, then said, "Welcome, nephew of Jake!"

His eyes lingered on Caroline, but she missed his appreciative look as she stared at Jake and Hank. Not his son, but his nephew! At last the mysterious relationship was explained. But she still had a million more questions. She recalled Hank's question about her name, "Were you born without a father too?" Jake's sister must have had . . . or perhaps Hank was Jake's brother's child.

George took a step toward her, bringing her out of her reverie.

"Jake, you have a very beautiful missus," George complimented.

"What?" she said, then "No, we aren't marr—" She stopped, flushing scarlet at her words and the implication of them.

"Miss Conal is my guest, George." Jake said, smoothly intervening.

"Ah . . . and British too. When you have been the Customs Officer for as long as I, you develop an ear for accents." He laughed as though he had said something terribly funny. His laughter was so infectious Jake smiled, Hank laughed, and Caroline smiled half-heartedly, her embarrassment easing somewhat.

"Now, you have passports, Jake?" His laughter was gone; he had become serious and officious at his business.

"Come down to the saloon, George," invited Jake. As the four of them went down, Jake asked, "Can I pour you a cup of coffee?"

"No, thank you, Jake." It was plain that George Mekeni's code of conduct was business, and nothing, not even an innocent cup of coffee, would detour him.

Jake and Caroline went into the master cabin, the first time they had been in the compartment together in six days. She stood awkwardly aside while he located Hank's and his own documents. He went out while she extracted hers from among the winking stones of her jewels. When she returned to the saloon, George was already stamping Jake and Hank's papers. She handed him hers.

He read, "Caroline Blythe Mary Elizabeth McPherson Conal, born Conal Keep, Wales, England, age twenty-four, hair blond, eyes hazel, height five feet six inches, weight one hundred seventeen. That's you, Miss Conal." He stamped her passport.

She was embarrassed and angry with this man for reading her passport aloud like a book with interesting episodes. Seeing that she was about to make an angry comment, Jake stepped alongside her, slipping a careless arm about her shoulders. With a gentle warning squeeze he effectively silenced her. Glancing at his amused profile, she knew he was silently laughing at her. Her anger at Mekeni transferred to him. How dare he patronize her!

Then in the next instant, she knew just how much more angry she could get with him when he said, "George, Miss Conal has quite a bit of valuable jewelry she wishes to bring ashore, and also a fur coat. I believe she's planning to sell some of it for her fare home to England."

The man's bright eyes turned on her. He was clearly surprised at the turn of events. Why would a woman want to leave a handsome devil like Jake St. Simon? "Do you have the customs receipt from when you brought them into the States at Hawaii?" The recent stamp on her passport hadn't escaped his notice.

"No . . . no . . . I haven't brought . . ." she said, puzzled. Her father had handled all these details in Hong Kong and Hawaii. She supposed he had the customs receipts.

"Do you have sales receipts or insurance statements of value?" he asked her patiently.

"No."

"Then I'm sorry, Miss Conal, but you can't bring them into the islands, unless you want to have them impounded for three months or more while checks are made around the world to verify that you are the owner—not that I think you stole them," he said quickly, "but it is the law."

"But, but—" she stammered, "what am I to do now?"

"You best keep them aboard and not tell anyone. It could be dangerous; some people aren't honest," he declared, plainly disgusted at the state of the world.

Jake's hand tightened again on her shoulder; he was warning her not to say any more. He could feel the rigid anger and frustration in her body. She turned her blazing green eyes on him and, if they had been alone, would have vented her barely contained rage on his dark, handsome head.

"George, would you be willing to take young Hank ashore and show him the Customs and Coast Guard operations?" Jake asked smoothly, knowing full well that the man would be delighted to have an eager audience.

"Sure," he answered. "Good-bye, Miss Conal, sorry your plans are ruined."

"Good-bye, officer," she said between suppressed lips. She watched helplessly while the three of them went topside. Moments later she heard the launch move away and Jake reappeared in the saloon.

"You bas—" she began her familiar retort, only to once more be cut short by a cool voice.

"I told you, *chérie,* never to swear at me or call me names." He advanced on her; she backed away until the bulkhead was against her stiff back.

"Why did you do it?" she cried, afraid. Her anger was so great it drove away her reason and made her rashly say, "You haven't a shred of decency in your body, you're an unprincipled, ruthless man, Jake. I suppose you want my jewels for yourself."

"No, I don't want your precious jewels, Caroline! I don't need to rob you!" he rasped out as he caught hold of her shoulders. "To answer your first question, I did it because you're not going to run away again!"

"I wasn't . . ." She hesitated, knowing it would be yet another lie. She was planning to run, run as fast and as far as she could from him, hoping that distance and time would work him out of her heart and mind.

"Caroline McPherson, or Conal, you're stuck here with me until I say you may leave," he said angrily before his lips descended on hers. His kiss was cold and unrelenting as his steel hard form crushed against hers.

When at last he drew away, she slapped his arrogant face. She had to lash out at this hard, unbending man, who for some perverse private reason of his own, wanted to keep her captive.

His blazing eyes gazed into her own for a long moment before he drew her back into his arms and kissed her tenderly with teasing, taunting passion. Her treacherous lips opened and became his; her rigid body relaxed itself in helpless compliance. He picked her up in his arms and carried her to their cabin. Suddenly, nothing stood in his way of making love to her.

While kissing her face, his hands tenderly and unerringly sought the pleasure points of her body. Soon the silk dress shirt that she had been wearing was on the floor, his tee shirt soon beside it.

Their bodies were touching in eager remembrance of their first time together—but this wasn't right—wasn't possible. Caroline couldn't forget the days of silence, anger and harsh words. She knew it wasn't love that Jake sought, but only a desire to humiliate her completely while slaking his own needs. Her love was too beautiful and strong to be used for just a fleeting moment of pleasure. She couldn't give herself to him willingly as she would have the last time they had embraced this way—when she had thought that he loved her.

Not being able to struggle against his superior

strength, she began to cry helplessly against this onslaught of passion. Tears rolled down her face into her ear, which Jake was slowly tantalizing with his tongue. At the taste of her salty tears he drew away, his passion-filled eyes questioning and puzzled, his dark face tender above hers. Caroline closed her eyes tightly in an effort to stem the tide of tears; she didn't see the emotion in his face that would have answered her questions and filled her heart with happiness. Instead, she begged in a broken voice, "Jake, please, don't do this to me."

"Carrie, I—" His voice was husky. Then with a disgusted groan, he rolled off the bunk, retrieved his shirt and stormed out of the cabin.

She lay cold and so very alone for several minutes, trying to regain her composure. Finally she stood up, slipped into the discarded shirt, brushed her tumbled hair and bathed her face. When she came out of the cabin, she found him waiting. Looking at him with a calm she didn't feel, she waited for him to speak.

"We've supplies to buy and Hank to pick up. I have to arrange for a slip at dockside, and I won't leave you here alone while I'm gone. It would be too easy for you to swim for the freedom you long for. Another master might take you aboard, but he would more than likely take his payment from you. Your tears wouldn't dampen the pleasure of some men—but I find women who tease, then protest, boring."

She gasped at his cold, cutting words, but couldn't find a suitable reply in her anger.

"Let's go ashore," he said flatly.

With all the dignity she could summon, she agreed quietly, "All right."

"Haven't you any shoes?"

"No, only evening pumps," she returned coldly. He knew she hadn't any shoes.

"Come on," he said, annoyance in his voice.

She followed. They swung down to the rubber dinghy. He rowed while she stared silently over his shoulder at the dock. After he rented the slip from the harbor master, they rowed back to the *Sunflower*. Jake weighed anchor rapidly and under auxiliary power took the sloop into the marina, where in minutes he was making her fast to the dock.

He took Caroline's arm with a proprietary grip and began firmly guiding her toward the open air shops that lined the streets. His hand on her arm tightened and pulled her hastily into a shoe stall. Before she could protest, he bought her a pair of sandals and a pair of deck shoes. Mentally she vowed to find the money to pay him back somehow. An angry thought raced through her mind—her hard labor of the past six weeks was more than adequate for the price of two pairs of shoes!

They went into a marine supply store, where they selected a wide variety of canned goods and other staples. Jake asked that the supplies be delivered to the sloop. Jake and Caroline silently proceeded arm in arm through the fresh produce, meat and fish markets. When they returned to the sloop, he helped her stow their purchases and started the refrigerator for the perishables. Neither had spoken since before tying the *Sunflower* to the dock.

They walked down to the customs shed where they

met Hank. He was flushed with excitement and, for the first time in a week, he seemed relaxed and inquisitive. He barraged Jake with questions and caught up Caroline's hand only to let go of it, dancing in front of them, pointing out the native structures and metal prefab buildings. Jake caught Caroline's hand and guided her around the traffic of people, bikes, motorbikes and small cars.

It was nearly dark when they returned to the sloop. Jake took a small brazier out of a locker and prepared to barbecue steaks, while Caroline prepared their first fresh salad in weeks. It was the first time in days the three of them had eaten together. Hank and Jake talked of the diving they would do soon, and the general flow of talk between the three of them resumed as though the silence of the past few days had never happened.

Hank went to bed early, tired from his exciting day. Caroline soon followed, but she could not sleep. She lay awake, trying to understand why Jake had forced her into staying aboard.

She had thought he was as anxious as she to be rid of trouble, and trouble was plainly what he thought she was to him. Wide awake, she searched her mind for a reason for his strange behavior. Perhaps he wanted to continue his taunting and humiliation, but the consideration he had shown her this evening wasn't consistent with that idea. Could he want her aboard simply to do the cooking and cleaning, thereby freeing him from these tedious chores? But he had always helped her with these chores, and she knew he accepted her as a member of the crew. Her mind refused to consider the possibility that he could want her because he cared for her. Too often he had been cool and distant, proving how little he cared. She heard him moving about overhead, then his footsteps were in the saloon and he was opening the door to the cabin. Her body tensed in panic; she closed her eyes. She heard him moving quietly about as he undressed. Then his bunk sighed softly beneath his weight.

Moments later the deep familiar drawl came across the dark, "Good night, Carrie."

"Good night, Jake," she answered with a forced lightness.

At length he slept, and it was comforting to hear his steady, even breathing in the night once more.

The glassy smoothness of the water around the Truk Islands was ideal for sailing. Jake explained that the waters around these islands were so calm that marine experts called them a lake in the middle of the Pacific. On the sail to Dublon Island, where the sunken fleet lay in shallow waters, the *Sunflower* was like a power boat before the gentle breeze, even and smooth on the water, the customary pitching and rolling gone.

It was dusk when they reached the exposed mast of the *Fujikawa Maru,* the wreck Jake wanted to explore first. The ship was sunk off the small island of Eten. Jake decided to make anchorage in a small cove off the island.

With the *Sunflower* secure, Jake again set up the brazier and cooked the fresh fish they had purchased that morning. After supper and the cleanup, all three watched a full moon rise over the calm sea, its

soft lumination dancing merrily on the surface ripples. Hank went below and in a moment they heard
the strains of Beethoven's *Moonlight Sonata*.

Jake chuckled and said, "Carrie, I believe you've
inspired the poetic soul in that boy."

She laughed low and said, "It's not hard to be
poetic on a night like tonight."

"Or forgive stupidity?" he asked quietly.

Caroline could hardly believe she had heard his
words correctly. Was he apologizing? And for what?
So much had passed between them. His anger over
her name? His anger at her tears when he attempted
to make love to her yesterday afternoon? Or his
simple distrust of her? She studied his face in the soft
light and found no answers there, only his usual
neutral expression. She answered truthfully, taking a
chance that he meant his words, "Yes, I can forgive.
Can you forgive me for not telling you who I was?"

"Yes." He paused, then reluctantly admitted, "I
know I'm sometimes too harsh and cynical. I've
been accustomed to living alone." His deep voice
stopped, as though he had realized how stunned she
was.

In six weeks together this was the first time he had
ever come close to talking about himself.

"Can you dive?" he asked, closing the subject of
past misunderstandings.

"Once I spent the summer holidays with a school
mate from the Bahamas. Her family snorkeled a
great deal and we did some diving. But it's been a
long time."

"It's like riding a bike, as the saying goes, once
you learn, you never forget it. Tomorrow I'll refresh

your memory, though technically you shouldn't be allowed to dive without being certified."

"I'd love to dive and see what you and Hank have been talking about for weeks."

"It's like nothing you've ever seen before." His voice was full of awe.

"Tell me," she breathed, her eyes caressing his handsome face and the length of his long masculine body.

"Down there among the wreckage you can almost feel and hear the day she was sunk: planes, tanks, bombs, deck guns—instruments of violence held in time by one of the tiniest organisms on the face of the Earth."

The reverence in his voice gave her yet another glimpse of one of the many facets that made this man so complex, a man who was admittedly a cynic, but who also stood in awe of nature.

Her love burned bright in her face and eyes. His voice was rough with desire as he said, "You'd better get some sleep, I've some things to check before I go to bed."

She knew he was trying to ease the awkwardness between them by not going to bed at the same time as she.

A long time later, when she had drifted into a light, hazy half-sleep, she heard him come into the cabin and whisper, "Good night, Carrie."

She murmured back sleepily, "Good night, Jake."

The next two days were so wonderful they were not to be believed! The three of them played and frolicked in the crystal clear depths of their private cove. They dove down to the *Fujikawa Maru* and witnessed a world of extraordinary beauty. As Jake had told her, the ship's cargo of deadly war munitions, fighter planes and drums of fuel was now frosted with coral. Caroline was reminded of a festive school dance where all the furniture had been decorated with pink, blue, green and yellow tissue flowers; only the gruesome shapes of the war materials underneath dissolved this notion.

Schools of small, electric blue damselfish darted among their home in the twisted metal of the artificial reef which this once proud war machine now created. Large groupers hid in the shadows, and everywhere hundreds of small silver fish flashed in and out of portholes.

After the required decompression stops were over, Caroline, with the help of the submerged mast of the *Fujikawa Maru,* finned up toward the bright yellow hull. The eerie light that filtered through the clear, warm water diffused the color of the hull in a million minisunbursts. She climbed aboard, her legs trembling for a moment, adjusting to the change from the weightlessness in the water to the full gravity of the ketch. Jake and Hank had worn dual tanks for diving, while she had worn a single. They could stay below another twenty minutes.

She stripped off her weightbelt, tank and wetsuit, exposing the new bikini Jake had provided. His practiced eye and intimate knowledge of her body had allowed him to purchase a perfect fit and the lime green color complemented her amber skin. She knew he had chosen the garment with care. Caroline smiled to herself. She had been very happy these past days, and Jake had too. He laughed and teased Hank, and even joined in on the playful fun of their afternoon swims in the clear lagoon.

After unbraiding her hair to allow it to dry, she lay down on the warm boards of the deck in the sun. Feeling too thirsty to relax, she went below to get a cold soft drink. When she returned and lay back down her peace was shattered. The sound of a boat approaching caused her to jump up in alarm.

Jake's emphatic warning concerning strangers caused a ripple of fear in her, but she remembered his careful preparations. She threw a balloon buoy overboard to alert him of the craft's approach. She pulled on her tee shirt and went to stand in the bow.

"Hello, there?" greeted a large, red-bearded man from the blunt bow of a diving support boat.

"Hello," she returned cautiously. She could see four or five people aboard the craft. In a brief second all the stories of modern day pirates flashed through her mind.

"Is this Jake St. Simon's ketch?" asked red-beard.

"Who are you?" she countered.

"We're friends of Jake," he yelled back.

She stared at them skeptically. The craft came to a stop and the red-bearded man commented, "I see you're flying your diver below flag."

"Yes."

"Is Jake below?" he inquired.

When she again didn't answer, he gave up with a shrug of his shoulders. Then a clear, lilting female voice called out, "Jake, Jake, it's Toni Mitchell."

"I'm sorry, Miss Mitchell, if you'll be patient . . ."

"So he *is* below," the woman said smugly.

Caroline couldn't see the woman who was speaking, but she hadn't cared for the caressing tone she had used when she called out Jake's name. Out of the corner of her eye she saw the *Sunflower*'s anchor chain on the starboard side move slightly. Jake was decompressing and would soon be coming up over that side, away from the other craft.

"You're English, aren't you?" asked the red-bearded man. His frank blue eyes moved freely over her body, intimidating her. "You don't talk much, do you?"

She didn't answer. She felt the *Sunflower* rock as Jake came over the side. She ran to help him off with the heavy tanks. She saw that Hank was remaining in the water hidden near the hull. As Jake dropped the tanks on the deck he zipped open the front of his wetsuit, exposing his broad brown chest. He slipped a protecting arm about her waist and drew her against him as they turned toward the diving launch.

"Jake!" cried the feminine voice of Toni Mitchell.

He dropped his comforting arm from around Caroline's waist and yelled back in delight, "Toni Mitchell!"

"And Terry the Pirate!" yelled red-beard.

"Come aboard!" invited Jake. His broad grin and the undisguised pleasure in his voice told Caroline that these people were welcome. The caressing tone in which he had spoken the woman's name filled Caroline with fear.

Soon the saloon of the *Sunflower* was overrun with Jake's friends. She had grown accustomed to the quiet companionship of Jake and Hank, and was slightly overwhelmed at the appearance of all these people on board at once. Her earlier estimation of only four or five people aboard the launch was wrong, there were seven.

Her eyes swept the saloon. Three Trukese divers were sitting on the deck, their backs against the bulkhead. They were talking to Terry, the red-bearded man. Two Australian divers were half-sitting, half-lying on the benches of the dinette. All were talking of their recent dives. Caroline's lips tightened when her eyes found the final member of the party, Toni Mitchell.

Toni and Jake were sitting together on the deck near the door of the master cabin, which had been opened to allow ventilation in the heavy, humid afternoon air. In the cabin Caroline could see her few clothes neatly folded on her bunk and, across the cabin on Jake's bunk, his carelessly dropped clothes. There was evidence of intimacy, but Toni Mitchell pretended not to notice it, *or* Caroline for that matter. After a barely civil introduction, Toni had turned her undivided attention to Jake.

Caroline's eyes burned with jealousy, an emotion she had never been subject to before. She looked at the object of her wrath. The woman was leaning forward in rapt attention, hanging on Jake's every word.

She reminded Caroline of a fairy tale description of a pixie, as she was only around five feet tall. Her body was lean, but Caroline knew that she was probably deceptively strong from years of diving and swimming. One of the Australian divers had indicated that Toni had received her doctorate in marine biology. Toni's blue eyes were spread wide apart above a short upturned nose, which was dusted with small freckles. Her pointed chin gave her face a heart shape, her mouth small and cupid bow perfect. All these features considered separately were nothing special, but under a cap of light brown, sun-kissed curls, she was very appealing. The all-American girl.

Caroline sighed as Terry crashed onto the floor beside the deck chair where she sat quietly alone in her thoughts.

As the afternoon had worn on, his consumption of beer had increased his boldness. His eyes roved over her as he greeted, "Beautiful lady."

"Thank you for the compliment, but I'm sure you make the same clever remarks to all the ladies." She tried to return his flirting with good humor, but her patience was wearing thin under the leers and frank appraisals.

"No. No, not really," he answered solemnly. Then his boyish face split in an impish grin as he added, "Only the pretty ones!"

She smiled but offered no further encouragement, hoping he would go back to his companions.

"What part of England are you from, Miss Conal?" Terry's voice was courteous and polite, but his brown eyes were not. Caroline felt as if he were mentally stripping her. She suppressed an urge to cross her arms over her chest as she answered with a slight degree of impatience.

"Wales."

"Wales!" he exclaimed. "I spent a summer there. How come I didn't run across you—before Jake had you!"

Caroline felt her face turn red at the crude implication, knowing she had no right to protest. Everyone probably assumed that she and Jake were lovers. Nevertheless she was still embarrassed and mad. Stiffly she asked, "How long have you been here in the Islands?"

"Two months." His eyes had begun a slow exploration of her uncovered legs.

"How did you know of Jake's return to Truk?" she asked, nervously tugging downward at the bottom of her tee shirt.

"Jake St. Simon's a legend in these Islands; word of his arrival spread quickly." His smile was wide in his red beard.

"Oh?" she questioned.

"When he was here two years ago he romanced every woman in sight, drank every man under the table and cleared out several bars—well, never mind," he mumbled at her shocked face.

Her eyes flew to Jake, her breath stopping as his stormy aqua eyes caught hers. On his face was a frown of displeasure at her conversation with Terry. She was instantly filled with anger at his obvious disapproval. How dare he be angry with her when he was engaged in an intimate conversation with Toni! She turned to Terry and smiled sweetly into his face.

He almost gasped at her sudden change. He smiled back and said, "Why do you stay with Jake?"

"I—" she began, blushing at the personal inquiry. Caroline chided herself because her smile had prompted continued boldness in him.

"You would be better appreciated by a man whose interest in a woman is more than just a tumble in bed."

"That's quite enough, Mr.—?" she rasped out.

"Mitchell. I'm Toni's brother," he supplied pleasantly.

"Mr. Mitchell, I don't need advice from you!" she said coldly. She was disgusted with Terry and extremely angry at Jake for putting her in this position. She did not like being cast as his casual lady friend. Caroline arose and went to sit by Hank on the companionway stairs.

Her eyes returned to Jake and Toni. Toni was leaning across Jake to accept another drink from a sullen-faced Terry. Her small firm breasts were rubbing against Jake's bare brown arm. Had there been something between Jake and Toni? She recalled the clinging kiss of greeting Toni had given Jake. It was certainly longer than just an ordinary colleague type kiss.

"Caroline?" said Hank.

"Hummmm?" she answered absently as she continued to watch Jake preening before Toni's adoring eyes.

"Caroline!" demanded Hank.

"I'm sorry, what did you say?" She turned to look at him. His chocolate brown eyes held a puzzled and bewildered look.

"Could we go for a swim? It's hot in here," he complained.

"I don't think we should go now, Hank." Her father had taught her too well how to entertain; one was never rude to a guest, even when they were rude to you. You hid behind cold dignity with the knowledge that you were above that kind of behavior. She didn't feel above that kind of behavior; she wanted to shout at them to leave, feeling ignorant and left out with all this scientific talk that no one would bother to explain, even though she asked questions. She felt like a child, present but not invited to participate in the adult conversation. She knew only about the small amount of underwater beauty Jake had introduced to her these past three days, but apparently there was so much more to learn. Suddenly Caroline found the overpowering heat unbearable and said to Hank, "Let's go for that swim!"

They slipped past the boisterous group totally unnoticed. After taking off the tee shirt, she stepped onto the gunwale and dove into the clear water. Her entry left barely a ripple on the placid surface, whereas Hank's joyous cannonball made a large spout of water and a small wake that rocked the ketch. No one on board seemed to notice or care. Caroline and Hank were already engaged in a race for the white sandy beach of the island. It was a daily game.

They finished the race in a tie, allowing their winded bodies to be washed ashore by the mild surf. Caroline gained her feet and waded out of the sea's reach onto the beach, while Hank scampered around in the surf collecting driftwood into a pile above the water's reach. He stopped now and then to investigate a shell or other bit of sea debris.

She walked down the beach to a point of land sheltered by a few stunted palm trees, which offered some protection from the prying eyes of those aboard the *Sunflower*. She had noticed this place yesterday, but hadn't really investigated until now. It was perfect. The rest of the beach was visible, allowing her to watch Hank. She could just see the tip of the mast of the *Fujikawa Maru* and an occasional flash of the bright yellow hull moored nearby, but they could not see her. The sand underfoot was so fine it reminded her of confectioner's sugar. She sank down into the sand's dry warmth and, for the first time today, felt at ease and alone.

She lay back and closed her eyes. The water and arduous swim had soothed her body, but her mind was still in a turmoil over Jake. What kind of friends had he and Toni been in the past? Hadn't Terry or someone said they had all been together on their exploration of these waters for six months? Six months was a very long time! She and Jake had been together only six weeks and he had—she blushed at the remembrance of his demanding kisses, his questing hands on her flesh and his hard masculine body burning against hers. Had he and Toni lain together as they had? Had they reached the ultimate physical pleasure?

The possibility was driven from her mind as she felt a large strong hand close about her ankle. She tried to sit up with a protesting squeak, but a familiar mouth, moist from a swim to the island, settled on hers and pushed her back into the sand. She relaxed and accepted the unexpected delight. Her hands stroked the wet muscles of Jake's back, then moved to touch the wet rough curls on his chest. He drew away from her body, stilled her hands with one of his, then rolled away from her completely. Her eyes opened; why had he stopped? Suddenly she remembered Hank and the party aboard the ketch! Were they watching this apparent lovers' tryst? Shame rushed through her, and she jerked upright and searched the beach; it was empty, even Hank was gone.

She looked at the silent man beside her, resting on

his right elbow, his aqua eyes studying her with curious intent. She flushed under this scrutiny. She couldn't meet his eyes, afraid her recent wishes would easily be read.

At last she stammered, "Where's Hank?"

"Back on the *Sunflower, chérie,*" he replied, his voice husky and low, the sweet rich southern slur of his words caressing her.

Her eyes were drawn to his as a strange excitement began in her. She nervously licked her lips, not knowing how provocative a gesture it was. His eyes never left her as he moved forward to claim her lips with his. His hand deftly dispensed with her bra and she gasped as his rough chest hair rubbed against the sensitive peaks of her breasts. His hands moved to cup them, and his lips soon followed. Flames of desire licked through her body, into her thighs, causing an aching need for him to take her and put an end to this torment. She whimpered deep in her throat.

"Carrie, love," he whispered at her throat.

"Am I your love, Jake?" she whispered back, instantly hating herself for asking the question. She had mindlessly forced Jake into a corner. If he was going to acknowledge that he cared for her she wanted him to **do** it without prompting. Her need was swept away in fear of what she had done. In horror she rolled away from him. With panic she reached for her discarded swim top and put it on with trembling fingers. She glanced at him lying there. He was just staring at her with amusement. His powerful body was relaxed while she was as tight as a bowstring, strained with unreleased passion and love for him.

"Carrie, what's wrong with you?" he asked; his eyes swept her body to fasten on her face.

"Wrong?" she whispered.

"Yes, damn it. Wrong. First you're passionate and wanting me as much as I want you. The next instant you're ready to run." He stopped, and his face became clear as a grim realization came to him. He ground out angrily, "Run, that's all you know, isn't it? When something doesn't suit you or becomes too difficult, you run away."

"I—I wasn't going to run, Jake," she denied. It was the second time in three days she had denied the charge. The first time she had been ready to run; now the only place she wanted to run was into his arms.

"Then what is all of this about?" His voice rose in frustration, his eyes demanded an answer.

"You . . . and I . . . together . . ." she stumbled out, ready to blurt out the truth, but the old habit of defending her pride forced her to say bitterly, "You have a lot of cheek asking that question! Why don't you lay Toni Mitchell on the soft sand and turn her on? I'm sure she would be a willing partner for your needs!"

"That's an excellent idea! Toni, at least, is a woman who doesn't play coy little games with a man. She gives herself without strings."

"And you would know! Did you have an affair on your so-called *last expedition* here?" she accused like a jealous shrew.

"Yes," he ground out cruelly, "Toni's a very passionate woman, and I find her refreshing after hot and cold little rich girls who play with a man as a pastime, whereas Toni . . ."

"Stop it, Jake." She didn't need to hear any more to confirm that Toni Mitchell was a woman and Jake was her lover.

"Afraid to hear the truth about a real woman's honest passion." He reached out and seized her trembling body.

The mouth that came crashing down on hers was not tender or teasing as it had been moments ago, but it was nevertheless just as devastating to her battered senses. She struggled to deny him her total surrender, but in the end her arms encircled his neck, her body arched into his and her lips parted under his.

When at last he raised his head, she was breathless.

She reluctantly opened her eyes. His handsome face was cold and hard with the success of his experiment in arousing her.

Her desire was drowned in a wave of bitter rage. With a physical strength she did not know existed, she pushed him away, scrambled to her feet and ran into the crashing surf. She swam with all the strength she could summon from her trembling body. When at last she pulled herself onto the ketch, her lungs were burning, her eyes stinging from the salt of tears and sea.

She padded below, not caring if she dripped water onto the polished decks, storming about the confined space of the saloon, picking up beer and soft drink cans, putting the pillows of the settee and dinette back into place, trying unconsciously to wipe away any traces of the group that had shattered her peace. Jake's words kept echoing in her ears, and they left no room for doubt—Toni Mitchell and he had been lovers, and their relationship would now pick up . . .

"Caroline?" called Hank.

"Hank?" she answered. "Where are you?"

"I'm in my cabin, Caroline." His voice didn't sound very strong or lively.

"May I come in?"

"Yes."

She found him on his bunk, just staring at the ceiling. His face was ashen and his eyes unnaturally glassy. The bubbly boy of just two hours ago was nowhere to be seen. Feeling that his forehead was hot with fever, she asked in alarm, "What's wrong?"

"I don't feel good, Caroline," he whispered.

"Mmmm, too much sun perhaps? I'll get a cool cloth and make you a light supper. When Jake comes back from his swim I'll ask him about aspirin tablets," she said reassuringly, trying to hide her worry.

"Thanks," he murmured.

She went into the head and returned with the cloth. He didn't open his eyes as she put it on his forehead but he whispered, "That feels good."

She swallowed the lump in her throat and said with false bravado, "I'll be right outside in the galley; if you need me, just sing out."

He smiled a little and replied softly, "Okay."

She went out and began preparing chicken soup. She once had a nanny who swore by the chicken soup treatment for any ailment, and another who swore by the tea, honey and lemon treatment. Just to be safe, she would try both. She wished she knew more about children's illnesses. She remembered the fresh oranges that had been stocked on Moen; she would try vitamin C as well! Quickly she squeezed them for juice.

She was preparing a tray with the juice and tea when she felt the ketch rock and heard Jake's feet overhead. Completely forgetting their scene on the island, she anxiously called out to him, "Jake."

He came down immediately to stare at her, his face cold, his eyes hostile. Ignoring his black mood, she said, "Hank's not feeling well. I think it's probably too much sun, but would you check him anyway, please?"

He said nothing as he brushed by her on his way into Hank's cabin. She followed with the tray.

"Caroline says you're not feeling well," he said, looking down at the pale boy.

"It's nothing. I just don't feel very good, Jake," he said, trying to put up a brave front.

Jake took the wet cloth off and felt his face. His own face immediately registered concern, but unlike Caroline, he seemed to know instantly what to do. He glanced over his shoulder at her tray and reached for the glass of orange juice, offering it to Hank as he instructed her to get the thermometer and aspirin out of the medical kit.

She put the tray down and went quickly as he ordered, glad that Hank was in capable hands.

At the evening meal, Jake ate sandwiches and chicken soup with Hank in his cabin, persuading him to drink some tea, another glass of juice and a cup of soup. He didn't speak to Caroline except to call her to do something for Hank, which she was only too happy to do.

As night came Hank's fever went down. Relief flooded her mind. But remembering Jake's thundercloud look, the memory of this afternoon on the beach caused a worry of another kind. Would Jake treat her as a slave again? Would he retreat behind a wall of silence? Would he rekindle with his lips and hard body the passion in her? A sigh escaped her. How much longer could she take living with Jake and not surrender to him? And if she did, would he leave her when he grew bored with her? She vowed not to become another Toni Mitchell, begging him to love her after he had discarded her. Or had he discarded her? This afternoon he had been more than willing to receive Toni's attentions.

Hank's cabin door opened. She asked, "How is he?"

"Better," was Jake's curt response. His sea green eyes studied her lovely body, still scantily clad in the swimsuit and tee shirt, her concern for Hank making her forget to change. She blushed under his intense look. His face was weary and strained. Despite her resolutions of a few moments ago, she felt a tender, overpowering desire to put her arms out to him, to kiss the lines of weariness from his face, to caress the tight tense column of muscles along his neck; but most of all, *she* wanted to be held in the protective circle of his arms. She took a step toward him, but his weary voice halted her.

"Go to bed, Carrie. I'll stay up awhile until Hank has settled down."

"All right," she whispered in a low voice. She went into their cabin, stripped off her clothes and slipped into bed. But so much had happened this day that she couldn't relax or sleep. Her mind saw again and again Toni Mitchell's face smiling into Jake's. Toni's small breasts touching his arm, her eyes caressing his bare torso. She remembered Jake's words about Toni's passion.

The door to the cabin opened quietly and Jake slipped in. She forced her body and breathing to remain still, even when he came near to the bunk and looked down at her. He reached out and lightly touched her silken hair. Involuntarily her eyes flew open at his touch. He mistook her startled expression and apologized for waking her.

"You didn't," she whispered as she sat up slowly, "I was just thinking."

"Carr—" he began, but the sheet covering her had fallen down, revealing her rosy breasts. She was so lovely and desirable he couldn't continue. Strangely, she didn't feel compelled to cover her body from his gaze. The dam holding back her resistance and self-control burst; she put her arms out to him and he came willingly into them.

"I need you so badly, Carrie," he muttered at the sensitive cord of her throat. She moaned as his tongue and mouth traced her collarbone. He demanded in a hoarse voice, "Make love with me, *chérie.*"

She didn't answer with words, but with her hands as she continued to explore his tanned, warm skin. With a boldness that once would have surprised her, Caroline tugged his shirt open so that her fingers could know every inch of him. Slowly, she helped him undress, massaging the muscles of his masculine form which were taut with longing. She could no longer deny that she loved him, and regardless of the consequences, she would have these moments of splendid, anguished love to relish and remember.

Answering the invitation in her eyes, he pulled the sheet aside and slipped into the bunk beside her. Their bodies melded in a fusion of white hot shattering delight; her breasts pressed against his chest, her thighs against his, she became aware of the steely strength of him against her soft, supple form.

She gasped with pleasure as his hands began a slow exploration of her sensitive breasts, circling each swollen bud with a motion that stirred feelings in the recesses of her being. They were both trembling with delicious need when his hands wandered lower, toward the smooth region of her inner thighs. She was aching with desire for him when she felt the slight pain of her initiation into womanhood, but it was quickly brushed away by the growing excitement within her, as they carried each other on wave after wave of pleasure. They rode the crest together, landing on a golden shore of contentment. Caroline felt moved by the perfection of their love. She had become one with him, and the warm, sweet feeling that enveloped her brought tears to her eyes.

"*Chérie*, I didn't know . . . I was the first." Jake brushed her eyes gently with his fingertips.

"Oh, Jake. I never thought it would be so beautiful," she whispered.

He stroked her shining hair, and for a moment she thought she a look of sadness in his eyes. "You're the one who is truly beautiful, *chérie*."

Still entwined in an embrace, they drifted off to sleep.

* * *

Reluctantly she removed her clinging arms as he went to check on Hank. Later as she lay in a dreamy contented sleep, she was aroused slightly as she heard him return. "Jake?"

"Yes, *chérie?*" he replied, his voice low and caressing.

She opened her eyes and saw his soft smiling face. She held out her arms to him. He leaned over until she could encircle his neck and draw him down to her. He kissed her lightly and she smiled against his lips and sighed sleepily. He tried to slip quietly away from her, but she presssed a kiss to his shoulder, tightened her arms around his waist, and held him close against her as he slept. Eventually his exhaustion and worry receded, his muscles relaxed, and with a heavy sigh he fell asleep in her embrace.

Chapter Seven

Caroline awoke slowly, stretching her body with the grace of a cat. She had a wonderful feeling of well-being in her body and mind. Suddenly she remembered why she felt this way! She opened her dreamy eyes to look at Jake's handsome face, but she was alone in the bed. Was last night a fantasy?

As if to confirm what she already knew, she looked across at Jake's neatly made bed. The clothes that had been heaped carelessly onto it yesterday were in the exact same place. She turned her face into the pillow next to hers. His masculine scent was faint on the pillow slip and she breathed deeply, filling her nose with his heady smell.

Last night hadn't been a fantasy. Jake had made love to her and held her through a night of soft slumber. She wondered briefly why he hadn't wakened her when he had left their bed this morning. She smiled with lingering contentment, hugging the pillow to her bare breasts and glowing with the radiance of a woman in love. The physical triumph of love added yet another satisfying dimension to their relationship—the mistrust and anger would be a thing of the past now.

Every fiber in her body was filled with vitality, wanting to greet the morning, to feel the sun on her face, to look at Jake's face. The memory of his face as he had taken her to the glorious heights of passion, and later as he held her tenderly, was vivid in her mind. Suddenly she wanted to be near him, to touch him with gentleness and be reassured that he was as happy and content as she was with the pleasurable new turn in their relationship.

She had surrendered completely, ready to stay with him and risk the consequences of the future. Gone were her own strict moral codes, and in their place was overwhelming love. Her happiness and well-being pushed away any ideas that Jake didn't return her love. Her thoughts instead turned to the hard sinewy length of the man who had lain next to her in the night.

As she slipped out of the bunk, her body somehow felt different from every previous morning of her life. She moved to the wardrobe and opened the door, selecting Jake's favorite outfit, the blue silk dress shirt and cutoffs. She raked her fingers through her hair to restore some order to the tumbled mass.

Caroline opened the cabin door with some feelings of trepidation and modesty, but she felt excitement too. The saloon was empty. Then she heard

Hank's voice coming from the deck, where he was talking to Jake.

Slipping into the head, she washed her face, brushed her teeth and combed her hair. As she smiled into the mirror over the pullman, Caroline was pleased with the reflection of the woman with dreamy eyes and rosy cheeks. She went into the saloon again, her anxiety and shyness gone, swept away by her need to see him. But only Hank was there to greet her. Still slightly pale, he was obviously feeling better.

"Good morning, Hank," she sang out. She couldn't seem to stop smiling.

"Good morning," he mumbled.

"How are you, Hank? You look better." She touched his forehead and found it to be cool. He ducked under her hand, embarrassed at her concern.

"I'm fine!" His questioning eyes studied her contented face. He remembered Jake's withdrawn mood. Since Caroline had come aboard Hank had learned that the two adults in his life were seldom at the opposite ends of the mood scale. When one was happy, the other was usually cheerful too, and vice versa.

She began breakfast, humming a happy tune under her breath. Hank mumbled that he was going to his cabin to read.

"I'll call you when breakfast is ready." She smiled tenderly at the handsome young face so much like Jake's.

"All right," he said slowly. He glanced up at the deck where he knew Jake sat staring out to sea. With a perplexed frown he watched Caroline's bubbly form for a moment longer. What was up? He shrugged his shoulders and went into his cabin.

When the coffee was ready she went topside. Caroline's heart was thumping in joyous anticipation of going into his arms without hesitation or shyness. They were lovers now; it gave her the right to initiate physical contact, but she was still strangely shy too. She smiled at this foolishness. After last night she had nothing to be shy of, their love was an established fact now. He knew her body perhaps better than she did.

She halted abruptly at the sight of him slumped in the deck chair. Her stomach tightened at his brooding posture. It brought back memories of the terrible days of isolation and bitter anger between them.

"Jake?" she whispered, a note of desperation creeping into her voice.

He stood and turned slowly, his face neutral. Her mind cried in pain at the lack of welcome. As his eyes searched her face, she did not attempt to conceal her confusion, shyness or love. Had last night meant nothing to him? Had he only sated his physical hunger? Doubts and fears began to pummel her already weak self-confidence.

"I came to tell you that the coffee is ready," she said, her voice sounding loud and shrill to her.

Several awkward moments passed, then he said, "Thank you, *chérie*." His eyes held hers; perhaps there was a suggestion of a smile in their aqua depths.

At the use of his endearment and the glint in his eyes, she ventured a weak smile. He responded with a slow gathering smile. His eyes swept her slender form in a silent breathless commentary of his intimate knowledge of her.

Relief flooded her. He reached for her. She needed no additional persuasion; she was back in those strong arms and resting against him with a familiar intimacy.

She tilted her head back to receive his kiss. A kiss which was slow and lingering, filled with sweetness instead of unbridled passion. They savored this caress as one does a gentle spring day after a long stormy winter.

Caroline felt a stab of regret when it ended. Now that she knew the physical delights of lovemaking and the spectacular passions possible between a man and woman, it only created a deeper yearning in her than she had known before, when lovemaking was a hazy unexplored aspect between them.

"Jake, I—" She wanted to say she loved him and much, much more. Instead she was tongue-tied with the inadequacy of words.

He seemed to understand as he drew her against him and whispered in her tumbled golden red hair, "Me too, *chérie.*"

"Hey, you guys!" yelled Hank from the companionway. His face was no longer bewildered but beaming with undisguised pleasure at the sight of Jake holding Caroline in his arms.

Jake muttered in her ear, "That boy has no sense of timing."

She laughed, her bubble of happiness suppressing the doubts and fears which were, for the moment, pushed to an insignificant corner of her mind.

Breakfast was a noisy affair with Hank babbling

over the dive they had planned for today. He was good-naturedly disgruntled when Jake vetoed the dive on the grounds of Hank's bout with fever last night. Caroline blushed as Jake added softly, his eyes traveling over her, "And mine."

"Didn't you feel good either last night?" questioned Hank. He looked from Caroline's scarlet face to Jake's gently teasing contented face. Jake's earlier mood seemed to have gone now that Caroline was around. He smiled at both of them.

"I've never felt better than I did last night, boy," Jake answered, his voice low and caressing as his aqua eyes devoured Caroline.

"Jake—?" began a puzzled Hank. Then he turned to Caroline, whose eyes were shimmering with delight at Jake's answer.

With the kitchen put in order, the three of them went about their chores. Jake refilled the air tank, Caroline washed clothes, and Hank did school work.

After a quick lunch eaten with banter and laughter, they took the dinghy and rowed for the island.

Caroline dropped onto the powdery sand and leisurely surveyed the sights of her private paradise: the *Sunflower* bobbing on jewel bright seas, the crescent-shaped white beach, the bronze figures of Jake and Hank as they walked along the beach at the surf line.

As her tanned body relaxed, her lazy sun-dulled thoughts drifted and she fell into a light sleep. Her dreams should have been filled with sugarplum enchantment, but the doubts and fears she was able to suppress in the waking hours now rose. Jake hadn't said he loved her. Jake hadn't said he wanted to marry her. He obviously desired her physically but did he care for her? Terry Mitchell's red-bearded face smiled knowingly into her dream saying, "Ask my sister. She'll tell you all about Jake St. Simon."

She awoke startled and shaken; the object of her dreams loomed over her. She gasped in fear and was immediately ashamed of that fear when his face was filled with tender concern.

"Oh Jake," she groaned. Her heart thumped in alarm, tears threatened to spill.

He took her into his arms and held her trembling body against his own. His warmth and strength seemed to shelter and protect her. He kissed her face and whispered in a low, rough voice, "What is it, *chérie?*"

"I—oh—" She couldn't tell him that he had caused her bad dream, that he was the dark brooding figure that loomed as a question mark in her mind. Instead she frantically kissed him, while her hands sought to reassure her troubled mind of his tangible presence as they moved over his bare back and strong neck to the soft black hair.

"*Chérie,* what has frightened you?" he demanded, the tenderness in his eyes taking the edge off his voice.

"It was nothing, Jake, just a bad dream." She pulled his head down to hers, silencing his words with an eager kiss.

Mutual passion exploded between them. Jake's questions were gone when their lips parted. His eyes roved over her bikini-clad figure, closely followed by his seeking hands. He sighed in frustration as he whispered, "Hank's just down the beach exploring a tide pool, *chérie.*"

"Oh—" She blushed and pulled away from him in alarm.

He laughed and said in a low teasing voice, "Your blush betrays you. He'll know I've been kissing you."

She smiled sheepishly but retorted, "And your wicked grin condemns you, sir."

His laughter reminded her of the same merry thunder she had heard on that first morning. She was reminded of his contemptuous mockery of her wealth and lofty attitude as he had executed his low, formal bow. That day seemed so long ago, yet it was only six short weeks ago. Her life had turned completely upside down since that morning.

"Where have you gone, Carrie?" he asked, his eyes puzzled as they traveled over her thought-filled face.

She answered truthfully, "I was thinking about my life up to now."

"Do you miss being a rich girl?" he asked half-serious and half-teasing.

"No," she answered slowly, then smiled as she added, "Although it would be nice to have a dress or two from my wardrobe."

"I like you in next to nothing." His eyes slowly traversed her body in a possessive look that took her breath and words away. Her eyes held his in a long, lingering, unspoken conversation.

He reached out and with one finger lightly traced her parted lips, smooth cheek and slender neck. A tingle of longing swept over her at these slow sensuous gestures.

"The sun's going down, *chérie*." His voice was heavy.

"Yes." Her own voice was choked and raspy.

"Dinner can't be over quickly enough for me." His eyes told her that with the close of this day she would once more be in his bed and arms.

Would this night bring the words she longed to hear?

"Come on!" yelled a completely forgotten Hank.

Reluctantly they stood and went to the surf line where Hank was waiting impatiently beside the dinghy for the short trip back to the ketch.

The evening passed in its established pattern, dinner, cleanup and the evening view of the setting blood red sun and rise of the icy white moon over the dark seas. She thought about the new Caroline, knowing that she'd always cherish this moonstruck voyage with Jake. The inner voice that had taunted her with doubts was overridden by the hope that Jake would silence it forever with a declaration of love.

Later as she lay in his arms, when his gentle even breath told her he was asleep, she felt silent tears trickle down her face. Their loving had been breathless and satisfying, but apart from endearments and encouragement, Jake had not said he loved her nor mentioned that he wanted to make their relationship permanent. Sleep was a long time in claiming her.

The dawn of morning was not as joyous as the previous morning had been when she had awakened refreshed and replete in the aftermath of loving. She felt drained and nervous as if she were walking a highwire of taut emotions. One wrong move would bring her crashing down into the dust of heartbreak.

Jake seemed to echo her nervousness. He eagerly accepted a radio invitation from Toni Mitchell's group to dive on the wrecks off Dublon Island.

The short voyage to Dublon Island took less than forty-five minutes. They anchored away from the diving launch, and soon after dropping anchor, a dinghy was launched from the cumbersome craft. Caroline did not rejoice at the thought of seeing Toni or Terry Mitchell again, but she smiled as Jake greeted them.

While Caroline was in the cabin changing into her swimsuit she heard Toni ask Jake in an arched voice, "Where is your friend, Jake?"

"She's changing for the dive."

"Are you going to allow a rank amateur on a deep dive?" she asked, her voice full of contempt and scorn.

"She'll be all right." His curt reply cheered Caroline, but the next words did not. "I'll stay with her and keep her from blundering into any of your experiments."

Their voices faded as they moved about the deck. Caroline's anger rose at his condescending remark, as if she were a child that had to be watched! He expected her to make mistakes, did he? She would show him and Dr. Toni Mitchell! She wouldn't make any errors! She wouldn't give him any reason to be ashamed of her inexperience!

After she struggled into the wetsuit that was required on this deep dive, she stormed on deck. Her smile was bright and frozen for the members of the expedition. Terry's joyous delight at seeing her again was displayed on his face. His boyish good looks were accented by the tight red wetsuit top he wore over navy swim trunks. His red hair was a curly shambles from the sea water and wind.

He came over to her and said, "I'm glad you're diving today, pretty lady."

"You're the only one," she muttered as she gave Jake and Toni a freezing glance. Jake's face changed from puzzlement to anger as she smiled sweetly at Terry.

Jake grasped Caroline's elbow firmly as they rolled backwards over the side of the launch's platform into the balmy water.

The underwater beauty she witnessed soon cooled her anger. The awe she'd felt during her previous dives on the *Fujikawa Maru* was multiplied a thousand times over. They explored the coral-encrusted relics of tanks, trucks and airplanes that were trapped inside an aircraft carrier. They poked among the litter of china plates, delicate sake cups and all sorts of other fragile objects that miraculously managed to survive intact during the storm of bombs.

When at last they decompressed and surfaced among the schools of small, brilliantly flashing fish, Caroline was aglow with a million questions. Jake's time was immediately claimed by Toni and Terry with a barrage of scientific questions that meant very little to her or Hank.

Later, Caroline and Hank slipped away in a dinghy and went back to the *Sunflower* to prepare dinner. But Jake's portion of dinner grew cool, then cold, and later was thrown into the garbage as the sun set on the fiery waters of the Pacific.

Jake's nonappearance confirmed her worst fears—Jake was growing tired and bored with her. She went to bed early to hide the sick despair she felt, but an astute Hank seemed to read her feelings no matter how carefully she tried to hide them.

It was well after midnight when she felt the ketch rock under Jake's weight. She heard the oars of the diving launch's dinghy slip quietly away in the night. Whoever had brought him home was trying to be quiet but she couldn't say the same about Jake. She heard banging and a mumbled curse, then another bump, another curse, this time louder and more distinguishable, having something to do with the ancestry of the offending winch.

Moments later the door to the cabin was thrown open. The rank smell of alcohol assailed her nostrils; she realized that he was drunk. After several unsuccessful attempts at undressing, he fell across their bunk in a stupor. She rolled over and switched on the dim night lamp. In the soft illumination she couldn't stop her eyes from traveling over his almost naked form as he lay sleeping. He really was a magnificent man! His body was lean, tough, and bronzed by the sun. Her eyes rested on his dark head against the white pillow. She reached out and pushed back the stray lock of hair. Like all people in sleep, he was so vulnerable and so desirable. At last she forced herself out of her reverence of him and placed a blanket over his long legs. She couldn't help wishing tonight were last night. She slipped beneath the blanket next to his comforting warmth and once again felt his possessive arm cross her body in sleep. She sighed deeply as she went to sleep. At least she could sleep now—he was safely home; for home was just what her heart and mind had labeled the *Sunflower*.

* * *

The steady hum of the auxiliary motor woke her. Jake's place beside her was still warm to the touch. He could not have been up more than a few minutes, yet he was already moving the *Sunflower*. What was today's plan, more diving with the expedition?

Once again, her inner voice assailed her. Had Jake tired of her already? Had her physical surrender ended the challenge for him? Was he merely giving her silent signals that they were finished?

Panic rose in her. She loved him, but she could not stay with him until he was forced to rid himself of her. Angry pride built within her. She would not allow him to cast her aside, *she* would be the one to go away! But before she went, she had to confront him, she had to know his true feelings.

With firm resolve she dressed, performed her morning grooming, and went on deck after checking on a still sleeping Hank.

Jake was at the helm. She stared out at the sea. They were moving away from the diving launch but were not sailing in the direction of Eten Island.

As she approached the cockpit her courage began to waver. Jake's face was closed, his lips compressed into a tight line, his eyes cool and unwelcoming.

She received only a curt not at her good morning greeting. When she asked where they were going she received yet another curt reply, "Moen Island."

She retreated to the saloon. Moen Island—where the airport was. Did he intend to dump her once they reached the island? Her mind cried out that she couldn't bear to hear those words. She would go ashore and wire her father. She would rather go home to her father and his prearranged marriage than live in this permanent purgatory with Jake!

Jake rented an isolated slip on a dock that was away from the hustle and bustle of the main wharf. Jake's mood did not improve with breakfast. He told Hank rather curtly to go ashore for a while, explaining that he wanted to speak privately to Caroline. Both the boy and the woman paled. What was the meaning of this? Was it the end?

Once the boy was gone, Caroline nervously began to clear the galley of the breakfast clutter, unwilling to face his trite explanations of the end of their relationship.

"Stop that," he snapped.

She turned to face him with a calm, cool haunting stare characteristic of the uncaring young woman he had first seen in Hawaii.

She thought she saw him physically recoil at her closed face, but as quickly as he had shown this small weakness, he stood straight, his own face cool and foreboding.

"Why did you leave the diving launch yesterday?" he demanded in a cutting voice.

"What?" she whispered stupidly. She hadn't anticipated the question.

"Didn't my friends meet your expectations? Were we boring you?"

"I—" She was not prepared to defend herself against his attack. She had been prepared to say good-bye.

"Caroline, I won't change my friends nor will I accept your blatant snobbery of them."

"I didn't mean—" she stupidly began to apologize but then anger filled her. She lashed out, "You're a fine one to talk about snobbery, Jake. When I brought your bored, tired and hungry nephew back here you were too wrapped up in your scientific discussion to care or notice that both he and I were odd-man out!"

"You've encouraged Hank to take on your rich girl attitudes!" he accused. His eyes were sparkling with blue fire.

This final accusation cut her to the quick. He had not changed his opinion of her at all! He still thought she was a shallow, callous woman with no heart!

She pushed past him and off the *Sunflower,* not bothering to look back. Had she done so, she would have stopped her headlong flight and returned to the dejected man who watched her disappearing into the crowded marketplace.

She found the telegraph office, where the man behind the narrow counter seemed somewhat reluctant to put her collect cable through. After several minutes of assuring him that the party on the other end would be more than happy to accept the charges, he sent the cable to her father's main office in London and to the *Caroline* in care of the marine operator in Hawaii. She prayed he was still aboard the yacht in Hawaii or cruising near there.

As she awaited acknowledgment of her cable she recalled the night of her first impulsive flight. The scene she had witnessed between Jean and her father came to mind, and she hoped something had come of their embrace. Perhaps her father could understand and forgive her with Jean by his side to temper his anger.

The cables were immediately accepted in both places; apparently Robert had alerted his offices around the world to accept any communication from her. Perhaps he cared for her after all—no, he cared only for a male heir to his fortune.

She wished it could be Jake's child, but she quickly stopped her childish thinking before it got out of hand. If she was lucky, she would be walking away from Jake with only a broken heart.

When she asked the clerk how long an answer would be in coming, he shrugged nonchalantly. "Hour or two, if the party on the other end wants to answer you." She felt panicked as she hadn't thought of that possibility! After two very long hours she was rewarded, much to her relief, by a tersely worded cable: Arriving there soonest by company jet. Robert.

Her hands shook as she tucked the thin yellow paper of the cable reply into the pocket of her cutoffs. How would she meet him without arousing Jake's suspicions? She turned to leave the office.

"Miss, Miss?" called the man behind the counter.

"Yes?" she breathed, half-afraid he would ask for some payment.

"You've forgotten your money." He was all smiles now.

"Money?" she echoed, confused.

"The man—Mr. Conal." He glanced down at his copy of the telegram. "He sent you a thousand dollars."

"A thousand . . ." She stopped in utter amazement. Leave it to Robert to have thought first of her finances.

"You just sign this voucher and take it across to the bank. Bingo! Money!" He grinned at her.

"Thank you," she said, signing the paper.

It was as easy as the telegraph agent had said. A young native girl with melting black eyes smiled cheerfully as she counted ten crisp, new one-hundred dollar bills into Caroline's hand. Only weeks ago she would have rejoiced at this money, but now she just tucked it into her pocket with the telegram.

Caroline wandered among the market stalls. She couldn't return to the *Sunflower* and her angry master. With the money she didn't need to, but what of her cape and jewels—she didn't care if she ever retrieved them, she thought angrily.

"Well, well, Ms. Conal," purred the voice of Toni Mitchell.

Caroline began to turn away from the woman, then as an afterthought, turned to face her. Caroline's pride would not allow her to let this woman think she had caused her discomfort. Toni had on a lovely, bright print sundress that put Caroline's very limited wardrobe to shame, but she equaled the sultry woman's stare as she said, "Hello, Doctor."

"Please, don't stand on ceremony, call me Toni, Caroline—or is it Carrie or *chérie?*" she drawled in a mock southern accent.

The shock of the woman's using Jake's words of endearment must have shown on her face because the woman laughed lightly and invited, "Come on, we'll have a drink, it's too late for lunch. I'll tell you more about Jake. That's what you'd like to ask but haven't the nerve, isn't it?"

Caroline suddenly realized somewhere in her subconscious mind that Toni was right. She wanted to hear from this woman's own lips what she and Jake had meant to one another and what kind of man Jake was. Caroline fleetingly wondered if deep within herself she hid some form of masochism. Why was it necessary to punish herself with the gory details of his past affairs? She was tempted to turn and run, but like a moth drawn to the flame that would most assuredly destroy it, she accepted Toni's invitation.

They sat facing one another across a small quiet table. The lighting was subdued in the nearly empty hotel bar. Silently they sized each other up like two pugilists about to begin a match. Caroline was tongue-tied and reluctant to begin the conversation. She felt slightly guilty, and somehow disloyal, at discussing the man she loved with this woman.

However, Toni Mitchell showed no sign of either of these discomforts as her small mouth curved upward and her eyebrows arched in mocking amusement. With a degree of frivolity in her voice she said, "Well, Carrie, what do you want to know? If I love him? If I've slept with him?"

Her blue eyes bored into Caroline's, which had widened in surprise. Much to her dismay Caroline blushed at the directness of the woman's words.

"My, my, I didn't expect a blush from a woman who has lived with Jake for months on end!"

"Months on end?"

"Don't tell me he just recently picked you up?" she asked with amusement.

"Picked me up?" she echoed again.

"Can't you do more than repeat my words?" Toni asked scathingly, her blue eyes now contemptuous of Caroline's naïveté. It was plain she had expected a more spirited fight than the one Caroline was offering.

"Yes, I can do more than repeat your words. It's

just that you haven't asked any questions that make sense, and I have some questions of my own, too," Caroline countered.

Leaning back in her chair, Toni seemed to be making a detailed inspection of the ceiling fan that whirred in the afternoon heat. When she did speak it was steady and deliberate. "Then I'll be perfectly clear. You want to know if I love Jake? Maybe I do. Jake certainly would be worth loving, if he loved you in return. Jake St. Simon will love only once in his life and it will be forever and as deep as the ocean!"

Caroline could not dispute the statement. Jake did everything with a singleminded intensity. She wondered if Therese, the woman who haunted Jake's dreams, had been the love of his life. Was she the reason he only had brief affairs? Couldn't he love again?

"You know, Carrie, I thought *you* were *that* woman, but then I've seen the two of you together, and I don't think you would be very good for him."

"Why not?" demanded Caroline.

"Jake's not a man who could be kept on a tight rein. Or who would be willing to play silly games to keep you happy! And you? You're just a high-class lady playing at slumming. Cooking, washing by hand, sailing around the world, they really aren't your idea of life, are they?" Toni's eyes had left the ceiling fan and were now piercing Caroline.

"I'm not playing at anything, Toni," Caroline retorted.

"Aren't you?" demanded the woman.

"No. I love him and I don't care what his life is like," Caroline answered quietly.

"Jake drank a great deal last night. He ran on

about you, Carrie, love. Your society life, your wealth."

"He spoke of my life?" she asked, amazed that he would even care about the kind of life he thought she led.

"Yes, he spoke of you and his own life."

"His life?" She couldn't stop the curious questions.

"Caroline, do you really think he can continue to be 'the most successful young head of America's foremost electronics firm in the state he's in?" she asked coldly.

Caroline sat in shock at this revelation. Jake? Her Jake? Jake was a business magnate like her father? My Lord, no wonder he was so contemptuous of her life! He was in the same position as she! His life had been full of users, hustlers, money grubbers . . .

"Don't you know who Jake is or what he does for a living?" It was plain Toni was surprised that Caroline knew so little of the man she lived with.

"No, I met him in Hawaii, quite by accident," Caroline stammered out truthfully, unable to find the words for pretense and fencing with Toni any longer.

"You really don't know a damn thing about him, do you?" she asked, her voice sharp.

"No—yes, yes, I do know him—better than you do!" Suddenly unwilling to hear any more about Jake from this woman, Caroline stood up. It didn't matter what Jake was, or what he had been in the past or how many women he had known. It was the future Caroline wanted, and there was only one way to find out what it held—from Jake! She must confront Jake. She realized that she couldn't leave tomorrow without trying one more time to bridge the chasm between them. She must make him understand that she didn't want the kind of life he thought she did! She would make him see that she understood why he had given up his life-style, and that she wanted the same kind of life-style he wanted.

"Wait a minute!" cried Toni as Caroline paid for her untouched drink and started toward the door. Over her shoulder, she called, "Thanks, Toni."

The sun was setting when she reached the *Sunflower*. She hadn't realized so many hours had passed since she had left Jake's hateful words. Would he be worried? Or mad?

Only Hank was aboard.

"Caroline! Where have you been?" he demanded with the same superiority as Jake would have.

"I'm sorry, Hank. I had some thinking to do," she apologized.

"You've been gone six hours!" he accused, although he seemed to be somewhat mollified at her explanation.

"Where's Jake?" she asked.

"Looking for you—there he is!"

Jake was coming down the dock as she said to the boy, "Would you please go below? I really need to talk to him."

"Sure." He disappeared before Jake was aboard.

She saw the relief flare in his eyes when he saw her standing on the deck. Her hopes soared.

Caroline looked up into his tender questioning eyes as he reached out and touched her face with a strong hand. The electrical shock of their physical contact never ceased to amaze her. The merest brush or bumping of their bodies in the close quarters of the ketch could momentarily halt their progress, until either or both of them reluctantly broke the spell and continued on their separate ways. Now neither wanted to move away.

He was wearing slacks and a white linen shirt with the top buttons open. The ruby glow of the late afternoon played on his dark hair and caught the shine of the gold medal around his neck.

The warmth of his chest beckoned her and she moved into the circle of his welcoming arms. Her nose came to rest in the open collar of his shirt. Idly she touched his skin, savoring the satin smoothness on her fingertips.

His hands were restless too, tracing the outline of her curving spine, pausing briefly to release the buttons of her shirt and push the offending garment open. Her nipples were hard and taut against his warm chest. He groaned softly as she arched against him. His hands resumed their roaming, running a slow finger around the top of her cutoffs. He stopped the light tantalizing and put his hands on her hipbones, drawing her to him. Her thighs molded against his, the smooth cotton cloth of his slacks failing to disguise his need for her.

"Carrie?" the husky whisper came at her temple.

"Hmmmm?" she answered, totally bemused by his nearness.

"Carrie, tell me what you want of me." His voice caressed her senses. His slow drawl flowed into her very heart.

She drew away, looking into his face. In the muted light his perfectly sculpted features were tender yet questioning, his sea green eyes were seducing her thoughts.

"Jake, I want only to be at peace with you," she answered truthfully.

"No more games!" His voice was rough, but tempered with a slow melting smile. His eyes were caressing her soft lips and lazily traveling from the hollow at her throat to the valley between her breasts.

Wordlessly, like a marionette, her arms came up to his head, her fingers threaded through his midnight black hair and drew his face down to hers. She could feel his ragged breath warm and seductive on her lips as he whispered, "I want you, *chérie,* but we must talk—" Then he groaned and gave in to the longing to kiss her.

After a long while he smiled against her moist mouth and withdrew his lips, putting them on her throat that softly whimpered. Suddenly, his hands stopped the tantalizing caressing of her body, he stilled the lips that had been making a fiery trail of kisses from her shoulders to the curve of her breasts.

She trembled against him as he held her next to him. He asked huskily in her windblown hair, "Carrie, what am I going to do with you?"

"Do?" she asked, trying to draw away; but his arms tightened to prevent her escape. She put her head down on his chest, her arms about his waist.

"We can't go on this way," came the raspy reply.

"No, we can't, I . . ." Her words were lost in the shattering sound of a deep demanding voice.

"Hello! Mr. St. Simon?"

This time he allowed her to draw away. They looked in the direction of the sound. She quickly sought to close her blouse, but her fumbling fingers were pushed away as Jake easily performed the intimate task.

They turned to answer the voice, their hands clasped, reluctant to break the physical contact between them.

Then Caroline's face went white and she turned a terrified face to Jake. The black pupils in his eyes dilated as he searched her face, demanding roughly, "For God's sake, what's the matter, Carrie?"

She whispered brokenly, "It's my father."

Chapter Eight

Caroline couldn't drag her eyes away from Jake's face as he turned to stare at the man approaching the *Sunflower*. A look which she could only interpret as fierce possession went over his face, only to be hidden behind a carefully controlled mask, void of any emotion. Only his blazing eyes were alive, wary, calculating and ready to concede nothing. Caroline shivered at the toughness in him.

"Mr. St. Simon?" came Robert Conal's voice from the dock. Caroline had forgotten how cold and flat his voice could be.

"Yes?" Jake's fingers tightened on hers.

"I believe my daughter is aboard your craft," came back the foolish statement. Robert could clearly see her standing next to Jake.

"If your daughter is Caroline Conal, she's aboard." Jake's voice was cold.

Caroline almost laughed out loud at the absurdity of the conversation between the two men. She felt that she had suddenly become an inanimate object on auction for permanent ownership.

"I wish to come aboard your vessel and speak with my daughter—in private," demanded Robert. It was plain to see that he was not going to accept anything but yes for an answer.

Caroline could barely see Robert's face in the waning light of dusk, but his words and voice were enough to chill her heart. Jake looked down at her, his face still void of any emotion, but there was a question mark in his stormy eyes. Her face must have shown fear because his cold mask slipped somewhat, but his powerful body was still tight and coiled as though ready to spring on his prey.

"I—Jake—" she began, her body trembling slightly, her skin dimpled with goose bumps.

Jake reached out and touched her arm with his warm fingertips, as though he were infusing strength into her. His voice dropped to a whisper, "You don't have to speak to him, *chérie.*"

She felt the crushing weight of indecision; how easy it would be to let Jake deny Robert permission to come aboard. She knew it would be impossible to hide behind him, and it would be impossible to hide from him that she had sent for Robert! She would have to tell him the whole story and hope he would understand, though she knew he would not. He would think she was running away again. She shook her head as she stammered and stumbled over the broken words she feared would push the man she loved away from her forever. "I must speak to him—you see, Jake, I wired him to come for me."

The face staring into her pleading eyes was a fearful sight as it burned with the fire of betrayal; suddenly a fleeting look of defeat covered Jake's face. His voice was grating as he accused, "You're tired of the dull life? So it's back to party time."

"No—"

He turned away from her, leaving her empty and lost without him.

"She will speak to you, sir. Come aboard," he said with careless casual words, and one might have thought he was discussing the color of the sunset from the tone of his bored voice.

Once aboard, Robert stood hands on hips, face hard, blue eyes contemptuously sweeping the man who stood beside her. The silence between the three of them was awkward yet charged with danger. Caroline was too stricken to break it, Robert too angry. Jake seemed reluctant to end the tense moments; in fact, he seemed to be enjoying the calm before the vortex of the storm came careening into them.

Then, incredibly, Jake smiled at Robert and announced, "Sir, your daughter owes me for passage to these islands. She stowed away on my vessel for reasons of her own."

Unwittingly he had twisted the knife in Robert's own heart with the guilt of the part he had played in sending his daughter into headlong flight from him, but he answered coldly, without a trace of his guilt.

"You are a vile and contemptible villain, Mr. St. Simon."

Jake laughed, though his laughter lacked humor. "It's been years since I've heard anyone called a vile and comtemptible villain; such a polite term for bastard."

"Villain is too good a term for you!"

"Your daughter has worked off only one-tenth of what it cost me to feed her."

Caroline gasped with anger at his arrogance. Her face had turned white and her knees felt ready to buckle. She turned away from him to Robert. He moved to place a protective arm about her shoulders. She turned her face into her father's solid shoulder, unable to return Jake's cold eyes. Robert's stare was glacial as his blue eyes silently condemned Jake over his daughter's head.

Jake responded, his southern drawl heavily laden with exaggerated charm, "I'm a little old to be terrified of an outraged father, but should you insist, I will *marry* your daughter, Mr. Conal."

Caroline stiffened in her father's arms at Jake's proposal. What was his game now? Did he want to marry her or was it that he didn't like the idea of losing her before he had broken and crushed her beyond repair. Couldn't he see that he had already achieved his goal?

She felt her father's arm tighten painfully around her shoulders as he said in his best lord of the manor voice, "I wouldn't have you as a son-in-law, Mr. St. Simon."

Jake shrugged carelessly, crossed his arms on his broad chest, tilted his head back and surveyed Caroline through veiled, half-closed eyes. She could almost feel the physical touch of him on her flesh. She shivered against her father.

Robert looked down at her tenderly, pressed a

light comforting kiss on her forehead and said gently, "Caroline, I suggest you collect whatever belongings you have, while I settle the amount of your fare with Mr. St. Simon."

She moved reluctantly past Jake, carefully avoiding contact with his body. Woodenly she went into the cabin. She drew a sobbing breath, moved to the wardrobe and dragged out her evening gown. She hurriedly took off the cutoffs and Jake's dress shirt and dropped them to the floor; she wouldn't take them or the shoes or the swimsuit. She wouldn't take anything to remind her of Jake. Her love and her heart might be broken, but her pride was rapidly recovering. She drew the black slip over her trembling body, shocked at the feeling of luxurious silk against her skin that had grown accustomed to cotton tee shirts and denim cutoff pants. She put on the evening gown she had fled in; it seemed a lifetime ago since she had this dress on. The flashing sequins, high velvet pumps and white ermine cape were so frivolous and silly.

While she was combing out her hair, a tap on the door startled her. She called out woodenly, "Come in."

Hank's bleak face came cautiously around the jamb. She motioned for him to come in. He did so with hesitancy, his eyes confused and tight with unshed tears, his face white and hurt.

"Oh Hank!" she cried, ashamed that she and Jake had caused such torment to this young innocent bystander.

"Caroline, I—you can't go!" he pleaded.

"Oh my darling, Hank, I can't stay. We both knew

191

when you first gave me refuge that it would have to end sometime," she said lamely as her own tears threatened to spill with his.

He rushed against her and hugged her close; his sweet voice was filled with youthful innocence. "Please, Caroline. I heard Jake tell your father that he wanted to marry you! Marry him, Caroline."

"Hank darling," she whispered against his dark head, searching her heart for the best words to explain the impossibility of what he was asking. "Hank, you didn't hear Jake say he *wanted* to marry me, only that he would. Jake, well, he isn't in love with me."

"But you love him!" he stated with frankness. It was clear to him that she should marry Jake regardless of the fact that he didn't love her.

"I just can't, Hank," she whispered helplessly, unable to deny his statement that she loved Jake.

"We could be happy, just the way we were."

"Hank," she pleaded, "don't torture yourself. We had fun and now it's time for that fun to end. I love you, and I'll always be your friend. I'll see you again."

"No you won't! You'll be just like my mother!" He ran from the cabin before she could stop him.

She ran after him but stopped at the threshold. Hank had catapulted himself against the solid bulk of Jake who was standing alone in the saloon.

"Jake, Hank, please," she begged, looking into Jake's unforgiving hard face. His eyes framed in black silky lashes were now dull and unrevealing. Not anger, not passion—nothing!

"Don't worry, Carrie, Hank will be fine. Your

father's waiting," he said tiredly. His eyes scanned her in the evening gown, and she remembered that he had never seen her in it. She felt like everything he accused her of being, vain, selfish and shallow.

She nodded dumbly and turned back into the cabin, picked up her bulging evening bag, draped the soft ermine around her shoulders and stepped into the high evening shoes.

In the saloon Jake was absently massaging the boy's sobbing shoulders. Caroline paused to say she would stay, she would marry him; but Jake looked at her and shook his head no, as if he knew what she was going to say and wanted no part of it. She left without another word—leaving the two people she loved most in the world hating the very sight of her.

Caroline didn't remember the trip to the hotel. She sat quietly in the car next to her silent father. She stared straight ahead with dry eyes, too shocked to cry. As the black night closed in around her, a crushing loneliness descended on her.

She realized she hadn't the slightest notion of what her father would require of her for coming to these islands at a moment's notice to rescue his runaway daughter. Would his price be a quiet unopposed marriage to Edward Ashford? Or would he consider her soiled now and unworthy of Edward Ashford? Instantly she rejected the idea. His conduct on the *Sunflower* reassured her of just how deeply he did care. If he still wanted her to marry, she would. She would become a model wife and mother.

When at last they stopped before a small but

elegant hotel, Robert took her arm and gently but firmly led her to their suite. As she passed through the door her father had opened for her she saw a woman turn from the window.

"Jean!"

"Caroline." Jean came forward and hugged the dazed girl. As Jean drew away and studied the face before her, her own face filled with concern.

"Jean, what are you doing here?" Caroline began, confused. Then the woman's appearance struck her; Jean was absolutely beautiful. Her sable hair hung softly about her face in a pleasant new style. She wore a stylish clinging jersey dress which fell gracefully around her womanly curves—here was the woman Caroline had always suspected existed. She looked into Jean's soft, serene eyes and then turned swiftly to her father.

Her unspoken question was answered. Robert's eyes met Jean's, and the love and respect he felt for her were there in his eyes.

"Your father and I were married," Jean said quietly. She turned to Robert and asked in a soft voice, "What happened, Robert?"

"My darling," he began, "I didn't demand that she return with me. St. Simon was abominable to her! He was totally detestable, abhorrent! Never in my life have I wanted to hit a man as much as I wanted to hit him."

"Robert, I think Caroline has had quite enough turmoil for one day. She needs a hot soak in the tub, a light dinner and bed."

"Of course, darling," he instantly agreed to her suggestions.

Before she could speak, Caroline found herself

ushered into a large bedroom. Her luggage was already there, filled with her clothes from the *Caroline*. She turned to Jean and said, "Thank you. How did you know I'd come back with father?"

"I didn't. In fact, I hoped you wouldn't come back with him, but either way, you would have needed your clothing," she stated practically.

"Why didn't you want me to come back with father?" Had Jean changed so much that she didn't want to share Robert?

"I had hoped you had found love with Jake St. Simon."

Caroline was instantly ashamed of her previous thoughts, and she answered slowly, "I did—I do love him, Jean, but unfortunately, he doesn't share that love." Her voice was without pity for herself.

"Are you sure he doesn't love you?"

"Yes," she answered with a curt voice that said she didn't want to discuss it any further.

"I see. I'll draw your bath and order some dinner. We'll sort this all out in the morning," Jean responded in a very efficient voice, although her sherry brown eyes were filled with unshed tears for the girl who was now her step-daughter.

"Jean?" she called out to the woman who was disappearing through the door.

"Yes, dear?"

"I'm so glad about you and father. I want to hear all about it," Caroline said, reluctant to be left alone with her thoughts.

"Tomorrow morning," Jean said with gentle firmness. She could see how close to the edge of hysteria Caroline was, even if she couldn't see it herself.

The hot bath helped somewhat to relax her tense body, but the dinner was wasted. She could not eat.

The hotel bed was soft, but Caroline didn't sleep until the early hours of the morning. When she awoke late in the morning, she heard a strong wind whipping a heavy rain.

Robert called the airport and found that the airfield would be closed until further notice. At present they could not, as Caroline so fervently wished, leave these islands behind.

"That settles that!" declared Jean with impatience.

"My darling, there is nothing to be done about it," answered Robert calmly.

Caroline couldn't believe the change in her father. Just two months ago he would have raged at the weather for daring to delay him.

"You're right, of course," Jean answered, then turned to Caroline. "Caroline, your father has a fairly good idea why you ran away."

"Caroline, sweetheart, can you forgive me?" asked Robert.

"Father, I—forgive you. I tried to understand. I'm sorry I caused you needless worry. I should have told you where I was . . ."

He interrupted, "I knew where you were all the time, Caroline."

"You knew? But how?"

"Jean suspected it and St. Simon reported to the Coast Guard in Hawaii that he had taken a Miss *McPherson* aboard." He smiled at her subterfuge.

"But . . . I don't understand. If you knew where I was, why didn't you . . ."

"Come drag you off his boat?" he finished the question for her. "I wanted to, but Jean seemed to think you needed this time alone with St. Simon, something about chemistry working at first glance and growing into lasting love," he muttered.

"You knew," she said half to herself, then suddenly she realized that her father talked as though he knew a great deal about Jake, probably more than she did! She asked, "Did you investigate Jake?" She knew full well his tactics of old. She couldn't believe he had changed that much.

"Yes," he answered truthfully, his blue eyes offering no apology.

"Did he measure up to your rigid criteria?" she asked harshly.

"Caroline!" reprimanded Jean.

She was instantly contrite for her outburst. Her father couldn't change from a lion to a lamb in one day. "I'm sorry."

"I am too." He smiled at her and added teasingly, "By the way, St. Simon has a very interesting dossier. Thirty-four years old, graduate of Massachusetts Institute of Technology with a degree in electrical engineering and one in marine biology, too. An old Creole family from New Orleans, no money though; St. Simon made it himself in electronics and computers. Chucked it all to take his nephew on a world cruise. The nephew is the illegitimate son of his sister, Therese. She's dead— drugs, wild life and all that, after he made money and could afford to put her into the jet set class."

His words were shocking and stunning. She breathed, "Therese!" The name from Jake's haunted dreams. She was his sister and Hank's mother.

Jake must blame himself for her death if he provided the money for her to have drugs and a fast life. Her heart constricted at the torment Jake must have gone through. Hank had told her Jake had prevented his mother from seeing him. Did he have to do it for Hank's protection? "Oh, Jake," she whispered, with pity and love for him.

"Did he tell you about her?" Jean asked, seeing her distress.

"No—well in his own way he did. He loathes the jet-setting life. He adores Hank and he's a very good parent."

"St. Simon?" Robert snorted.

"Father, he'll make a wonderful father," she blurted out. Instantly she was sorry; only yesterday she had speculated along these same lines.

"Caroline!" exclaimed Robert; it was plain he was speculating himself. "You aren't . . ."

"No!" she denied, strongly praying it was a true denial.

But he hadn't heard her denial. "How could he seduce an innocent girl in his care? What kind of man is he?"

"Please, Father, don't—"

"Why didn't you accept his proposal yesterday if you're carrying his child?"

"I'm not having a child, Father," she answered calmly.

"I'm sorry, Caroline," Robert said.

"I am too." She walked out of the room, unable to continue this discussion.

For two days the weather was reluctant to cooperate with the tense and nervous threesome. Nothing more had been said concerning Jake or Caroline's weeks aboard the *Sunflower*.

Caroline turned away from the window, tired of watching the heavy sheets of rain bounce off the street below. Jean stopped her needlework and smiled at Caroline. "I don't suppose it has stopped raining?"

"No such luck," she declared. She dropped into a chair beside Jean and in a small voice asked, "What has become of Sir Edward Ashford?"

"Edward left the yacht and headed for England after making a cursory show of concern for your disappearance.

"When you left, your father and I realized that you must have overheard our argument concerning his plans for you. For two days we searched the Hawaiian Islands for you. Mr. St. Simon had radioed the Coast Guard and reported a young woman aboard his vessel but we didn't learn of it right away. When we did, your father raged that Mr. St. Simon had lied to him about your presence on his vessel. Robert was ready to have him charged with kidnapping until it was pointed out that you are twenty-two years old and above the age of consent. Since no ransom had been demanded—why would a multimillionaire such as Mr. St. Simon kidnap someone for personal gain? The authorities pointed out, not too gently, that you had probably fallen in love with Jake, who is by all accounts handsome, young and rich, the same being true of you. They insinuated that Robert should be happy with such a perfect match."

"Father must have wanted to strangle me," Caroline admitted in a small voice. "I'm sorry for running away, you'll never know *how* sorry," she added under her breath. If she hadn't dashed recklessly onto Jake's ketch in the first place she wouldn't have fallen in love with him. Or would she? From the first moment they had locked eyes across the water on Hilo Bay, there had been an undeniable attraction. Chance or fate, whoever or whatever governed these things, had arranged the nurturing of this attraction; but like two burning objects they had met and fought for the fuel of love and had destroyed everything. She smiled bitterly at her fanciful imaginings. Jake hadn't loved her. He had only appeased his need to torment her and her kind. Now he could move on to greener pastures, leaving her behind as ash on the hearth of hollow love.

"Caroline?"

"Yes?" she choked.

"Would it be so hard to swallow your pride and go to him and tell him you love him? Perhaps if you told him you might have a common ground to . . ."

"No, Jean. It would only give him perverse pleasure to see me beg," she retorted with bitterness. "I wish this bloody damn rain would stop so we could leave here!" Caroline jumped to her feet and went to the window to stare out into the rain again.

Caroline crossed the lobby of the hotel with long graceful strides. She bumped into a man emerging from the cocktail lounge.

"Caroline."

"Hello, Terry," she greeted coolly.

"This is great! Jake said you had gone home! What are you doing here?" he rushed out in a tumble.

She could see by his flushed face he had been

partying, and for some time too. His shirt was crumpled and his tattered Levi's had seen better days. "I might ask the same of you, Terry."

"The damn weather forced us in, and Jake too," he answered, smiling crookedly at her. She knew this forced respite on shore wasn't a hardship for Terry.

"That's too bad, Terry. Is Jake with you now?" she asked, hoping he was not. If she ran into him now, she wasn't sure if she could maintain her composure.

"No, he and Toni and some Trukese buddies are at George Mekeni's house discussing old times," he answered.

In a burst of forwardness his hand came out to caress her bare arm.

"I don't appreciate your uninvited touch, Terry," she said coldly. He was just like his sister, always touching and forcing his way into people's lives. But in reality she wasn't angry with Terry, he was just a target for the anger she felt at Jake, who apparently hadn't missed a beat before he replaced her with Toni. He was probably in Toni's arms right now.

"Caroline, I'm sorry. How about having some drinks and dinner with me. No touching, I promise."

"I'm sorry, Terry, but I can't, I'm having dinner with my family." Looking at her watch in what she thought was a reasonable coverup, she excused herself. "I must run, I'm late. Good-bye, Terry."

She turned and walked swiftly away, leaving him to stare at her retreating cloud of swinging golden red hair. The yellow cotton sundress that stirred sweetly around her slender form and her shapely tanned legs below the hemline were more than enough to turn the head of a passing waiter. Under his breath Terry mumbled, "What a fool you are, Jake St. Simon. If a woman like that were mine, I'd never let her get away."

After another endless night during which Caroline had snatched only a few fitful hours of sleep, the morning sun rose, unobstructed by the gray clouds. Sometime during the night the storm had passed leaving the threesome free to leave.

The handling of the luggage at the airport was slow and tedious as they moved along the slow line of customs. Caroline gasped sharply as she recognized the short, broad form of George Mekeni behind the customs counter. When it was her turn, she reluctantly handed over her papers to him. She stared at a sign over his head, not really reading the instructions to declare any purchases over five hundred dollars.

"Ah, Miss Conal, it's a pleasure to see you again." He gave her papers the same inspection he had two weeks ago.

"Thank you, Mr. Mekeni." She smiled at him.

"Do you still have your jewelry and ermine?" he asked in a businesslike manner.

"Yes, in my case."

"I've the papers, sir, on my daughter's jewelry," interposed Robert. He didn't like the turn this routine check through customs had taken, especially since he could see the distress on his daughter's face.

George's eyes widened slightly as Robert identified himself, but he was still purposeful and determined to do his job. He said, "Very good, sir. If I might see them."

As George returned the papers to her father, he said, "Good-bye, Miss Conal. I'm sorry about Jake's nephew. I hope he is better this morning."

"What?" cried Caroline. Her face whitened, her knees weakened; had it not been for the supporting arm of her father, she would have fallen.

Chapter Nine

*G*eorge, please tell me," she whispered brokenly, "not Hank. What about Hank?"

"Jake left my house about twelve last night. This morning I heard that when he returned to his boat, the boy was very sick. The ambulance came and took him to the hospital."

"How serious is it?" asked Robert who had tightened his supportive arm around his weak daughter.

"I don't know, I thought you might know."

"Father, I must go to the hospital. I'll fly back to England alone. You go ahead."

"No," said Jean. "We'll return to the hotel and wait for you."

"Thank you, Jean."

"I'll return to the hotel; you go to the hospital with Caroline," Robert told Jean.

Caroline came to many decisions on the terror-filled trip to the hospital. Among her prayers for Hank, she had swallowed her pride. They were a family: she knew she belonged with Jake and Hank, just as her towel and toothbrush had hung beside theirs. The bonds had been forged. Hank needed two parents, and while she couldn't pretend to be his mother, she loved him and knew he loved her in return. She would accept the proposal Jake had made to her father—if he still meant it. If not, then she would live with him.

The taxi had barely slowed to a stop when Caroline exited from the rear door and fairly ran into the hospital, leaving Jean to handle the ordinary, mundane things such as paying the fare.

A nurse, apparently accustomed to incoherent conversation, directed Caroline to a waiting room at the end of the hall. Her run slowed to a stop when she saw Jake. He sat with his elbows resting on his knees, his dark head in his hands. She choked out, "Jake?"

He looked at her a long time and finally rose slowly to his feet. She gasped at his appearance. His face was a sickly gray above the beard stubble. His eyes were red with fatigue and haunted with worry. His dark hair was mussed as though he had run his fingers roughly through it time and time again. His clothing was rumpled as if he had no time to look after himself.

Jake crossed the space between them and took the hands she offered. She returned his grasp, comforting him with her eyes and the solid touch of her fingers.

"Did Toni and Terry send you?" he asked as he drew away.

"Toni and Terry?"

"I sent them to look for you. Hank's been asking for you," he answered. Clamping down on his emotions, he pushed her away from him. Not to be put off, she reached out and brushed an errant curl off his forehead, her fingers lightly caressing the side of his weary face. It broke the ice between them. He took her hand away from his face, holding it in his own instead of dropping it.

"If Toni or Terry didn't send you, how did you find out about Hank?"

"From George Mekeni as I went through customs this morning. Jake, I had to come."

"Thank you for coming, *chérie.*"

"Jake, what's wrong with Hank?"

"His appendix burst. It's my fault. I should have recognized the symptoms; instead I went off to drown my sorrows."

"I don't understand." She had never seen such loathing and self-contempt in a human being. "He's going to be all right, isn't he, Jake?" she cried in alarm.

He dropped her hand and began to pace the narrow room. Her hand reached out to stop him, but even though he tried to pull away, her fingers gripped his arm, the nails dug painfully into his flesh, forcing his anguished eyes to meet hers.

"I don't know, Carrie."

"No, Jake!"

"Mr. St. Simon?" called a man standing in the doorway.

They pivoted sharply, together, Jake's arm coming to rest unconsciously around her waist. Her own arm slipped around his narrow waist in mutual support.

"Yes, Doctor."

Caroline's hold on his waist tightened. She involuntarily held her breath, dread filling her throat with a black, bitter, metallic taste.

"Your nephew has made no progress either way. I've ordered intravenous antibiotics to fight the infection, but they still take some time to work."

"How long?"

"Maybe ten to twelve hours. If he pulls through this crisis period his chances become better and better."

"He will," Caroline vowed.

"Are you the young woman Hank's been calling for?"

"Yes, she is, Doctor," Jake answered.

"Please come with me."

The door to Hank's room was opened for them by a nurse. Caroline didn't notice her, she only saw the boy so still and white in the bed. He seemed to have shrunk since she last saw him; perhaps it was only the enormity of the white room, hospital bed and equipment surrounding this one small boy.

"Oh, my darling." Dropping Jake's hand, she rushed to the bed. She touched his forehead gently and groaned at the feel of the dry, blazing fever in his body. She took his limp hand in hers and squeezed gently, reassuring him of her presence. She called out to him. "Hank, we're here with you. You don't have to worry anymore."

Later in the day the floor nurse came and ushered them out while they changed the bed and sponged Hank's fevered body. As Jake and Caroline came out into the hallway Caroline was surprised to find

Jean sitting in the waiting room. Her dark head was bent over her needlework.

"Jean, you didn't have to wait," said Caroline, ashamed that she had forgotten her altogether.

"I wanted to wait, dear. How is he?"

"The same," answered Jake, his jaw clenched in tight control over emotions that had been stretched to the limit.

"Could I bring you anything? Food? Cold tea? Coffee?"

"No, thank you, er—?" Jake answered politely.

"Jean. I'm Robert's personal aide," she identified. Now wasn't the time to go into new family explanations.

"And his new wife," Caroline added proudly, linking her arm in Jean's.

"You have my deepest sympathies," retorted the Jake of old. Then he smiled crookedly at Caroline's shocked face at his rude remark. "I apologize, that was uncalled for, Mrs. Conal."

But Jean only returned his smile. "Please call me Jean, Mr. St. Simon. If we're to be friends, and I think we shall, you may always speak your mind as I intend to. Robert is too much like yourself for the two of you to be friends."

"You're probably right," he agreed. Then he moved to stare out the window at the shimmering heat causing steam to rise above the mud puddles on the street below.

In Hank's room again they stood, paced, and sat in the hard chairs next to Hank's bed throughout the long, agonizing hours of the afternoon and early evening. Once or twice Hank stirred restlessly in his deep sleep, bringing them hopefully to his side, but he did not awaken.

At dusk the doctor returned and insisted that both go to the small cafeteria in the hospital and eat, although neither of them was hungry. Despite all the coffee he had drunk, Jake was thoroughly exhausted. Having had no sleep the previous night and no rest today, he was close to total exhaustion. The doctor arranged to have a bed made available for him, threatening him with expulsion from Hank's room unless he rested. After Caroline assured him that she wouldn't leave Hank's side for a moment and would call him if there was any change, he went to rest.

At about two A.M. Hank stirred and seemed to recognize her, but immediately her hopes that he had improved were dashed as he lapsed back into his deep sleep.

She leaned back in the chair, her muscles cramped and stiff. She put a hand up to rub the taut muscles of her neck which felt as if they were pinching her tired brain. Her hands were pushed aside. A pair of familiar hands replaced hers and rubbed away the sore stiffness.

She smiled at him over her shoulder. She could tell that he had slept some, although he still looked tired. He had taken a shower, shaved and changed his clothes.

"Better?" he asked in a low drawl that sent shivers through her body. She nodded.

She stood knowing she couldn't take much more of his gentle touch. Stretching her legs and emitting a tired sigh, she turned to him and asked, "Did you go back to the *Sunflower?*"

Knowing why she had asked the question, he looked down at his clothes. "No. Your step-mother must have. My razor, toothbrush, paste and fresh clothes arrived in a morocco leather bag while I was asleep." He smiled wryly at being managed this way.

"She's a very efficient person." She paused, then ventured tentatively, "I'm sure you're accustomed to efficient people like Jean, Mr. Business Tycoon."

"So, your father did his homework on me? I'm not surprised. I would have done the same in the old days of Jacob David St. Simon, young corporate superstar and wealthy man about New Orleans," he declared cynically. His crooked smile went straight into her heart.

"How's Hank? I saw the nurse outside and she told me he came around and seemed to recognize you." He paused. "I suppose your father told you about Hank's mother?" He moved to look down at the small boy in the bed. His light eyes were tender, yet somehow fiercely protective.

"Father said that Hank's mother was your sister and that she had led a tragic life." Her voice trailed off helplessly.

"Therese was very beautiful. She had dark hair, the same cocoa brown hair and melting eyes Hank has. Those eyes could charm the birds right out of the trees, as the saying goes. I guess it was my misfortune to inherit my mother's cool blue eyes when I had to grow up with a sister whose eyes . . ." He shrugged his shoulders. "I couldn't deny her anything any more than anyone else who knew her could."

She almost laughed. If he only knew that he could seduce a woman with one glance of those green eyes. Cool? They could be alive with burning fire, whether in anger or in passion. Now they were subdued in pain. Caroline turned to touch his arm in comfort, but somehow she had turned into his arms.

He kissed her hungrily, drinking deeply from the well of her love. They knew it wasn't passion they were seeking, but something deeper—mutual comfort in one another.

When the kiss ended, he looked down into her face and was rewarded with a soft smile which said she was sensitive to his need to be healed of the past.

"Hi, you two!" called a weak voice from the bed. They jumped apart and eagerly rushed to the bed.

Hank's eyes were clear, his forehead was cooler and his smile, though weak, was in place for them.

"Hi, yourself, boy," drawled Jake, his own smile wide, his blue eyes filled with grateful relief.

"Jake?" he croaked through parched lips.

"Yes?" he prompted.

"Could I have some orange juice?" he groaned.

"I'll go and find a nurse and get you some." Jake squeezed Hank's hand and winked at Caroline, as if to say he's asking for something to drink, food can't be far behind.

"Caroline?" called Hank.

"Yes, darling?" She took his hand in hers, her hazel eyes filled with love.

"Are you staying?" he asked. Fear that she would go away was in his white face.

"Yes, I'm staying," she reassured.

"No, I don't mean right now. I mean after I get out of here. You won't leave Jake and me again, will you?" His voice was strained, agitated.

She leaned over him and pressed a kiss to his

cheek. She vowed in a firm, clear voice her commitment to him, "I will not leave you ever again."

"Thank you." He sighed and closed his eyes.

She flinched as she heard Jake appear behind her with Hank's juice. Not saying a word to either of them, Jake slipped an arm under Hank's shoulders while Caroline held the glass to his lips. Jake's look penetrated her from across the bed. He had heard her statement to Hank. Now he knew that she wasn't going away with her father but was staying with him, and she was glad.

Doctor Randle came at breakfast time. With a smile, he told the anxious pair that Hank would be fine in a couple of weeks. Then he ordered them to go away and rest.

As they went into the hall, Jake gave her another penetrating look. She blushed, unable to stop her rampant thoughts of the time she had spent in his arms, the kisses and love they had shared.

"I must be a mess," she stammered out. In an attempt to tuck away stray hairs, she put a hand to the coronet of braids she had wound her hair into yesterday morning. Her fingers were nervous and the hair wouldn't obey. She ran her hands down the sides of her blouse and skirt, not realizing how this innocent gesture stirred desire in the man beside her.

"You look like a young schoolgirl with your hair up like that; I'm almost ashamed of the thoughts that come to mind. When you're standing beside me, I can't think of anything but taking you to my bed," he said.

She trembled at the sudden interjection of intimacy into their conversation. She was drawn to look into his eyes, at the twin flames of passion burning in their depths. He put his hands on her shoulders, his thumbs moving in light caressing circles on the smooth thin silk of her blouse just over the starting swell of her breasts. Shivers of delight and longing licked through her body.

"Jake," she whispered, her breath lost to the supercharged moment between them.

"Come with me to the *Sunflower,* we have to—"

"Caroline?" Her father's voice obliterated the rest of Jake's words, destroying whatever they had been on the verge of discovering.

They turned sharply to face Robert and Jean. Jean's face was happy, but not Robert's. His blue eyes were sparks of fiery disdain for the man who had a familiar but careless arm around his daughter.

"How is Hank, Mr. St. Simon?" Jean asked, deep concern in her eyes.

"He is improving, Jean. What's this Mr. St. Simon stuff? After a woman's been through a man's closet and dresser drawers she can hardly call him Mister. Thank you for the things you sent over. They helped a great deal."

Robert stood frustrated and bewildered at the unexpected jocularity between his wife and the despicable man who had broken his daughter's heart. Caroline hardly seemed the picture of dejection and sorrow she had been two days ago. Her cheeks glowed with beautiful, delicate color; her hazel eyes were shimmering with luminous happiness; and her entire body seemed to radiate with joy. It was as if she belonged in the circle of Jake's arm, where she was at peace. Robert wasn't about to trust this man who had displayed such blatant disregard for her feelings such a short time ago. His eyebrows beetled in disapproval at Jake.

"You look tired, Caroline," commented Jean.

"I am tired," she admitted, but although she was physically weary her mind was racing. She had a thousand unanswered questions, and she wanted very much to be left alone with Jake to seek the answers.

"Perhaps you should tell young Master Hank you'll be back after you've had some rest, Caroline. Come back to the hotel and go to bed," Robert suggested, eagerly seizing the opportunity to get her away from Jake.

Robert's tactics weren't overlooked by Jake. His face tightened, as did his grip on Caroline's shoulder. At first he wasn't going to release her, but then he looked down into her face and saw for the first time how fatigued she was. He felt her sway slightly against him on unsteady legs.

"Hank's better now, Carrie. Your father is right, you should go to the hotel and sleep." Jake's reply took Robert off guard.

"You need rest too." Her hand went out in an unconscious gesture and touched the tiny lines of fatigue around his sensual mouth.

And just as naturally as she had touched him, he turned and kissed her fingertips. Then he took her hand away from his mouth and held it in his own.

This short scene wasn't lost on Robert, whose fatherly patience had been stretched to the limits when the younger man touched his daughter. He stepped forward and said, "I have the car waiting to take you to the hotel, Caroline."

Jake shrugged his broad shoulders, dropped her hand and without a good-bye walked away, leaving her to stare at him in hurt surprise at this sudden change in mood. His face was blank with indifference, a mood he so often reverted to without warning, and she remembered too well the days of black bitterness that usually followed. She felt a rushing tingle of panic up her spine; he had pushed her away once again. Feeling terribly alone and frightened, she couldn't suppress the shiver that shook her body.

Jean moved to link her arm in Caroline's and said for her ears alone, "He's avoiding an argument with your father."

"Do you really think so?" she said grasping at the thin ray of hope Jean offered.

Chapter Ten

It was early evening when Caroline awoke from her exhausted slumber. She quickly showered, dressed and slipped from her room, not wanting to disturb Jean and her father, knowing that they too had gotten very little rest in the past two days. She went directly to the taxi stand in front of the hotel and hailed a cab for the drive to the hospital.

She walked down the hall to Hank's room, her arms filled with items she had purchased from several shops on the way to the hospital, much to the dismay of the taxi driver who only sighed loudly when she asked him to stop every few blocks as still another shop caught her eye. She was hoping to pique Hank's interest and curiosity while he convalesced—a task she knew would be very difficult!

"Hi, Caroline," greeted an entirely different Hank. His bed was raised into an upright position and he was eating. His color was still pale but his eyes were bright and lively.

She bent forward to kiss his forehead, dumping the bundles on the bed and into a chair. He suffered her kisses and hugs with patience, returning her hug tightly with one of his own.

"Where's Jake?" she asked with all the nonchalance she could infuse into an unsteady voice.

"He's gone to the *Sunflower* to get some sleep. He was here all afternoon. He said he wouldn't be back until tomorrow morning."

She couldn't suppress the sigh of disappointment —or was it relief? She was afraid of what their next meeting might bring—cool contempt or loving warmth?

Hank was excitedly eyeing the bundles on the chair and bed. She smiled and moved to the chair and began handing him the packages one by one until there was a large pile of gifts surrounding him.

"Go ahead, open them," she urged.

He exclaimed with delight over every book, shell, model kit and fragment of native coral he unveiled from the wrappings. "It's like Christmas!" he exclaimed.

"In the summer!" she answered.

His excited chocolate brown eyes caught a movement behind her. "Jake," he cried.

She turned to face him. Jake smiled at Hank. His eyes were cool as they swept her slender form in the clinging white sundress. A sardonic flame in his aqua eyes told her he hadn't forgotten his remarks about her innocence as those eyes paused at the fresh coronet of braids.

She felt her skin flush with embarrassment but couldn't stop her own eyes from sweeping his virile body. The snug tailored jeans hugged his muscled thighs and the black silk shirt did the same to his wide shoulders and narrow waist. The buttons had been neglected down to the middle of his chest, exposing his dark chest hairs. Her eyes traveled up to his face, following his throat, strong chin, the full curve of his lips; his eyes were clear and rested and now amused at her appraisal. She blushed deeper and thought, My Lord, he's too handsome for his own good!

"Jake, see all the things Caroline brought me?" Hank said, breaking the gaze between them.

"She's spoiling you rotten!" he retorted, a teasing smile on his face. After admiring each item eagerly proffered for his inspection, Jake turned to Caroline and asked, "Have you eaten?"

"No, I'm not—"

"Well, I am and I want some company," he interrupted, squelching further protests.

They ate sparingly of the meal he ordered at a small uncrowded restaurant. Their talk was reserved too. Each seemed to be testing the other before daring to speak of the subject that lay between them like an ominous cloud—the future.

When the silence finally became unbearable, Caroline screwed up her courage to speak. Her voice was strained and forced. "Jake, I need to talk to you."

"Come with me to the *Sunflower*. I thought we

could talk here, on neutral ground, but we can't." His voice sounded cool and commanding.

Her heart took a plunge at the unemotional flat look in his eyes, but she whispered, "All right."

The twin masts of the *Sunflower* were readily apparent among the vessels that still crowded the wharf from the recent storm. The bright yellow hull seemed to welcome Caroline, and she felt more at ease. She didn't wait while Jake paid the taxi driver, instead walked quickly down to the craft rocking gently in the slip. Stepping lightly onto the deck, she waited for Jake.

"Let's go below." His voice was rough and low in the moonlight.

She reached out with familiar surety in the dark, found the chrome safety rail on the top of the cockpit and went below.

Jake switched on the small single light over the dinette, and the saloon was filled with soft, seductive light. Her hair caught the light, making her coronet shimmer like a golden sunset. Her peachy skin was delicate and delectable, as was her curvaceous body in the white dress. She heard Jake take in a hissing, swift breath after he turned to her. For an instant she thought he would take her into his arms and everything would right itself. But he turned sharply away from her.

A pain stabbed at her, a tremor of fear showed on her face as she stared at his stiff back. She was forced to wait several moments before he demanded in a blunt husky voice, "Did you mean what you said to Hank—about staying?"

She looked down at the deck, whispering an

answer, unable to meet the fierce eyes he had suddenly turned on her.

"Look at me!" he commanded angrily.

She brought her head up proudly, her hazel eyes unflinching as she declared in a firm, clear voice, "Yes, I meant what I told Hank."

His face was still hard and taut, but his eyes softened a little, the anger dying slowly. His voice was flat as he said, "We can't go back to the way we were. I don't think either of us found the old relationship enjoyable. I'm too old-fashioned for an unsettled living arrangement, and I don't think your father would allow it—not that he worries me one bit, but I don't want to be constantly wary of him either. Hank doesn't need any more insecurities, either. If we told him we were married he would see through that ruse immediately; he's very astute."

His words were falling like well-placed blows on her mind and body. She said stupidly, stumbling over the words, "Are you suggesting that we marry?"

"Yes, what else?" he said sharply, continuing in a flat voice, "I'm reasonably well-off, although not in the same league as your father, but you'll never know poverty. We'll finish this cruise if you like; if not we'll go back to New Orleans, to our home. You'll have the kind of life you want.

"Hank will live with us; I'm not the boarding school type. *Grand-mère* will probably want to return to France. However, should she wish to stay, she will have her own apartment in our house, independent of ours and with her own servants. My home is a large plantation mansion which isn't too difficult to manage with its trained staff. If you find you need more help, then you can hire it." Jake's voice was stern to the point of being over-bearing.

"It was never my intention to give up my business forever, just proceed at a much slower pace. I won't be involved with the financial end of it, just the creative side, that's always been my interest. You will have some business entertaining to do, but not on a large scale. For three months out of every year, you'll have to suffer a cruise or some other form of extended vacation with Hank and me, and I must warn you that we avoid the fashionable and chic resorts!"

She stared at his probing eyes, not really believing this was the same man who had held her close in his arms last night, giving her warmth and strength; this man was a cool stranger.

"Well?" he demanded.

She turned away and heard an angry curse under his breath. The hope in her heart soared at the hint of emotion in his reaction, but when she turned back to him, there was only burning anger and steady challenge on his face. She was so tempted to throw his cold marriage proposal back in his handsome, arrogant face. But the thought of Hank's white and gaunt face begging her to stay told her what the answer must be.

"I will marry you, Jake," she said quietly, her eyes as cool as his.

She saw the anger in his eyes fade at her accept-ance. In a flat, egotistical tone he said, "Good. My *grand-mère* is flying in tomorrow. I called her when Hank was so ill. We will be married at the end of the week, if that's agreeable."

"In just four days?" She couldn't help being surprised at the swiftness of his plan.

"Hank will be out of the hospital within two weeks and after that we'll sail again as soon as he's strong enough."

It was clear this was the way it was to be, whether she had objections or not. She thought of her father and how he, too, had planned her marriage with such cool deliberateness—Robert was going to be livid with anger. Not only was she marrying a man he could not endure, but she was getting married on foreign soil without the pomp and circumstance befitting Lady Caroline of Conal Keep. She didn't care if she missed all the splendor of a big formal wedding, but a grubby little civil ceremony didn't appeal to her either. She had always imagined that when two people loved one another and decided to join their lives it should be done with the help of a happy family and friends. Caroline smiled with a cynicism that matched his. What did it matter? It was clear this was to be a business arrangement for Jake, with his occasional lust to be sated on the side. That he desired her physically she did not doubt, she had seen that clearly in his eyes. With a lifeless voice she nodded to his dark shadowy figure. "Whatever you wish, Jake."

He nodded curtly, and said, "I'll take you back to your hotel now."

"No! I'll find a taxi," she retorted. She wanted to be alone.

"No, you won't," he said firmly, "I want to be there when you tell your father that we are getting married."

"Why?" she whispered. Did he want to taunt her

father with the knowledge that he had won his daughter away from him?

"I don't want him talking you out of marrying me," he snapped. His features sharpened as he turned out of the shadows into the light.

Although she gasped at the fierce possessiveness in his burning eyes, she answered with fortitude, "I make my own decisions and I stick to them."

"You're inclined to be impulsive and softhearted where your father is concerned," he returned patronizingly.

"No, Jake, I'm not impulsive." She had thought very carefully about marrying him. Softhearted toward her father? Jake apparently didn't know their history as well as he thought he did.

"You've demonstrated that impulsiveness over and over," he said coldly.

"What?" she cried.

"You have a conveniently short memory. You didn't exactly plan to be aboard the *Sunflower* three months ago, did you?"

"You've never once considered that I might have had good cause to flee my father, have you?" she lashed back. Her eyes flashed with spirit, outraged that he was once again prejudging her.

"What reason? Too small an allowance? A man?" He rasped the last out.

"Never mind!" she flung back, unwilling to justify her actions. Let him think whatever he wanted.

A muscle in his taut cheek began to twitch with anger at her bold rebellion. His eyes narrowed into remote sparks of dark blue, which shattered her courage into a million fragments.

"Caroline, don't ever run from me! I'll hunt you

down and drag you back with a ruthlessness that will make your father's efforts seem tame!" he threatened. His voice was low and menacing.

She shivered and wildly doubted her sanity for agreeing to marry him, but she promised in a weak tremorous voice, "I will not run away, Jake."

"We'll go and talk to your father now," he said, seemingly satisfied at her response. He reached out and turned off the light over the dinette.

Caroline's fleeting impression was that his hand was unsteady on the lamp, but then the saloon was plunged into blackness and the fingers that took her arm were as steady as a rock and warm enough to send the familiar fires of passion up her arm and into her heart.

As they reached the door of Robert and Jean's suite, Caroline turned to him. Her lovely eyes shimmered, pleading as she requested understanding for her father. "Please, Jake. He's my father and I love him, despite the things he's done or said."

"Carrie, I'm not totally insensitive to his feelings. I would be possessive too, if my daughter chose to marry a man I couldn't stand. I regret my boorish behavior of the other night. If I had been more tolerant of his outrage and less intent on venting my own indignation, then perhaps the three of us could have prevented some needless grief." His voice was low and filled with a humble and compassionate sincerity she could hardly believe came from Jake St. Simon.

"Oh Jake." She felt the lock on the cold box she had put her love in begin to open.

"You need not worry, *chérie.* I will be the very model of politeness and courtesy."

"Jake, do you think we—" she began, taking a step toward him, ready to tell him of her love. Her eyes were filled with tears of hope and longing, but he was blind to the overture.

Instead he told her, "If you don't take that forlorn look off your face, *chérie,* your sharp step-mother will know you're not marrying me because you love me but because you love my nephew. Is your reputation so precious to you that you'll marry a man you can barely tolerate, just because of a physical desire?"

"What?" she cried. How could he be so blind? Couldn't he see that she loved him? Wide with confusion, her eyes searched the planes and angles of his face, which were taut with cynicism; the mouth that could turn into easy crooked smiles was hard and compressed.

In a small low voice she said, "Jake, I wanted you to make love to me." She blushed as she continued, "I don't care a snap for my reputation."

"I know you feel a certain amount of desire for me physically. I woke the natural hungers of passion in you, while you . . . you pleased me too." He smiled wickedly at her. "We are very good in bed together."

"No, I—" She was appalled that he was implying their married relationship would be built on sex alone, without the tenderness and companionship they had shared. Had their last week together on the *Sunflower* been an elaborate charade on his part? Did he feel nothing but physical need?

Suddenly his arms came around her and his lips descended on her startled mouth. At first she struggled in surprise, but then with a contented whimper in her throat she surrendered again to his exploring lips. It was a bitter acknowledgment on her part, she could not deny that her physical desires overrode all her other needs.

Her arms went around his narrow waist, her hands seeking the warm skin of his back and the ripple of his muscles through his thin silk shirt.

At the sound of a door opening behind her, she stiffened, but Jake didn't seem to notice. He simply deepened his kiss and tightened his hold on her slender form. Slowly, as he raised his head and loosened his hold, she drew back in the circle of his arms.

"Good evening, Mr. Conal," he drawled lazily. His eyes were friendly but filled with challenge.

He had kissed her deliberately; he heard Robert about to open the door and kissed her for Robert's benefit! He *was* trying to provoke her father. Anger raced within her, killing the passion and love she had felt only moments ago. Caroline tried to wrench away from him but his grip tightened, forcing her to relax against his hard chest.

"Mr. St. Simon," she heard the clipped threatening voice of her father.

With a brief warning glance, Jake turned her around to face her father but kept an arm across her shoulder. His long fingers toyed lightly on her bare upper arm.

"Hello, Father," she rushed out, then couldn't think of another word.

It didn't matter, as Jake stepped neatly into the

226

breach, "Forgive us, Mr. Conal, for disturbing you, but we would like very much to speak with you."

"Please, Father," Caroline added.

"Very well. Jean has retired for the evening."

"I'll get her, Father." There was a slight break in her voice. Jake caught her arm lightly and squeezed gently, forcing her to meet his eyes. His look was warm, reminding her that they were supposed to be in love and about to announce the happiest moment of their lives. She smiled up at him, but her battered emotions were veiled behind a cheerful facade. To her father this appeared to be a very loving exchange between them; it was faintly reminiscent of the morning at the hospital.

"Please come in, Mr. St. Simon," Robert invited, somewhat reluctantly.

Jean opened the bedroom door at Caroline's tap and stepped fully clothed into the room. Caroline guessed that Jean must have heard their voices and dressed.

"Good evening, Mr.—Jake," Jean greeted warmly, her eyes sweeping from him to Caroline, then to Robert.

"Good evening, lovely lady," drawled Jake, his face open with charm and genuine warmth. Caroline could easily see that he felt respect and admiration for Jean. Somehow, he and Jean had developed an instant rapport with one another.

"Are we going to stand here all night?" Robert asked, irritated at the turn of events.

Jean smiled fondly at Robert and led the way to the small sitting room. She asked graciously, "Could

I order anything from room service for either of you?"

"A bottle of champagne and four glasses," Jake answered casually.

Caroline gasped at his direct approach to the matter they had come to discuss. She turned her alarmed eyes on his dark face. He in turn just smiled and reassured her silently with light caressing eyes.

"I don't find you amusing, St. Simon," Robert ground out harshly.

"I'm sorry, sir," Jake apologized. He reached out and took Caroline's hand, his eyes full of tenderness and love.

Caroline stiffened at the convincing act, wishing that she had the courage to accuse him of hypocrisy. Instead she forced herself to relax and return his smile with equal tenderness and love.

"Carrie and I are going to be married on Friday, and we would like very much for you to be present. I know I've earned your dislike, Mr. Conal, but I am more than willing to meet you halfway for the sake of family harmony. I will take excellent care of your daughter." He paused and smiled with irony at Robert. "As you already know, I'm not exactly a pauper and I intend to return to my business at the end of this cruise, in about a year's time."

"Why couldn't you wait until then to be married?" interrupted Robert, grasping at anything to stop this union.

"Carrie and I don't think that it would be advisable to live together aboard the ketch without the ties of matrimony." Jake's voice was dry, his implication clear to Robert—they could not keep their passions under control.

"You are saying you're going to take my daughter with you on this cruise, regardless of marital status?"

"Father, please," Caroline interposed gently. She didn't want a terrible breach between her father and her future husband. She couldn't start her married life in hatred and bitterness.

"Caroline, do you really want this man?" demanded her father.

"Please don't drive a wedge between us and force me to choose between the two of you," she pleaded.

His eyes searched the beautiful face—her eyes, blue gray with unshed tears, her trembling lower lip, and her chalky white skin. He sighed, his voice tired and defeated. "All right, sweetheart, if this is what you want, I'll arrange a small but suitable wedding here at the hotel on Friday."

"Father, I don't want—"

"Thank you, sir." Jake stood and offered his hand. Slowly Robert stood and took it, shaking hands very solemnly.

Jean came forward and Jake kissed her smooth cheek. "I'm sure we'll be happy with whatever you plan for Friday, Jean. My *grand-mère* will be here tomorrow. I'm sure you will indulge her and allow her to fuss and help with the planning."

"Of course, Jake." She smiled in return, sure in her heart that once the barriers were down between them, they would really find each other.

"I'll order that champagne now." Robert picked up the phone.

Jake smiled down into Caroline's upturned face, and his eyes held genuine admiration for her handling of the situation. He dropped a light kiss on her astonished lips before he shuttered the expression on his face. She relaxed slightly and accepted Jean's best wishes.

Chapter Eleven

The midafternoon sun shimmered on the runway, the wavering heat waves rising from the asphalt, distorting the image of the jet taxiing toward the tarmac where the small air terminal building of Moen and the Truk Islands stood. A rented white Mercedes Benz was waiting at the private side entrance of customs to receive one of the jet's passengers.

A couple stood in the small snatch of shade afforded by a window awning. They didn't speak to pass the time; she looked down at her handbag and he looked down at the top of her golden red head.

As the passengers began to unload, Caroline raised her head and searched the crowd for Jake's *grand-mère*. There was a young couple, very much in love and from all appearances on their honeymoon, next, a native couple with two fretting children at their heels, then finally a very striking silver-haired lady whose face and figure seemed much too young to be the *grand-mère* of the man beside her.

"She's very beautiful, Jake."

He didn't answer, but softly reached out and brushed a red gold curl away from her face. There was a long, searching look in her hazel eyes as he drew in a sharp breath and pulled her into his arms. His lips were gentle against the curve of her cheek, and his stormy breath tickled her ear as he whispered, "Put your arms around me, *chérie.*"

She obeyed instantly, sliding her arms about his narrow waist and resting her cheek against the broad chest where his heartbeat sounded in her ear. Her hands felt his back muscles constrict powerfully under the thin material of his tan polo shirt. A large warm hand came up to cup her face. He tipped it up to meet his descending lips.

Under his expert lips her mouth molded itself to his. The promise of fulfillment that his lips elicited from deep within her made her quiver against him. He drew away slightly and smiled gently at her and said in his sweet, husky drawl, *"Chérie,* why do you have a penchant for making me want to make mad love to you at the most inopportune moments?"

"I didn't mean to," she cautiously retorted at his light teasing. Why did he turn his charm and tenderness on and off like a water tap?

"Jake, *chérie.*" A musical voice chimed out from among the crowd.

He squeezed Caroline's hand lightly, then dropped it and moved into the outstretched arms of the silver-haired woman Caroline had seen minutes earlier. The youthful glow Caroline had observed at a distance had been no illusion. At close range Caroline could see that the woman used no subterfuge to appear young. Her gold slack suit hugged her trim figure, while her glorious silver hair was cut in a short, soft style, framing an oval face with only the tiniest of telltale age lines visible. Her long inky lashes were perfect frames for her midnight black eyes. The twin lights of love for her grandson shone out of those eyes like a beacon.

"That's *grand-mère, chérie,*" Jake whispered as the woman approached.

"I received your telegram in Hawaii about Hank's improvement. Tell me quickly, how is he now?"

Jake smiled at her. "He's improved so much he has the nurses dancing a merry jig to keep up with him."

"Excellent!" She laughed; it reminded Caroline of tinkling bells. Caroline then found herself the object of the woman's attention. Her black eyes smiled kindly as she said, "You are very beautiful, my dear."

Caroline blushed at the compliment and returned her smile as she whispered, "Thank you, madame. So are you."

Jake chuckled at both women. He took Caroline's arm and drew her to his side. *"Grand-mère,* may I present Lady Caroline of Conal Keep in Wales. Carrie, Madame Judalyn Bossette."

Caroline's face was frozen with shock at Jake's use of her title; he had never before even hinted that he was aware of her title or her father's.

"I'm so pleased to know you, Carrie." Madame

Bossette had abandoned the use of her title for Jake's pet name.

"Thank you, Madame Bossette. Hank and Jake have both spoken of you often," she returned with warmth, grateful that the woman was easy to like and talk to.

"Please call me Judalyn, or perhaps *Grand-mère* would not be too wrong a title for me?" Her dark eyes shifted from Caroline's blushing face to Jake's sheepishly grinning face.

"As usual you are right, *chérie*. Carrie and I are to be married on Friday," he announced proudly.

"I'm so pleased!" she cried with delight.

At a gasp from behind them all three turned to find Toni Mitchell, her face white with shock. "I'm sorry, Jake, your—er—news startled me. Congratulations, Caroline." Toni's voice dripped with bitter venom.

"Thank you," Caroline said quietly.

"Well, Jake, I'm off to Hawaii. Kiss me good-bye?" Without waiting for his answer, she threw her arms around Jake's neck and delivered a long, lingering kiss. Jake was cool but didn't protest.

"Look me up sometime, Jake," Toni said as she slung her flight bag over her shoulder and strolled away. Three pairs of eyes watched her exit.

"*Chérie*, could we be on our way, now?" said *grand-mère* after a moment or two.

"Of course," answered Jake absently, reluctantly taking his eyes off Toni.

Caroline and Jean spent the afternoon before the wedding searching the island for a suitable wedding dress. Caroline decided on a simple, short, cream silk dress with a high lace collar and tight sleeves. It wasn't exactly a designer gown but it was lovely all the same. She decided to wear a wreath of native flowers instead of a veil. When everything for the wedding had been arranged, they just wandered among the shops. On impulse Caroline selected a gift for Jake, a very beautiful native artist's painting of the lagoon where they had spent their happiest days together.

After their initial meeting at the airport, Caroline saw little of Madame Bossette, but then she hadn't expected to. She knew the lady was exhausted from her hasty travel and worry over Hank.

Over the past two days she had also seen very little of Jake. When she had encountered him, he was cool and indifferent to her, giving her light, preoccupied kisses and murmuring vague excuses about business to attend to. Caroline was left to speculate about whether or not he regretted having set this union in motion. Did he want out of it now?

On the eve of the wedding day, the families had arranged a dinner party in the hotel dining room. At the appointed hour of dinner Jake still hadn't arrived. Madame Bossette dismissed it lightly, saying he had worked all day catching up on business papers he had received from his company. Upon seeing the frown on Caroline's face, Madame Bossette amended that he was upstairs dressing for supper right now and would be down very soon.

As if on cue, he appeared in the doorway. In brown tailored slacks, deep burgundy silk shirt and tan sports coat, he was by far the most handsome man in the room. His gaze embraced and held her fast and her heart accelerated. His eyes were appraising her slender form and approving the clinging blue dress she wore. A slow smile creased his face as he made his way across the space that separated them.

The smile on his dark face faded as his lips descended on her upturned face. His brief kiss was gentle, and as he drew away he whispered in a low voice for her benefit only, "I've just now realized how much I've missed you these past days."

"Did you?" she accused, suddenly remembering the doubts and uneasiness he had caused.

"Of course." He drew away, his eyes turning hard.

She couldn't suppress the jealous anger she felt, however foolish, toward his business. "How is your company?"

"Wonderfully managed in my absence."

She knew she had been unfair and was instantly sorry she had allowed it to happen, "Jake, I—"

"You don't look well, *chérie*. Perhaps prewedding nerves?" He took her upper arm in a tight grip and drew her against his hard chest. In a harsh whisper he said, "Be in my hotel room tomorrow morning before the wedding. I've taken room 728."

"But it's bad luck to see each other before—" she began foolishly.

"Be there."

He released her and turned to join their families

236

on the garden terrace where they were toasting the union of families. Woodenly, Caroline moved to join them, but before she could reach the side of the man she was to marry, he had left the dining room under the pretext of more business to attend to.

Chapter Twelve

The morning of her wedding dawned bright and beautiful, as all wedding days should. Caroline dressed in a pair of faded jeans and a blue tee shirt. She brushed her hair with impatient strokes, anger building by the minute at Jake's rude behavior of the past evening, though she admitted that part of the blame was due to her own stupid jealous behavior.

She knocked timidly on the door, and was answered with a curt, "Enter."

There were stacks of files and papers on a makeshift desk. She smiled slightly and said ironically, "You're not so different from my father."

"They are simply reports and account statements," he answered, his voice flat, his face cool and closed.

"Jake, I—" she began, wanting to apologize for her behavior, but he did not let her finish.

"I've decided to cut this cruise short. Hank,

grand-mère and you will fly home to New Orleans when Hank leaves the hospital next week."

"But what about the wedd—you?" she stammered.

"I'm leaving this afternoon after the wedding. I'm sailing the *Sunflower* to Hawaii, so I can hire a crew there to sail her back to the States for me."

"You're leaving this afternoon?" she echoed stupidly, her white face blank with shock.

"Yes," he affirmed quietly.

She searched his hard face for any sign of weakening, but his jaw was tight and his mouth was set in a firm line. His eyes were as cold and remote as a frozen lake. She breathed in sharply, a pain stabbing her. She whispered, "Why, Jake?"

"I want you to have these next months to get used to my home, being Hank's surrogate mother, and most important of all, I want you to prepare for becoming my wife."

"But how can I do that if you're not with me?" she cried, unable to believe that he could be serious.

"You will do well to think about what kind of marriage you and I will have. It will be a normal marriage! You will live in my house, you will eat at the same table as I do, you will take vacations with the family and you will sleep in the same bed as I do. You will be my wife in every sense of the word."

"How dare you tell me . . ." she interrupted heatedly at his dissertation on what her life would be; but he was having none of it, he interrupted right back.

"I will tell you, Carrie. Our children, and there *will* be children, will not grow up as you and I have, without the love and security of two parents. They will not grow up with self-doubts about what they have done to deserve a lonely and different child-hood from all their friends."

The truth of each word was like a well-placed dagger in her heart. She knew he was not only thinking of her childhood and his own, but of Hank's as well. She had known all along that one of the reasons he was marrying her was to give Hank security; that he wanted children of his own was something she hadn't thought of. Children. Oh, how she wanted children—his children!

She had to harden her heart to keep herself from running into his arms and showing him the softer emotions she wanted to give this hard, ruthless man she had the misfortune to love. Instead she said in a meek voice, "I'll do whatever you wish, Jake."

"Good." He turned away from her and said in a tired voice, "I suggest you go dress for the cere-mony."

"I, Caroline Blythe Mary Elizabeth, take thee, Jacob David, to be my lawfully wedded husband, to love, honor and cherish, to have and to hold from this day hence, in sickness and in health, for richer for poorer, till death us do part." She looked into the face of the man who had just given these same vows to her. She couldn't find one scrap of emotion in his eyes, only cool business as usual.

A heavy, cold, plain, gold ring was slipped onto the third finger of her left hand and she did the same to him. The priest, beaming from ear to ear with happiness, pronounced them man and wife and urged Jake to kiss the bride.

His arms were bands of steel as they encircled her, his lips warm on her cold lips. When he released her, she swayed and he drew her against his large body to steady her as they turned to accept the congratulations of their family.

The cake was cut, champagne drunk in toast and the dance of the bride and groom over, when suddenly Jake disappeared into the hotel garden. Caroline wondered if it was his plan to leave her alone in the middle of their wedding celebration to cope with the explanations of his whereabouts.

Then a thought so terrible occurred to her. Toni was in Hawaii—was Jake meeting her? Had he planned this tryst before he came home to settle into marriage? Hatred filled her. She would demand an annulment of this folly of a marriage before it had gone too far! She fairly ran into the garden searching for him. She called, "Jake?"

"My dear, Carrie," called Madame Bossette from a bower of trellised purple bougainvillea vines.

"Have you seen Jake, Madame—*Grand-mère?*" she corrected, as she joined her under the shade.

"Yes, my dear, and he's just now told me the distressing news of his departure." It was clear she was very angry with her grandson.

"Why is he doing this, Madame?" she cried, begging for some reasonable explanation. "Oh, *Grand-mère*, is he going to see Toni?"

"Toni?"

"The woman at the airport?"

"Good heavens no! My dear, has he told you that he loves you?" she asked gently. Caroline shook her head.

"He doesn't love—it's only business."

"He loves you *very* deeply. So deeply, he's scared of losing you. He had some foolish notion that you need time to yourself before he demands that your marriage begin in earnest."

"I don't want time, I want him!"

"Then don't let the *Sunflower* sail without you!" she urged, her black eyes filled with determination.

"How can I get him to let me—"

"How did you get aboard the first time?"

"You know?" she breathed.

"Of course, Hank tells me everything." She smiled slyly.

"You are suggesting I stow away? He would be furious!"

"Wouldn't he just? Now my dear, I will occupy Jake with good-byes while you sneak aboard—"

"But what about Hank?"

"I'll take him home with me. He'll be delighted. He's mature enough to realize newly married people need time alone. Here comes Jake to take you to your room. Call a taxi instantly or better still have your father's car take you to the waterfront. I'll hold him thirty minutes. Good-bye, darling, and good luck."

"Thank you, *Grand-mère*. I'll never forget how kind—"

"Hello, Jake, *chéri*. Are you leaving now? Please come up to my room before you leave. I have some things for you to attend to."

At the farewell, Robert gravely shook Jake's hand and embraced Caroline with tenderness and affection. Jean smiled radiantly at both of them. Caroline hadn't the heart to tell them earlier that Jake was leaving her behind, and now she was glad she hadn't spoiled the wedding day they had planned so wonderfully at such short notice.

Caroline took Jake's arm and let him lead her smiling demurely into the elevator. In the corridor before her door, he said grimly, "Good-bye, Carrie, I'll see you in three months' time."

He turned to leave. Caroline's hand caught the sleeve of his jacket. "Jake, aren't you going to kiss me good-bye?"

His eyes narrowed slightly at her request but he roughly drew her against him. His hands tumbled her lovely russet hair, and the wreath of flowers on her head fell to the floor unheeded as he held her face tipped to his. The mouth that descended on hers drank deeply of the sweet surrender he found there. His hands moved from her silken hair over her pliant body, seeming to commit her to memory. His hard thighs pressed into hers, and she leaned against him in loving surrender, her hands and lips caressing his throat, his hair, his lips.

With an impatient groan he pushed her away, turned on his heel and strode away from her. She smiled after him. If he had turned and seen the purely feline look of intrigue on her face he would have trembled knowing he was the object of such plotting.

She slipped quickly into her room; his ardent embrace had only endorsed her plan. She would be on the *Sunflower* if she had to swim after it! She hastily packed a small bag, grabbed the gaily wrapped painting she had purchased for him and raced down to the lobby where her father's driver waited.

Hank's cabin hadn't been cleaned or aired in the eight days he had been in the hospital; in truth the entire ketch was untidy. Jake had apparently procured spare parts and fresh provisions, but hadn't bothered to stow them. She smiled to herself; she would not have a shortage of dirty jobs when he found her stowed away this time.

Caroline went into the master cabin, and saw that Jake's smaller bunk was tumbled but hers was still neatly made. She doubted that he had slept in it since she had left. At the end of the bed were her clothes, folded with care. Jake must have been readying these things to be sent to her because an empty box was beside them.

She was startled out of her daydreaming when she heard activity from the dock. She had to hide! She ran back into Hank's cabin and rolled onto the bunk just as he came aboard. Her heart raced when she heard his footsteps in the saloon, fearing that he would check Hank's cabin, but he didn't. The auxiliary motor started and the ketch was soon underway.

The minutes ticked by into an hour, then two. And still he hadn't shut off the motor and hoisted the sails. What could he be doing? The motor suddenly became silent, the anchor winch was activated. A glance out the skylight told her that he had sailed into their tiny cove off Eten Island. An incredible feeling of joy surged through her. Jake had been happy here too! She had thought to give him a painting of this wonderful place but he had unwittingly given her the real thing.

The late afternoon sun kissed the sea softly with ribbons of shimmering gold when she heard Jake's body knife into the water. She came out of the cabin and onto the deck just in time to see him gaining the beach of the cove. For an instant she struggled with doubts but when her mind cleared she went below, pulled on her bikini, and followed him.

He stood on the white sand, arms crossed on his wide chest, thunderclouds in his light eyes. For once she wasn't intimidated by his anger, she just smiled in supreme confidence at him and said, "Mr. St. Simon, I presume?"

"Carrie, what is your game now?" His face was tight and stern.

"Jake, I've no games to play. I just offer you a stowaway, yours to do with what you will. And from the condition of the *Sunflower* I'll be very busy." She gave him an impish smile.

"You're going back." His eyes blazed.

"No, Jake, I am not!" she answered softly, her determined jaw tipped to meet his anger with a stubbornness equal to his own. Her eyes were bright with purpose.

"If I say—"

"Then don't say it, Jake! It will only be the gauntlet of challenge thrown down between us and one of us will feel bound to pick it up!" She smiled. Her eyes were serious and she was rewarded by a sudden light of mocking admiration in his eyes.

"It would be an interesting spectacle, wouldn't it? I can see the headlines now. HUSBAND FORCES WIFE OF ONE DAY TO PUT ASHORE." He laughed at himself.

She answered his laughter with flippancy. "Besides, you hate to stand night watch. Now you have a willing stowaway."

"That's true. And I have *all* those dirty jobs," he warned her in mock threatening tones. He grinned lazily but his eyes were tender and caressing, touching her heart and stirring a tight yearning in her.

She asked in a husky voice, "What payment for my passage did you ask of my father? If it's too steep I'll have to sell my jewels at the next port."

He laughed. "One thousand dollars to the Marine Foundation on Moen. But *I* pay my wife's fare."

"I want to see your canceled check," she laughed.

"Before the sun sets let's race for the *Sunflower*, slowpoke."

At his words she turned and ran toward the mild surf. Her headstart was to no avail, his powerful easy strokes far outdistanced hers. His strong arms lifted her from the water onto the deck, her golden body coming to rest against his warm brown chest. Her trembling hands burrowed into hair, seeking comfort and love as his arms swept around her. She was rewarded by the tremor of love that shook him.

His lips began a slow trip down the side of her wet face. As his mouth approached hers, she turned her quivering lips, seeking, then finding his. Their kiss was deep, their mouths playing, warming, until passion threatened to spill over into raw desire.

His hands caressed the curve of her back, her ribs, the swell of her breast held by her bikini. The clasp of that garment yielded instantly to his other hand. Groaning, he pushed it aside and cupped her naked breast in his hand; his mouth soon followed, teasing the nipple into a stiff peak.

He lifted his head to stare deeply into her violet

passion-filled eyes and seeing the answer he sought he whispered roughly, "Carrie, I've got to have you." Gazing into the depths of the twin aqua pools, she slowly reached up with silken arms and drew his head down to her. Her tongue followed his in exploration, searching the recesses of his heart. Gently he lifted her into his arms and carried her to his bed.

The remainder of their clothes fell away, victims of eager hands. Words weren't necessary, the fury he was stirring in her almost burst inside as he kissed the hard tips of her breasts. His lips traced her collarbone with light kisses, his tongue licked off the beads of saltwater. As he buried his face in her neck, she felt his breathing, hard and stormy as her own.

When she thought she could not stand another moment of waiting, he rose above her. The surge of fulfillment was so intense that it swept her away into incredible splendor.

She cried to him, "Jake, I love you."

"And I love you, *chérie,*" he answered hoarsely as fulfillment came to him.

Later, in the sweet aftermath, she whispered in a tender but accusing voice, "Why didn't you ever tell me you loved me? Why did you try to leave me behind?"

"I would label myself a fool every time I wanted to say those words to you. I waged a battle within myself and every time the dark side won. I didn't believe you would give up your carefree life to be my wife, my lover and my friend." His voice, lazy and deep, was filled with spent passion and tender love.

"My husband, lover and friend, I'm not, to quote

your words to Hank, that type of woman." She mocked him tenderly, her heart heavy with contentment.

He rolled onto his elbow and looked into her face, bathed in the brightness of a full moon rising to the east to softly touch their perfect world with silvery light. His hand lightly traced her moonstruck face, the line of her throat, the swell of her breast, the flat stomach, down to the curve of her soft thigh.

Slowly he said in a husky voice, "I knew you weren't that type of woman when I made love to you the first time and found you were a virgin."

"Jake!" She was indignant.

"But I knew it before then, *chérie*. However, it salvaged my pride to think of you as a plaything, then later a spoiled brat. The day you apparently decided to cable your father, I had decided to sail back to Moen and make you decide if you would marry me or go running home to your father. I was going to tell you I loved you and take my chances, but my pride got in the way and I couldn't seem to stop arguing with you." He kissed her nose.

"I was equally foolish, Jake. I let you believe the worst of me." She couldn't let him shoulder the blame that was partially hers too.

"Why did you run away from your father?" he asked.

She suddenly stiffened in his arms. Would he believe her? To plead a reason that was so archaic in this day and age—forced marriage for family gain. She took a deep breath and said bluntly, "My father wanted me to marry a distant cousin to keep the Conal earldom and all its properties from passing away from his direct control."

"Damn him!" he exploded.

She snuggled closer to him and giggled with relief, "Don't be too hard on him, Jake. Without his diabolical plan I would never have made it aboard the *Sunflower*." She kissed his tight jaw and felt it relax under her lips.

"For that I am grateful, *chérie*. But he will not interfere with our lives; our children will not be burdened with the crushing weight of history. I know too well what it does to a child to be constantly measured to some illustrious or infamous ancestor."

"Oh Jake, if only I had swallowed my damnable pride sooner and said what was in my heart. We very nearly lost each other." Her voice choked at the terrible thought!

"I love you, Carrie. I was preparing to follow you. I was going to fly Hank home; then I was coming to England to tell you I loved you and wanted to marry you. When I told your father I would marry you, I wanted him to accept. Nothing or no one will ever come between us," he whispered with possessiveness as his lips descended on hers. He admitted, "You very nearly drove me to the brink of insanity with your games."

"You deserved insanity! Most of the time you were very cynical and cold to me."

"Yes," he agreed slowly. "I think I knew all along you weren't the hard little witch I noticed that morning on Hilo Bay. And then two mornings later, you came out of Hank's cabin in my clothes and offered me your jewelry and fur, as if I were some peasant to be bought and sold to do your bidding. Well, *chérie*, you angered me so deeply I was afraid I would strangle you where you stood. So I kissed you and taunted you instead. When you took on every job I gave you and didn't complain, but became an indispensable member of the crew, I knew I couldn't break your spirit but that you had broken mine."

"Jake, I was scared to death of you at the start, then so crazy in love with you, I didn't want to be anywhere else but aboard the *Sunflower* with you and Hank."

"I was scared of me too. Something clicked in my mind at the sight of you. The thought that you belonged to someone else didn't quell the instant desire I had to make you mine. I had never before wanted anyone or anything as badly as I wanted you. I left Hawaii so I wouldn't have so see you so aloof and unattainable." His voice was low and sheepish as he told her of his secret inner thoughts and longings.

"I love you, Jake, and if it's any consolation, I couldn't get you out of my mind either. I was angry at you for laughing at me. When I fell against you on the wharf I wanted to melt against you and . . ."

He interrupted her story with a kiss. Then he whispered, "Did you bring that alluring little white thing you were wearing that morning?"

"Yes," she breathed, her head reeling with an intoxicating yearning for him.

"Sometime, in perhaps a week or two I may let you put it on . . ." he teased.

She nipped him playfully on the shoulder as his aqua eyes roved over her slender form.

He growled at her throat, "I want you, *chérie*."

"What's stopping you?"

"Nothing. . . ."

If you enjoyed this book...

...you will enjoy a Special Edition Book Club membership even more.

It will bring you each new title, as soon as it is published every month, delivered right to your door.

15-Day Free Trial Offer

We will send you 6 new Silhouette Special Editions to keep for 15 days absolutely free! If you decide not to keep them, send them back to us, you pay nothing. But if you enjoy them as much as we think you will, keep them and pay the invoice enclosed with your trial shipment. You will then automatically become a member of the Special Edition Book Club and receive 6 more romances every month. There is no minimum number of books to buy and you can cancel at any time.

MORE ROMANCE FOR
A SPECIAL WAY TO RELAX

$1.95 each

1 ☐ TERMS OF SURRENDER Dailey
2 ☐ INTIMATE STRANGERS Hastings
3 ☐ MEXICAN RHAPSODY Dixon
4 ☐ VALAQUEZ BRIDE Vitek
5 ☐ PARADISE POSTPONED Converse
6 ☐ SEARCH FOR A NEW DAWN Douglass
7 ☐ SILVER MIST Stanford
8 ☐ KEYS TO DANIEL'S HOUSE Halston
9 ☐ ALL OUR TOMORROWS Baxter
10 ☐ TEXAS ROSE Thiels
11 ☐ LOVE IS SURRENDER Thornton
12 ☐ NEVER GIVE YOUR HEART Sinclair
13 ☐ BITTER VICTORY Beckman
14 ☐ EYE OF THE HURRICANE Keene
15 ☐ DANGEROUS MAGIC James
16 ☐ MAYAN MOON Carr
17 ☐ SO MANY TOMORROWS John
18 ☐ A WOMAN'S PLACE Hamilton
19 ☐ DECEMBER'S WINE Shaw
20 ☐ NORTHERN LIGHTS Musgrave
21 ☐ ROUGH DIAMOND Hastings
22 ☐ ALL THAT GLITTERS Howard
23 ☐ LOVE'S GOLDEN SHADOW Charles
24 ☐ GAMBLE OF DESIRE Dixon
25 ☐ TEARS AND RED ROSES Hardy
26 ☐ A FLIGHT OF SWALLOWS Scott
27 ☐ A MAN WITH DOUBTS Wisdom

28 ☐ THE FLAMING TREE Ripy
29 ☐ YEARNING OF ANGELS Bergen
30 ☐ BRIDE IN BARBADOS Stephens
31 ☐ TEARS OF YESTERDAY Baxter
32 ☐ A TIME TO LOVE Douglass
33 ☐ HEATHER'S SONG Palmer
34 ☐ MIXED BLESSING Sinclair
35 ☐ STORMY CHALLENGE James
36 ☐ FOXFIRE LIGHT Dailey
37 ☐ MAGNOLIA MOON Stanford
38 ☐ WEB OF PASSION John
39 ☐ AUTUMN HARVEST Milan
40 ☐ HEARTSTORM Converse
41 ☐ COLLISION COURSE Halston
42 ☐ PROUD VINTAGE Drummond
43 ☐ ALL SHE EVER WANTED Shaw
44 ☐ SUMMER MAGIC Eden
45 ☐ LOVE'S TENDER TRIAL Charles
46 ☐ AN INDEPENDENT WIFE Howard
47 ☐ PRIDE'S POSSESSION Stephens
48 ☐ LOVE HAS ITS REASONS Ferrell
49 ☐ A MATTER OF TIME Hastings
50 ☐ FINDERS KEEPERS Browning
51 ☐ STORMY AFFAIR Trent
52 ☐ DESIGNED FOR LOVE Sinclair
53 ☐ GODDESS OF THE MOON Thomas
54 ☐ THORNE'S WAY Hohl

Silhouette Special Edition

MORE ROMANCE FOR
A SPECIAL WAY TO RELAX

55 ☐ SUN LOVER Stanford

56 ☐ SILVER FIRE Wallace

57 ☐ PRIDE'S RECKONING Thornton

58 ☐ KNIGHTLY LOVE Douglass

59 ☐ THE HEART'S VICTORY Roberts

60 ☐ ONCE AND FOREVER Thorne

61 ☐ TENDER DECEPTION Beckman

62 ☐ DEEP WATERS Bright

63 ☐ LOVE WITH A PERFECT STRANGER Wallace

64 ☐ MIST OF BLOSSOMS Converse

65 ☐ HANDFUL OF SKY Cates

66 ☐ A SPORTING AFFAIR Mikels

67 ☐ AFTER THE RAIN Shaw

68 ☐ CASTLES IN THE AIR Sinclair

69 ☐ SORREL SUNSET Dalton

70 ☐ TRACES OF DREAMS Clare

71 ☐ MOONSTRUCK Skillern

72 ☐ NIGHT MUSIC Belmont

LOOK FOR *AN ACT OF LOVE*
BY BROOKE HASTINGS AVAILABLE IN MARCH AND
ENCHANTED SURRENDER BY PATTI BECKMAN
IN APRIL.

SILHOUETTE SPECIAL EDITION, Department SE/2
1230 Avenue of the Americas
New York, NY 10020

Please send me the books I have checked above. I am enclosing $_____
(please add 50¢ to cover postage and handling. NYS and NYC residents
please add appropriate sales tax). Send check or money order—no cash or
C.O.D.'s please. Allow six weeks for delivery.

NAME _____

ADDRESS _____

CITY _____ STATE/ZIP _____

Coming Next Month

Season Of Seduction by Abra Taylor

In keeping her tennis pro sister out of trouble, Michele Haworth ran into a problem of her own: Damon Pierce— and Damon played to win no matter what the game!

Unspoken Past by Linda Wisdom

Unspoken, but not unremembered. How could Anne ever forget the brief hours she had shared with Kyle Harrison—or his anger when he discovered that she wasn't free to love?

Summer Rhapsody by Nancy John

Nina was leery of British tycoon Dexter Rolfe. But gradually she learned that the fire she found in his arms would warm the years ahead and secure their future together.

Tomorrow's Memory by Margaret Ripy

Cole's vengeful tie to Lacey's past held them together. But the passion they found soon melted their anger and had the Kentucky couple racing toward the future.

Prelude To Passion by Fran Bergen

Operatic set designer Nydia Lear was intrigued by world famous maestro Kurt Klausen. But she had a job to do and no time for love—until Kurt taught her otherwise.

Fortune's Play by Eve Gladstone

In the heat of the Arabian desert, Nicki's marriage to Steve had shattered. But now in Montana, Chinook winds swept across the plains to bring them together . . . this time forever.

15-Day Free Trial Offer
6 Silhouette Romances

6 Silhouette Romances, free for 15 days! We'll send you 6 new Silhouette Romances to keep for 15 days, absolutely free! If you decide not to keep them, send them back to us. You pay nothing.

Free Home Delivery. But if you enjoy them as much as we think you will, keep them by paying the invoice enclosed with your free trial shipment. We'll pay all shipping and handling charges. You get the convenience of Home Delivery and we pay the postage and handling charge each month.

Don't miss a copy. The Silhouette Book Club is the way to make sure you'll be able to receive every new romance we publish before they're sold out. There is no minimum number of books to buy and you can cancel at any time.

This offer expires June 30, 1983

Silhouette Book Club, Dept. SRSE 7D
120 Brighton Road, Clifton, NJ 07012

Please send me 6 Silhouette Romances to keep for 15 days, absolutely free. I understand I am not obligated to join the Silhouette Book Club unless I decide to keep them.

NAME_____

ADDRESS_____

CITY_____ STATE_____ ZIP_____

READERS' COMMENTS ON SILHOUETTE SPECIAL EDITIONS:

"I just finished reading the first six Silhouette Special Edition Books and I had to take the opportunity to write you and tell you how much I enjoyed them. I enjoyed all the authors in this series. Best wishes on your Silhouette Special Editions line and many thanks."

—B.H.*, Jackson, OH

"The Special Editions are really special and I enjoyed them very much! I am looking forward to next month's books."

—R.M.W.*, Melbourne, FL

"I've just finished reading four of your first six Special Editions and I enjoyed them very much. I like the more sensual detail and longer stories. I will look forward each month to your new Special Editions."

—L.S.*, Visalia, CA

"Silhouette Special Editions are — 1.) Superb! 2.) Great! 3.) Delicious! 4.) Fantastic! . . . Did I leave anything out? These are books that an adult woman can read . . . I love them!"

—H.C.*, Monterey Park, CA

*names available on request

She tossed and turned, then sat up on the bed and sighed restlessly. What was wrong with her? There were times when she felt so irritable and tense, and others when her body ached. She lay back down disgustedly, knowing full well what was the matter. Lizette had already informed her, and she'd been right. If she could only go to Roth. To feel his hands on her again.

Her body ached with longing. How could she survive without him? She needed him. Not just any man; she needed Roth. Love was like a tonic to her, and without it she felt only half alive, and she loved him so much. But she couldn't. She had no right to him. She'd given him up for Quinn, and there was no longer any room for her in his life. She couldn't go crawling back to him. Besides, by now he might have found someone else.

Suddenly she heard a noise in the passageway outside the cabin that wasn't caused by the creaking ship; then the door opened and she held her breath. A lantern was hanging on the wall, and there was no mistaking the familiar stance of the man in the doorway.

She sat bolt upright, staring at him, and her heart turned over inside her. "Roth!" she cried, and her voice broke.

He stepped into the cabin and shut the door behind him, then stood staring at her. He looked so ruggedly masculine, the way he had that day back in England when she'd gone to bring him back to London, and she felt the same warm quickening deep inside.

His eyes sifted over her from head to toe in the dim lamplight. She was lovely, her hair loose, falling onto her shoulders, and the flimsy nightgown she wore hugged the firm outline of her breasts.

"You wouldn't come to me, so I came to you," he said huskily, and she shook her head.

"You shouldn't . . ."

He walked toward her, stopping at the edge of the bed, his eyes looking directly into hers. "You don't want me?" he asked, and she groaned.

"Oh, God, yes . . . I want you," she gasped breathlessly, her voice trembling. "I want you so much I ache inside," and she reached up toward him.

He sat on the edge of the bed, taking both her hands in his. "Why didn't you come?"

"I couldn't," she whispered, her eyes searching his. "I

couldn't come crawling back to you after what I'd done. You know why."

"Sometimes you're stubborn."

"I know."

"And unreasonable."

"I know."

"You don't want me to take his place?"

She shook her head, her eyes filled with love. "No, Roth. Not that. Not ever . . . not his place. You'll take your own place. You've always had your own place in my heart, you know that. I don't want you to try to take his place. I want you to be yourself with me, like it was before. Like it was in England."

He reached up and touched her face, his fingers caressing her cheek lightly, sending shivers to her toes. "You mean you don't intend to send me away?"

She sighed and lay back on the bed, her body alive, warm sensations pulsating through her. "Never," she groaned breathlessly. "I'll never send you away again," and he stared at her, his heart pounding.

He reached out slowly, grasping her flimsy nightgown, pulling it up her body, and she wriggled beneath his hands, stretching as he drew it up over her head, pushing it to one side, her naked flesh as smooth and soft as a ripe peach, inviting him to take her.

He undressed slowly as she waited, his eyes never leaving her face; then he crawled in beside her on the narrow bunk barely big enough for one, and her body thrilled to the feel of him close beside her. She laughed lightly, sensuously as she tried to make room for him; then he leaned on one elbow, looking down into her face as she lay almost beneath him.

He lay partially on his side, partially on his stomach, pressed close to her, and she could feel him hard against her, and her body began to throb.

He leaned down, putting his mouth to her breast, his tongue teasing as his hand ran the length of her body from thigh to breast, to stomach, then rested in the patch of dark hair he knew so well, and she trembled at his touch.

"Dicia, Dicia, I love you," he whispered eagerly, and lifted his head partway, his lips moving to kiss her neck, the hollow at the base of her throat, and then her lips, lightly at first, provocatively, then growing more urgent.

Her lips answered his kiss hungrily; then he raised his head, his eyes darkening with desire. "I've waited so long," he whispered passionately. "Just to touch you like this without feeling guilty," and she felt his hand moving in her soft hair, then moving up her body to caress her breasts, the nipples hard and firm now. "Just to love you, Dicia, to make you mine once more for always," he whispered, and kissed her again, and she felt the blood rushing through her veins like liquid fire, her flesh hot beneath his hands as she responded to him passionately.

His body pressed against hers hard, and she felt him enter her, a sweet warmth spreading into her loins, and he moved slowly, rhythmically, every movement a caress as he made love to her. Then, as her need for him became more urgent and he felt her body answering him wantonly, he moved above her, his thrusts more demanding, his mouth still on hers, and as she arched to meet him, climaxing wildly, he thrust hard, exploding inside her, and she moaned beneath him, trembling at the savage release that shook her and made her cry out with rapture.

Her arms were around him, and she felt his skin soft beneath her hands, the muscles relaxing as he lay spent, his breathing heavy.

His lips softened on her mouth as he drew his head back and looked down into her face, his body still throbbing savagely. "You amaze me, woman," he whispered softly, and she sighed as she reached up, running her hand through his hair.

"How's that?"

"Because you still make love the way you did when we first got married, wild and wanton," and she frowned.

"But we're not married," she whispered, her eyes on his, and he sighed.

"On the contrary, my love. You've always been my wife as far as I'm concerned. I thought you knew that," and she stared up at him as he went on. "Tomorrow we'll have Beau make it official again before we go ashore, and I'm taking you to live with me at the Château, where we won't ever be separated again, and I intend to spend the rest of my life making love to you," and he kissed her long and hard, and she felt it deep inside, stirring her loins violently, making her tremble.

She smiled to herself as she lay beneath him, warm and

contented, his lips on hers, feeling the rapture of the love she'd always had for him. She knew now that Quinn had been right. Here's where she belonged now, in Roth's arms, and the world seemed right again.

THE END

FOR YOUR FUTURE
PLEASURE—A PREVIEW
OF THE THIRD NOVEL IN THIS
ROMANTIC AMERICAN TRILOGY OF
ADVENTURE AND PASSION,

THE WILD STORMS
OF HEAVEN

Here, printed in full,
is the opening chapter of the
mighty saga that brings
June Lund Shiplett's great drama
of the American past to a
stirring conclusion. Watch for
the complete novel coming to you
soon in a Signet edition.

THE WILD STORMS
OF HEAVEN
by June Lund Shiplett

1

Port Royal, South Carolina, May 1794

Moonlight crept into the shadowy folds of the furled
sails and made strange patterns take shape like· ghosts
through the rigging, as a full breeze gently rocked the
ship. The night was warm and humid, the scent of mag-
nolias from the plantations along Port Royal Sound filled
the air with their sweet fragrance, and below the quarter-
deck, in one of the cabins, two figures lay·pressed close
in a narrow bunk, unmindful of the heat or the late hour.

Roth stirred, feeling Loedicia's softness against him,
and once more he was aroused. She was life to him, and
he could hardly believe that after all these years she
would finally be his again. In the morning he'd have the
young man who captained the ship—the one they called
Beau—he'd have him perform the ceremony making her
Mrs. Roth Chapman, then he'd take her to the Château
on the banks of ·the Broad River, his home, where she
belonged, and this time it would be forever.

Loedicia moved as ·he stirred against her, and she
nestled even closer in·his arms. She hadn't really been
asleep, only dozing..Her body was too alive·for sleep, her
senses too keen. She was content in his· arms, yet so
aware of him. She felt his bare skin next to her, the soft
hairs on his chest brushing her face· as she turned her
body all the way toward him, snuggling close.

Nineteen years earlier she had married Roth, thinking
her first husband, Quinn Locke, was dead; then Quinn
had miraculously turned up alive barely two months after

the nuptials, making her second marriage void. But she had become pregnant before Quinn's return and had given Roth a son. A son her first husband had resented and almost grown to hate over the years. Quinn saw the boy as a symbol of the love between Loedicia and Roth that had never died. Although Loedicia had loved her husband fiercely, she'd loved Roth too and had always kept a special place in her heart for him. The tortuous years between her brief marriage to Roth and the present had been wrought with anguish as she'd tried to rationalize her feelings for the two men, but now Quinn was dead. He'd been killed by a bullet intended for Roth's son. The son Quinn had thought at one time was his but against whom he had turned as the child grew and he realized the truth. With Quinn's death a part of Loedicia had died too. A part that could never be replaced. Yet at the same time, a new peace was born within her. She'd given Quinn her love unashamedly from the depths of her heart, putting all else aside, but now her love was free again. Free to be given to Roth.

Roth's arms moved up her back, his lips pressing against her forehead. "Are you awake?" he asked, whispering in the dimly lit cabin, and she sighed.

"I haven't really been asleep."

He held her closer, paying little heed to the sweat that stuck to their bodies, only conscious of his need for her. "Sometimes I think I'm dreaming," he said as his hand moved down over her hip, feeling its velvet smoothness, and she lifted her head lazily, her violet eyes gazing into his handsome face, and she reached up slowly, touching the slight frost at his temples that made him look even more attractive, running her hand through his dark, almost black hair.

"You told me once you never wanted to see me again," she whispered softly, and he frowned.

"Did I say that?"

"Emphatically."

"That's because I couldn't have you."

"And now?"

"I'll never let you go," and he kissed her deeply, letting his hands caress her once more, bringing her to life.

Suddenly she felt his muscles tense, and his hand stopped on her breast, caressing it hesitantly as he became distracted. "Did you hear anything?" he asked soft-ly, his lips against hers, and she stared into his dark eyes, wanting only to kiss him again, but instead she listened, straining her ears.

"Only the waves," she replied, but he jerked his head suddenly, looking at the ceiling.

"Listen!" he cautioned, and she tuned her ears toward the ceiling of the small cabin.

Now she could hear scuffling noises, soft but firm, on deck. "Could it be morning?"

He shook his head. "It couldn't be later than two or three."

"Then who?"

Suddenly there was a knock on the cabin door, and Roth stirred, startled. He reluctantly took his arms from about her and slid from the small bunk, slipping into his underwear and breeches, and hurried to the door as she pulled up the lone blanket to cover herself.

He unlocked the door and opened it hesitantly until he saw his son's worried face. The boy was eighteen now. No longer a boy, but a young man far older than his years, and for Roth, looking at him was like looking into a mir-ror. He had the same dark hair and dark eyes. So dark it was hard to see their true color.

"What is it?" he asked, whispering, and Heath frowned.

Heath was second mate on the *Golden Eagle*, a French privateer, at the moment anchored off the coast of Port Royal disguised as the *White Dolphin*, a merchant ship.

"Beau wants to see you above deck," Heath said softly. "It's urgent," and his face reddened. He'd met his father for the first time only the day before, and although he'd warmed to him, the thought that he was spending the night with his mother in the cabin without having the convenience of a marriage ceremony embarrassed him. Mothers weren't supposed to do things like that. But then, his mother was different. She was beautiful and unpre-dictable, and he'd seen more than one man look at her with hungry eyes.

"I'll be right up," Roth said, and closed the door as Heath turned away; then he walked back to where Loe-dicia waited. He dropped down, sitting beside her on the bunk. "I don't know what's happened," he said. "But Beau wants me on deck. I shouldn't be too long." He leaned over, kissing her long and hard, hating to leave her like this.

She watched him leave the cabin barefoot and shirtless, and she sighed contentedly.

Heath was waiting at the end of the passage, and Roth followed, feeling the warm breeze as he stepped on deck. Beau was at the rail in much the same attire as Roth, only he was staring toward shore, a grim look on his swarthy face.

"What is it?" asked Roth as he addressed the younger man, and Beau straightened, nodding off beyond the jib.

Roth followed the motion of his head until his eyes distinctly made out the outline of a ship some four or five hundred yards away. It was silhouetted in the moonlight, the rigging gaunt, like picked-over bones, with the sails furled.

"British," stated Roth, and he turned back to Beau. "How long has it been there?"

"Long enough to send a boat in to shore."

"In the middle of the night?"

"They called from shore a few minutes ago, and insist on coming aboard."

Roth frowned. He was certain he knew the ship. Only yesterday morning he'd been in Beaufort with its captain signing some papers the captain had brought to him from his businesses in England. Roth lived in Port Royal, owned a shipyard in Beaufort, a shipping company in Charleston, and still ran the shipping and shipbuilding companies his father had left him in England. He continued frowning as he glanced at Beau.

"You think they're suspicious?"

"I know they are. Why else would they want to come aboard?"

"They can't touch you in these waters."

Beau sneered. "May I ask who's to stop them?" and Roth flushed.

Beau was right. There wasn't an American ship in sight, not even a merchant. They were looking at a British ship in American waters without any jurisdiction, but the fact that the whole British Navy was looking for Beau made him uneasy. If the British captain learned the truth, he'd overlook protocol, apologize to the Americans later, and Beau and Heath would hang for sure.

"I'll go talk to them," suggested Roth. "Maybe we're wrong assuming they're suspicious of who you really are. I know the British captain. Maybe I can talk him out of wanting to come aboard."

Beau's eyes relaxed momentarily as he quietly gave orders for the men to get a boat ready and Roth headed back to the cabin.

"I have to go ashore for a few minutes," he explained to Loedicia as he stood below in the cabin a few minutes later, putting on his shirt and boots. "There's a British ship lying off the port bow with a nose for trouble, and I think her captain's smarter than we think. He wants to send out a boarding party."

She raised up on her elbows, watching him, then sat the rest of the way up as he talked.

He leaned over the bed, and she laughed as he pulled her into his arms, his body warming her. "I wish they hadn't disturbed us."

"I know," she answered.

"I love you."

Her eyes shone. "I love you too," and he kissed her sensuously, his mouth devouring her, reluctant to leave, hating to be away from her even for a short time.

"I'd better go before he sends Heath back down," he said as he released her and left the cabin.

Men were scurrying about in the darkness as he reached the deck, and Beau was fully dressed now as he waited next to the rope ladder. The longboat was already in the water, bobbing up and down like a cork, and Roth stopped, glancing over the side.

"I'd better go alone," he said as he saw a man waiting for him in the small boat, and Beau looked at him sharply. "Under the circumstances, I think it's best, just in case," and Beau stared at him a minute, then agreed, so the man in the boat climbed back aboard and Roth started over the side, confident it was nothing to worry about and praying he was right.

On shore, Captain Horace Marlin paced the small dock, then stopped, looking abruptly at the three sailors standing a few feet from him. All three had been aboard a frigate captured by Captain Beau Thunder a little over a year earlier, but they had managed to escape from the French prison they'd been thrown into. On returning to

England, they'd been reassigned and were now part of the captain's crew.

"I hope you three are right about this," the captain said as he faced them. "I don't relish instigating an international incident, then finding out we were wrong."

All three men stood patiently as the captain fussed about, glancing at the rest of the men he'd brought to shore with him; then finally the sailor in the middle spoke.

"We couldn't be mistaken, sir," he said. "I'd know the lines of the *Golden Eagle* anywhere. She rides different in the water. There's just something about the ship. Once you see it, you never forget it. That is, if you're a sailor and know your ships. I'll swear that ship's the *Golden Eagle*."

The captain straightened, then glanced toward the ship again, in time to see a small boat leave its side and head for shore, and he scowled. "Now, who the devil could that be?" he said, and reached next to him where his aide stood, and asked for his spyglass.

One man was silhouetted in the boat, and he was rowing toward them. But it was too dark to see who it was. The captain kept his eye on the small boat all the way in until it was just a few yards away; then he cursed softly as he recognized Roth Chapman.

Roth swung the boat into the pier and called out, "Tie up!" then he tossed the rope to a sailor standing near the edge, and when the boat was secure, he climbed ashore. "Are you insane?" he began as he faced the captain, his face dark with anger. "It's three in the morning! What the hell are you trying to do, anyway?"

The captain blustered, licking his lips. He'd had no idea Roth Chapman was aboard the ship, and he was as startled to see him now as he would have been to see the King of England. "Mr. Chapman!" he exclaimed, and his face reddened. "I had no idea."

"Surely you've an explanation," snapped Roth, and the captain flushed.

God damn! Now what could he do? This was probably one of Roth's private ships. Roth was not only one of the richest men in England and America, but a close friend of the King of England and grandson of the late Earl of Cumberland, and a privileged guest in British society, even though he'd chosen to live in America. But yet . . .

the men were so determined, all three of them. He glanced at them quickly, then back to Roth.

"I have three sailors over there, sir," he said formidably, "who were once part of the crew of a ship captured by the notorious Captain Thunder. All three, I'm afraid, claim that the ship you just left is his ship, the *Golden Eagle*."

Roth's eyes narrowed, and he turned, looking at the three men. The pier was dark and their faces were hard to read. He turned back to the captain. "And when did they come to this conclusion?" he asked.

"Two of them work night watch, the other's the cook."

"Night watch? You mean they've only seen the ship in the dark, yet they think they can identify it?"

"They're good sailors," explained Captain Marlin. "They know their ships."

"Not as well as they should," said Roth. "That ship is the *White Dolphin* out of Jamaica."

"Excuse me, Captain," interrupted the sailor in the middle, and the captain turned to him, his face still flushed.

"Well?"

"Sir," the man began, "the *Golden Eagle* has a scroll design along the side, hiding its gun ports when they're not in use, her jib boom is extra long, and she doesn't carry a figurehead. I realize it's dark, but I suggest you look through your spyglass."

The captain still held the glass in his hand, and he frowned, then put it to his eye. He took his time scrutinizing the ship, the glass moving across every inch as it lay quiet in the water. He scanned the jib, his eyes taking in its length, then moved to where there should be a figurehead; there was none. He moved the glass to the side, where the faint outline of a scroll design was visible in the moonlight, then back again toward the jib, just to make sure before taking it from his eye.

He turned to Roth, his eyes wary. If this was the *Golden Eagle*, what the hell was Roth Chapman doing aboard? And if it wasn't the *Golden Eagle*, why did it fit the description?

"I think we'll take a look aboard anyway," he said, his curiosity aroused. "It shouldn't do any harm."

Roth's jaw set angrily. Of all the luck. He glanced toward the ship. He could barely make out figures moving about on her deck, and he bit his lip. If Captain Marlin and his crew set foot on board, anything could happen and probably would, because Beau wouldn't give in without a fight. Beau was three-quarters Indian, although he looked like his French grandfather, but Heath said he could be savage at times, and Loedicia and Heath would be right in the middle of it.

"Captain," said Roth stubbornly, trying to argue him out of it as the captain and his men began heading for their boats, "these are American waters. You can't just board any ship you want because you think something's wrong," and the captain stopped, looking about him at the quiet night.

There wasn't another man on the dock except his sailors, and not another ship in sight. "Mr. Chapman, sir," he said, pretending politeness, "I don't give a damn what waters I'm in. I've been hunting that bastard for months. If that ship isn't the *Golden Eagle*, I want to know why she fits the description my men have given me, and if she is the *Golden Eagle*, I intend to take her, American waters or no American waters!" He eyed Roth suspiciously. "And if she is the *Golden Eagle*, sir," he stated boldly, "I'd sure like to know what the hell you were doing aboard her," and Roth's face went white as the captain turned and continued getting into the boat with his men.

Now what could he do? Beau had been doing him a favor bringing Loedicia to him, and now look at the mess he was in.

The captain stopped and turned, looking at him. "Are you coming with us, sir?" he asked, and Roth hesitated as he stared at the captain. It was so dark he could barely see his face, but he didn't like what he saw. Captain Marlin was a crusty old goat who'd been on the seas too long for his own good and was too used to having his own way, and he liked nothing better than a battle to prove his worth.

"I'll take the boat I came ashore in," he answered, and climbed into the longboat by himself, his hair bristling at the captain's arrogance. He had to think of something by the time they reached the ship, but as he swung out from the pier behind the captain's two longboats, he realized they were leaving him behind, and he tried to row faster.

Suddenly he heard a shout from the captain's boat and glanced up, his oars stopping in midair as he gazed across the water at the *Golden Eagle*. He watched, fascinated, as the sails began to unfurl one by one, and slowly, luxuriously caught in the night breeze; with a creak and groan the *Golden Eagle* heaved forward and began moving, inching across the water. And as each new sail unfurled, his heart beat all the faster and he sat still in the boat, holding tightly to the oars, a sickening feeling in the pit of his stomach as the ship picked up speed. Loedicia was still on the ship, and here he was in this goddamn boat!

His eyes followed it as it moved through the water, each new sail that unfurled lengthening the distance between them.

"Row toward the *Fortress*," yelled Captain Marlin, seeing his prize begin slipping from his hands, and the British longboats turned in the water, heading for the sleeping man-of-war, increasing their speed as the captain shouted angrily.

Roth cursed as he sat helplessly in the drifting boat, watching the *Golden Eagle* slowly melt into the darkness; then he turned his head, watching as the longboats reached the British man-of-war and the ship came to life. Within a few minutes sails were unfurling, the anchor had been weighed, and she began moving slowly forward.

Roth watched solemnly, his hands still clenching the oars as the ship moved along in the dead of night, giving chase to the *Golden Eagle* until it too disappeared from sight.

For a long time he sat motionless, staring off into the darkness that surrounded him, hearing only the gentle lap of the water hitting against the side of the boat, his heart not wanting to believe what had just happened.

The night was exceptionally quiet now, not another soul in sight, and he cursed disgustedly as he dipped the oars back in the water and began turning the small boat toward shore. He was angry, upset, and frustrated. Of all the stupid things to happen. He shouldn't have stayed the night. He should have gathered Dicia and her baggage together and taken her back to the Château last night when he'd first arrived, but he'd been so thrilled at being with her again that nothing else had mattered.

He should have remembered that Captain Marlin and

the Fortress were at Beaufort, but he hadn't dreamed
they'd set sail before Beau could leave, and besides, who
would think anyone would recognize the Golden Eagle in
her disguise? Heath had explained that they'd used it
successfully dozens of times when they were in neutral
ports.

Roth maneuvered the small longboat in at the dock,
tied up, and climbed ashore, standing alone in the darkness, the breeze ruffling his hair. He took a deep breath,
then turned abruptly and headed for the livery where
he'd left the horses earlier in the evening.

His son, Heath, Heath's half-sister, Rebel, and Rebel's
husband, Brandon Avery, the Duke of Bourland, had ridden inland early in the day to fetch him, and he and
Heath had come back alone, leaving Rebel and her husband at the Château. They were there now, waiting for
him to bring Loedicia back.

No lights were on in the livery, it being almost four in
the morning by now, as he stood deciding what to do,
then walked up and began pounding on the door.

It was some minutes before the bleary-eyed stableman
swung the door open and held the lantern up to stare at
him.

"What the devil . . . Mr. Chapman!" He rubbed his eyes,
then blinked. "Somethin' wrong, sir?" he asked, and Roth
stepped inside, not offering an explanation.

"I need my horse, Tom," he said, and headed for the
stall where the horses he and Heath had used were
bedded down for the night. He searched about, finding
the saddle, and began saddling the horse quickly as the
man stared sleepy-eyed.

"It ain't even light out," Tom protested, but Roth paid
little attention as he finished saddling one horse, then
went to the other.

When both horses were saddled, he walked them outside, Tom shuffling behind in his nightshirt, and the last
Tom saw of him and the two horses was their backsides
as they headed inland.

"Now, if that don't beat all," he exclaimed, shaking his
head; then he shuffled back inside, wondering what had
happened to the young man who'd been with Mr. Chapman earlier.

He set the lantern down and blew it out, then went to

the window at the back of the room he kept next to the horses' stalls, and he leaned over, looking out. The back of the livery overlooked the water, and he squinted as he gazed out over the sound. There was nothing in sight, only the faint moonlight on empty water, and he wondered where the boat was that Mr. Chapman had rowed to earlier that evening. Oh, well. He shrugged, stretching lazily, then scratching his stomach. 'Tweren't none of his business anyway, and he crawled back into bed.

Roth slowed the horses to a walk as he left the sleeping town of Port Royal behind. What was the use of tiring the horses when there wasn't a damn thing he could do? By now Beau Dante, known to the British Navy and his crew alike as Captain Thunder, was probably past Hilton Head, heading out to sea.

He thought over events of the past few hours. He'd been in the fields at his plantation yesterday afternoon, seeing how things were progressing, when he'd caught a glimpse of a carriage coming up the drive to the house. He'd left the field on horseback and ridden to the house to discover Heath, Rebel, and the duke. He'd met Rebel and the duke in London the year before, and as he rode along now, he thought back to those days.

He'd been on a business trip to Portsmouth, England, and had had to ride into London for an audience with the king and some of his naval advisers when he'd run into Loedicia, her husband, Quinn, and their two children, Rebel, a beautiful girl almost nineteen, and Teak, a tall strapping blond boy of fourteen who looked every bit of eighteen and was the image of his father.

He remembered seeing Loedicia for the first time after so many years of separation. He'd come to a ball given by the Duchess of Bourland, Brandon Avery's aunt, her first ball since the death of her husband the year before, and he'd found himself staring across the ballroom floor directly into Loedicia's warm violet eyes, and the same yearning sensations had flooded through him that he'd felt twenty years before when he'd first fallen in love with her. He'd tried to forget her over the years, but Loedicia wasn't a woman any man could easily forget, especially after having once been married to her. She was a sensuous woman, beautiful and earthy, with dark curly hair, violet eyes, and a natural warmth that always thrilled him, and he'd never been able to find a woman to take her place in his heart.

Years before, when they both thought her husband, Quinn, had been killed by Indians, Roth had married her, supposedly to keep Lord Kendall Varrick, Quinn's cousin, from marrying her. She'd been betrothed to Lord Varrick before running away and marrying Quinn, but she was deathly afraid of the man. When Kendall learned of Quinn's death, he'd been determined to get her back, and she'd turned to Roth.

At first her feelings for him had been mixed, Roth knew, because she'd loved her husband very much. But shortly before Quinn's unexpected return, she'd given herself to him, loving him as she once had Quinn. Then Quinn had returned, and he'd lost her.

It had been both an agony and an ecstasy to see her again in London, for he'd learned, from her own lips, that, unknown to him, she'd given him a son, Heath, and because of this her life with Quinn had been less than ideal.

London had been a fiasco in more ways than one, and as he rode along now, with the sky beginning to lighten to dawn, he remembered another dawn when he'd held Loedicia in his arms and she'd confessed her love for him. It had been at a small inn on the English downs.

Quinn had been thrown into prison by the then Earl of Locksley, Lord Elton Chaucer, whose title Quinn had put claim to. He'd been arrested on a trumped-up charge of murdering Kendall Varrick almost twenty years before, when in actuality, although no one but Roth and Quinn knew it, Loedicia had shot Lord Varrick, trying to save Quinn's life. Loedicia knew that Roth was the only one besides herself who knew the truth, and he could save Quinn because he was a friend of the king, and King George would believe him. Unfortunately, however, Quinn and Roth had almost come to blows when Roth had lost his head and kissed Loedicia at a lawn party and been caught by Quinn. The only thing that kept Roth from accepting Quinn's challenge at the time was his inability to hurt Dicia any more than he already had. So when Quinn ordered him to leave London and never see her again, he'd complied, but then there she was in the salon at his home in Portsmouth begging his help, and how could he

refuse? She'd come all the way alone to plead with him.
What was he to do?

They'd been caught in a storm on the way back to
London from Portsmouth and been forced to take shelter
in a small inn, and it was a night so vivid, even now he
could close his eyes and see her sitting looking at him
with her warm eyes. Her body soft and wanting, begging
him to love her. It was as if the years between had never
been, and he'd died a thousand deaths when morning
came.

He remembered the look on her face that morning when
she'd realized it was time to go, and he thought of what
she must be feeling now. After all these years they were
finally free to love, and suddenly this. . . .

There were tears of frustration in his eyes and an ache
in his heart as he felt the first tender rays of the warm
sun in his face and smelled the fresh morning air. She
should be here by his side, enjoying it with him—not
miles away.

When he reached the Château it was shortly before
ten, and although he should have been tired from lack of
sleep, the anger and frustration of losing her again refused to let his eyes close. He turned the horses over to
Jacob, the stableman, a big black he'd bought when he'd
first come to the state three years before. Jacob had
worked his price off and was now his own man and
stayed on working for wages. Paying wages to a Negro
was a practice Roth was condemned for by many of his
neighbors, but a practice that pleased him.

Jacob rubbed the horses' noses as Roth handed him the
reins, and he frowned at the sadness in Roth's eyes, but
he didn't say anything, only watched, shaking his head as
Roth headed for the house, where work still progressed.

Roth stopped for a minute and stared at the place,
listening to the hammering and sawing, watching everyone scurrying about trying to get things done. The
Château wasn't finished yet. When he'd bought the land,
he put in indigo and put up a small place to live. The
indigo crop had been good that first year, convincing him
to stay, so now he was going ahead with the manor house,
and this year they had in a crop of cotton. Last year a
gentleman named Eli Whitney had made a machine he
called a cotton gin that took the seeds from the cotton so

much faster than could be done by hand that cotton had begun to flow on the market, and Roth was taking advantage of it. He'd even sunk money into a cotton mill he was having built along the Broad River at the back of the property, not far from the wharf.

He sighed as he looked at the house in its half-finished stage. He'd told Dicia all about it last night as she lay in his arms, and he'd been pleased at the prospect of showing it to her this morning and letting her help with the finished product.

He swore softly and exhaled disgustedly as he started toward the house, then saw Rebel standing in the doorway watching him, a puzzled look on her face. She was a beautiful young woman, looking much like her mother, with big violet eyes but with hair the color of faded dandelions, as her father had had. Quinn had been a strikingly handsome man, tall and blue-eyed. A renegade by all rights. A backwoodsman and Indian fighter who was also an English earl, a title he managed to claim while he was in England. Roth had liked him, and that was strange too. He should have hated him. But he was the kind of man a person couldn't help but admire. He'd been a violent man in some ways, and Rebel had inherited some of his wild rebelliousness. Her name fit her well.

She stepped out onto the veranda, the spring wind blowing her long flaxen hair. "Where's mother?" she asked, frowning as he approached, and he stopped, his eyes darkening.

"She's on the *Golden Eagle* somewhere out to sea by now," he explained, and took her arm, turning her toward the door. "Come inside and I'll explain."

He ushered her to the drawing room, sparse with furniture and minus a carpet, and made her sit and listen while he told her what had happened. She could tell how distraught he was as he finished.

"Maybe they'll head back in when it gets dark again," she said.

"Not a chance. If I know Captain Marlin, he'll make sure he haunts the waters off Hilton Head, unless he catches them, and in that case I hate to think what might happen. He had two other ships waiting for him off Hilton Head, and the *Golden Eagle*'s no match for three ships."

Reb bit her lip. He was right. The *Golden Eagle* was heavily armed, but three ships against one . . . it'd be a slaughter. "They won't catch them," she said confidently as she stared at Roth. "The *Eagle*'s the fastest ship afloat. I know. She'll get away."

"Then what?" asked Roth. "They won't dare try to even sneak back in."

She stood up. "But these are American waters. They have no right to lay in wait for them."

"That's what I told the captain of the *Fortress*, but he ignored it." He walked over and stood looking out the huge bay window that overlooked the river and the bottomland. "I'll tell you what's going to happen. If the *Golden Eagle* gets away, the *Fortress* will turn tail and come back to the sound with its sister ships in tow. They'll spread themselves around the area, faking repairs or business or some such, and lay in wait for the *Eagle*, and who's to force the issue?"

"Aren't there any American ships around at all?"

"Private merchants at Beaufort and a few in the sound toward Hilton Head, but they won't chance an incident that could have international repercussions." He turned to face her. "And to top it all off, Captain Marlin's going to ask for an explanation from me, and what do I tell him? That my son is Captain Thunder's first mate?" He took a deep breath. "My shipbuilding firms in England supply the British fleet. My shipping companies deliver arms to the British Army. My father was the fourth son of the Earl of Cumberland, and King George considers me a friend, and I'm supposed to tell them that my son is fighting on the side of France? The situation's awkward, to say the least."

Rebel's face reddened. "I'm sorry," she said regretfully. "We shouldn't have come," but his eyes softened as he looked at her.

"Nonsense! If you hadn't come . . . Rebel, I love your mother very much."

"But now we've gotten you in a mess."

"I'll get out of it somehow."

"Get out of what?" asked a voice from the doorway, and they both turned to face Brandon Avery, the Duke of Bourland, Rebel's husband of only a few weeks. He was tawny-haired, with gold-flecked brown eyes. Handsome in a foppish way, his appearance elegant.

Roth hadn't gotten to know him too well while in London, but what he did know he disliked. The man had never done him any harm, but his attitude left much to be desired. He was arrogant, as if he looked down his nose at everyone, and Roth wondered what a girl like Rebel could see in him. Heath explained that they'd been married aboard the *Golden Eagle* with its captain officiating, but Heath seemed none too pleased with his half-sister's choice of a husband.

"I'd have sworn she and Beau were in love," he'd told his father as they'd ridden toward the *Golden Eagle* the afternoon before. "But then, I never could tell what either Reb or Beau was thinking, and they're both so damn stubborn. I think she married Brandon just so she could be a duchess and to spite Beau." Roth remembered Heath's words now as he glanced first at Rebel, then to the tawny-haired man standing in the doorway.

"We had an unfortunate encounter with a British man-of-war," he stated. "I'm afraid the *Golden Eagle*'s miles out to sea by now, and Loedicia's still on it." He explained the whole incident, and the duke watched Rebel closely as Roth talked.

When Roth finished, there was a slight twitch at the corner of the duke's mouth and his eyes looked amused.

"You think it's funny?" asked Rebel angrily, and now he actually smiled a vicious smile.

"I hope they catch the bastard and hang him!" he stated boldly, and Roth's face darkened as Rebel snapped back.

"My mother's on that ship, and my brother!"

"Nobody'll hurt your mother, Reb, don't worry," he answered. "If I know the countess as well as I think I do, she can talk her way out of anything, but I'm sorry, Reb . . . Heath may be your brother, but he's just as guilty of crimes against the crown as Captain Thunder is, and I'm afraid I have no love for either man."

"You're talking about my son, sir!" said Roth as he stared at Brandon, but the duke never flinched.

"I realize that, sir," he answered, "so perhaps under the circumstances it might be best if I rode to the nearest town to inquire about lodgings for myself and my wife until we can find a ship heading for the Indies and we can finish the journey to Grenada that Captain Thunder so inconveniently interrupted. After all, I do still have my post as governor there to think of."

Roth glanced quickly at Rebel. Her face was flushed with anger as she looked at her husband, and he sensed rather than saw the disgust she felt, and he felt sorry for her.

"On the contrary," he said sternly, not wanting to hurt her any more than he felt she'd already been hurt. "I said the two of you were welcome here, and I don't go back on my word."

Brandon glanced about at the unfinished room devoid of the comfortable furnishings he was used to, then cocked his head back, listening to the sounds of the hammers as the men worked outside. "I'm not really sure I want to stay," he ventured, sighing. "I hadn't realized when you suggested it last night that the incessant noise and confusion would get on my nerves so," and Rebel glanced at him quickly, her eyes narrowing.

"A little noise won't hurt you."

"I detest it," he said haughtily, and he glanced around the room at the bare walls and at the floor without a carpet and she knew what he was thinking, but he'd better not say it. He'd said enough last night after Roth and Heath had left.

He'd confirmed to her his dislike of living in what he called crude circumstances, with the house only partway finished, and he also disliked the familiarity of the servants, who were all black. "Blacks have only one place in life," he said as they'd prepared for bed. "If this were my plantation, they'd be in the fields, not the house. I feel uneasy with them around," and Rebel had learned another facet of her husband's complicated personality. One that hadn't come to light before, and one she didn't like. She stared at him now, praying he wouldn't say anything further.

"I'm sorry the noise disturbs you, your Grace," apologized Roth stiffly, his eyes still dark with anger at the man's insolence, "but I'm afraid the work has to be done. As I said, you're welcome to stay, as you wish, whatever suits you," and he sighed. "Now, if you two don't mind, I'm going to order a bath and clean up, then take the ship out and see what I can learn."

"You have a ship?" asked Rebel.

"Down on the river. She's a small three-master, specially made. I can't catch up to them, they've got too much of a head start, but I can meet the *Fortress* if she tries to come back in."

Reb stepped forward anxiously. "May I go with you, Roth . . . please? I can't just sit here and wait."

He looked at Brandon. "And you?"

"Anything would be better than this," he said, and he closed his eyes, listening to the hammering, as Rebel glanced quickly at Roth, her eyes apologizing.

An hour later they boarded Roth's private ship, the *Interlude*. The Château overlooked the Broad River, and a pier had been built to accommodate the ship. She was a trim vessel, but with extra sails fore and aft, and narrower than her contemporaries.

Roth had given orders, and the crew was waiting to shove off the minute they stepped aboard. Rebel was surprised to hear Roth shouting orders.

"You captain your own ship?" she asked.

"When I can. And I work in my own fields when I get the chance, and I guess I do a lot of other things most folks wouldn't approve of," he answered, his eyes wandering to Brandon, who was standing away from them against the rail looking up at the sails as they unfurled.

"The man who drove us out here yesterday was telling us," she said. "It seems you don't believe in owning slaves, either."

"Oh, I own them. For a while, that is. I buy them, then set a wage for them and let them work off their sale price. When they've paid me back for my initial investment, they have a choice of staying and working here at the Château or leaving. Most of them stay." He turned and headed for the wheel, while she followed, and Brandon's eyes left the sails, watching them from the railing.

"You don't believe in slavery?" she asked.

"Do you?"

"No."

"But your husband does."

She looked uncomfortable. "Yes," she murmured; then her head went up stubbornly. "But it doesn't matter."

He turned to her, looking deep into her eyes as she stood beside him, and she blushed under his scrutiny.

"You don't have to apologize to me, Reb," he said softly. "What your husband does or doesn't do is none of my business . . . unless he intends to cause trouble for Heath," he added. "Then it matters very much."

Her eyes fell; then she glanced furtively toward Brandon, and back again to Roth, her lips trembling. "When we arrived yesterday, I was so happy for you and Heath," she said softly. "I love my brother dearly, and he's been so upset since he learned the truth about you being his father. I was pleased that he'd finally found you, but now . . . Brandon says he's going to inform the King of England and anyone else who'll listen that Heath's your son, and he doesn't believe that you and Mother were married once. He thinks Heath is the result of an affair."

Roth's forehead wrinkled into a frown.

"Especially because of my father's reaction to you when we were in England," she explained.

Roth took the wheel from his helmsman, and as the sails caught the wind, he maneuvered the ship out into the river. They talked, and he listened intently to Rebel's revealing conversation.

"Brandon hates Heath and Beau," she went on. "I think he hates them because of the kind of men they are." Her eyes came alive, watching ahead as the ship moved downstream. "You met Beau," she said. "He's a dynamic person. He commands his men out of respect, not fear, something Brandon wishes he could do. And there's a warmth and sincerity about Heath that draws people to him." She turned to look at Roth, watching the way he handled the wheel, his face determined. "Something he inherited from you," she added, and he looked pleased.

"I wish I'd had a chance to get to know Heath better," he said as he watched the river ahead, turning the wheel slightly to catch the swifter current; then he glanced over at her. "He told me that he and Beau Dante grew up together at Fort Locke," he said, and her eyes narrowed as she glanced quickly toward her husband, who was still standing at the rail, then back to Roth again.

"Shhh . . ." she cautioned, putting a finger to her lips. "Brandon doesn't know Beau's real last name. All he knows is that he's Captain Thunder—Beau Thunder, as his crew calls him. Someday he intends to quit privateering for the French and settle down and become respectable, and the fewer people who know his real name the better."

"Heath said he's the son of an Indian chief."

"His father is Telak, chief of the Tuscarora at Fort Locke, but he's one-quarter French. His mother is one of Telak's four wives, and her father was a Frenchman." She turned again and watched as the ship cleared the mouth of the river and moved into the sound. "Fort Locke is on the shores of Lake Erie by the Ashtabula River, and we all grew up there together, even my brother Teak, who's still back in England. My parents treated Beau almost like a son. Mother was very partial to him, and they even sent him to a school in Philadelphia."

Roth watched Rebel's eyes as she talked of Beau. They were alive and warm, her face glowing. Heath was right: she was in love with him. He glanced quickly at Brandon, who had left the rail and was walking toward them, and he wondered. If she was in love with Beau, why the hell had she married Brandon?

Brandon stretched, then walked over, putting an arm about Rebel's waist possessively, and Roth saw her stiffen at his touch. "Your ship seems quite sound, sir," he said, addressing Roth. "Why do you have to stop at Hilton Head? We could perhaps scout the coast."

"It's a big ocean," answered Roth as he maneuvered through the sound, which at the moment was dotted with small fishing boats. "We could miss them too easily. I don't know if the *Golden Eagle* would have headed out to sea, or north, or toward the gulf. We could end up on a wild-goose chase."

They reached Hilton Head, furled the sails, and dropped anchor a few hundred yards offshore, where they couldn't miss a ship approaching from any direction. The afternoon was hot but windy as they settled down to wait.

Three American merchant ships passed into the sound, and two moved out, one sailing north, the other south, but the *Interlude* still held its position. There was food and drink aboard, and to while away the time they played whist in Roth's cabin. But his mind wasn't on the whist game. Too much had happened since yesterday, and he excused himself time after time to pace the deck, watching the horizon.

It was well after dark when they finally gave up and

weighed anchor, heading back for the Château, and later, in their bedroom, as Rebel and Brandon prepared for bed, Brandon stared at Rebel hard, watching her brush her long flaxen hair.

"How can you like the man after what he did to your father?" he finally said as he slipped into his nightshirt, and she stopped the brush halfway down her hair, staring at her reflection in the mirror.

"I don't expect you to understand," she answered, then continued brushing. "You don't believe anything I've told you about Roth and my mother anyway, so how can I expect you to understand?"

He frowned as he walked over and stood behind her, looking down at her hair. It was like burnished gold in the candlelight. She was a sensuous woman, her whole body, every movement, every gesture a natural invitation, yet he was sure she was unaware of it. Sometimes his desire for her nearly drove him mad, but she was still edgy and held herself back. If she'd just let herself go . . . just once. They'd been married only a few weeks, true, but by now she should have come out of her shell.

She was wearing an emerald-green satin dressing gown, and he reached out, pulling it off her shoulder, the strap on her nightgown moving with it; then he leaned down, kissing her velvet skin, and he felt her muscles stiffen beneath his lips.

"Why do you do that?" he asked angrily, and she tried to laugh it off.

"Do what?"

"You know very well what I mean. Every time I touch you, you tense up, as if you can't stand it."

"Don't be silly, Bran," she exclaimed as she set the hairbrush down and stood up, walking toward the bed, pulling the shoulder of her dressing gown back up. "I'm just tired. It's been a long day and I've got a headache, that's all."

"You've had quite a few headaches since we've been married, haven't you, Reb?" he said as he stared at her. "Last night, the night before, the night before that."

"I can't help it . . . really . . . my time of the month was due a week ago and it's not here yet. Maybe that's what's wrong . . . I don't know."

She glanced back at him furtively as she stood beside

the bed, and she saw the expression in his eyes suddenly change as he stared at her, and he scowled.

"You think . . . already?"

"I don't know . . . I'm not sure yet." Her voice was strained. The thought of carrying his child sickened her. She stared ahead at the picture on the wall opposite the bed, not even seeing it, her mind miles away. Why had she ever married him? Why? Her mother had warned her. She'd been right. You couldn't pretend love. For a while you could put on a good show, but deep inside, you knew. It was always there. She hated his hands on her, and every time he claimed his right as her husband, she cringed beneath him, hating the feel of his body against hers. His lovemaking, as he arrogantly called it, was a one-sided affair with no thought to her needs or wants. It didn't really matter, though, because no matter what he did, it couldn't arouse her enough to make her want him. She'd thought it would be so easy. What a fool she'd been.

Brandon walked over to her and took her by the shoulders, turning her to face him. "Why didn't you tell me?" he asked. "I had no idea."

"I'm not sure," she said hesitantly, her face flushed. "It may be nothing. It might start any day."

"And if it doesn't?"

She shrugged. "Then I guess I'm pregnant."

His hands dropped from her shoulders. "You don't seem too happy about it."

"Am I supposed to be?"

"Most women would be pleased to give their husbands a son."

She flicked the hair back over her shoulder belligerently. "Do I have to be like most women?" she asked, and his eyes sifted over her, to the outline of her full breasts concealed by her dressing gown, then to her throat, soft and smooth above them, and up to the stubborn tilt of her chin and the sensuous depth in her eyes.

"That you'll never be," he answered emphatically. "But don't you want children?"

She bit her lip; then her mouth closed stubbornly. "I didn't want them now," she said softly. "Not now." Nor ever, she thought. Not your children, anyway.

She turned from him and walked to the window that overlooked the river at the back of the house and closed her eyes, ignoring Brandon, who was watching her curiously, and all she could see were a pair of green eyes beneath a crop of black wavy hair, the lips smiling at her cynically from his bronzed face. Why couldn't she forget Beau Dante? He'd done nothing but break her heart from the moment she'd become aware of him. How many times those eyes had haunted her over the past few years. Eyes that could stir her like no others. Was it any wonder she succumbed to him? She thought back to that night. The night before her wedding. She'd been unable to sleep, and had gone up on the deck of the *Golden Eagle*, watching the stars, wondering if maybe she'd made a mistake by saying she'd marry Brandon. But then, she'd promised herself that she was going to be a duchess. Besides, she'd vowed never to give her heart to anyone ever again. That no man was ever going to make a fool of her as Beau had before, when he'd mocked her protests of love and left Fort Locke three years before. She'd been young then, yes, but not too young to know what her heart was telling her, and as she stood by the rail that night, she'd been more vulnerable than she'd ever been before. Maybe that's why Beau's arms had looked so inviting. Maybe that's why, when he found her on deck alone, she'd melted against him without any inhibitions. And when he carried her to his cabin and made love to her, she'd given herself to him shamelessly. How was she to know as she lay beneath him, surrendering to him, that he had no intentions of marrying her?

"You're an earl's daughter and I'm an Indian with a price on my head," he'd said afterward, shattering her illusions, and a tear rolled down her cheek now as she remembered the ache in her heart the next day as she and Brandon had stood on the deck of the *Golden Eagle* and Beau had said the words that had made her Brandon's wife.

Brandon watched her now from across the room. The rigid stance, apparent preoccupation, then he saw her tremble slightly. "What's the matter?" he asked sharply as he shortened the distance between them, but she shook her head.

"It's nothing," she answered, her voice breaking as she continued to stare out the window.

"It's that Indian, isn't it?" he said savagely, his eyes

blazing, but she shook her head, still refusing to face him.
"No!"

He reached out and spun her around. "Don't lie to me!"
His eyes flashed angrily. "Something was going on between you two on board ship, wasn't it? I saw it. I'm not
stupid. Don't think I didn't see the looks that passed between you!"

There were tears at the corners of her eyes, but she
lifted her chin stubbornly.

"What is he to you? he cried as he stared at her, but
she didn't answer.

She couldn't, because she didn't know herself. She
hated Beau for what he'd done to her. For giving her a
taste of heaven, then plunging her into the hell she'd
found in Brandon's arms. Yet she couldn't forget him.
She'd never forget him.

"I asked you," he said again viciously. "What is he to
you?" and she inhaled quickly, holding back tears.

"He's nothing," she said softly, breathlessly, but his
eyes narrowed.

"Then it's time you remembered this," he said heatedly,
and reached out, pulling her into his arms. "You're mine,
Reb, only mine, do you understand?" he said passionately.
"Even if he wanted you, he could never have you . . . you're
my wife now . . . mine!" and his mouth crushed down on
hers brutally, bruising her lips; then he picked her up,
heading for the bed.

"Brandon, no," she pleaded, her mouth still hurting
from his kiss. "Not tonight, please, Bran. I don't want it
tonight. I don't feel good, please," but he paid her no
heed as he dropped her on the bed, ripping the dressing
gown open against her violent protests. "Stop, Bran!" she
cried, her heart pounding as she tried to keep him from
taking her nightgown off, but it only infuriated him more,
and he ripped the wrapper and nightgown from her.

"You've said no for the last time, Reb!" he snarled as
he threw the clothing aside, then stared down at her as
she cowered naked on the bed. "I'm through trying to
humor you. I married you because I wanted you, because
I had to have you. You do things to me, and by God I'm
going to have you whenever I want, do you understand?"
and Rebel gulped back the tears, wanting to die as she

saw the bulge beneath his nightshirt; then he quickly pulled the nightshirt off and was on the bed with her.

"Brandon, please," she begged tearfully, "not tonight . . . please," but he grabbed her hair, his eyes darkening, and she winced.

"Tonight and any other night," he answered hotly, his face flushed, eyes frenzied with his desire for her. "And if you fight me, that's all the better, my love," he whispered. "It only makes the taking all the better," and Rebel groaned agonizingly against him as he forced his way into her. He took her savagely, against her will, and that night she learned another shocking facet to her husband's character. Brandon Avery, the Duke of Bourland, and newly appointed governor of the island of Grenada in the West Indies, was not beyond raping a woman, even his wife, enjoying it immensely, while down the hall in the master bedroom, Roth stood by the open French doors of the balcony that overlooked the river, unaware of the misery to which Rebel was being subjected. He stared off into the star-filled night, praying that Captain Marlin and his ships had been unable to catch the *Golden Eagle*, and wondering what the hell he was going to do about the whole damn mess in the morning.

ABOUT THE AUTHOR

The granddaughter of an old-time vaudevillian, Mrs. Shiplett was born and raised in Ohio. She has been married to her husband, Charles, for thirty years, and has lived in the city of Mentor-on-the-Lake for twenty-five years. She has four daughters and two grandchildren.